THE HEART GUIDES YOU HOME

THE LITTLE BELITON SERIES
BOOK ONE

CAROLINE SCOTT COLLINS

Published in the United Kingdom by:
MoorPublishing

Content copyright © Caroline Scott Collins 2023
Illustrations copyright © Caroline Scott Collins/SueC 2023

Copyright © 2023 by Caroline Scott Collins
All rights reserved.
No part of this book may be reproduced in any form or by any electronic or mechanical means, including information storage and retrieval systems, without written permission from the author, except for the use of brief quotations in a book review.

The right of Caroline Scott Collins to be identified as the author of this work has been asserted by her in accordance with the Copyright Designs and Patents act 1988.

A CIP record of this book is available from the British Library

First printed 01/11/2023

Layout and design by MoorPublishing

Available in print and ebook formats
Paperback ISBN 978-1-838 4594-3-7
ebook ISBN 978-1-8384594-2-0

❀ Created with Vellum

For my family, friends and readers who have encouraged and supported me to follow my dream of writing and publishing stories. Thank you.

CONTENTS

Chapter 1	1
Chapter 2	11
Chapter 3	21
Chapter 4	29
Chapter 5	39
Chapter 6	49
Chapter 7	59
Chapter 8	69
Chapter 9	77
Chapter 10	85
Chapter 11	93
Chapter 12	103
Chapter 13	111
Chapter 14	119
Chapter 15	127
Chapter 16	135
Chapter 17	143
Chapter 18	151
Chapter 19	159
Chapter 20	167
Chapter 21	175
Chapter 22	183
Chapter 23	193
Chapter 24	201
Chapter 25	209
Chapter 26	219
Chapter 27	227
Chapter 28	235
Learn and Move On	243
About the Author	245
Also by Caroline Scott Collins	247
Caroline Scott Collins A Charming Bequest	249

CHAPTER 1

Sat nav: In 500 metres, turn right.

It was early April 2022, Marc was driving from London to Devon and he was close to the end of his journey. He considered himself lucky that his phone still had a signal in the heart of Dartmoor. He was on quite high ground but he could see, glancing around, even higher ground surrounded him with rocky outcrops on some of the hilltops. He thought, *they must be the infamous tors*.

He slowed down and turned into the junction, heartened to see the black and white fingerpost indicated Little Beliton. The lane no longer had centre white lines and was quite narrow, but the verges of moorland were quite flat and level with the road to pull onto, if something came the other way.

Sat nav: Continue for 2 miles.

He drove cautiously as the road descended and changed to a tunnel of trees, with high banks and hedges on both sides of the road. The moor changed too and morphed into hedged fields, some containing cattle, sheep, pigs, or ponies. He passed a picturesque farmhouse tucked away up a short track.

He muttered to himself, 'Jeez, these lanes are so narrow, I'm not used to this.' Marc continued cautiously along the road, hoping that nothing would come towards him. However, he had noticed wider bulges periodically designed into the lane. He made a mental note as he passed each one thinking they must be there to allow vehicles to pass each other.

He passed a farm gate standing open with a tractor in the field approaching it. The driver gave a friendly wave. Marc acknowledged the greeting and carried on slowly along the lane. Next, he passed a terrace of quaint thatched cottages with front door porches opening straight onto the road. Then turning a corner, what must be the heart of the village appeared before him. A village green, a small church with a stunted square tower, a village store with a thatched conservatory attached to one side, and a T-junction ahead.

Sat nav: You have reached your destination.

'Have I indeed? Hmm, left or right at the junction?' Marc muttered. He decided to pull into the car park he'd noticed, next to the church, to try and track down some guidance to his destination. He parked and got out, and pressed his key to lock the door. He wrestled himself into his hoodie that he'd picked up as he got out of his car and looked for the pay point. There wasn't one. *Free parking!*

He walked back out to the road and looked around; up the lane from the direction he'd driven, and across the village green. There was a small river running through the green with a humpback bridge over it, needed if turning to the right, to get to the shop and one side of the village. He looked up the lane to the lefthand turning and saw a terrace of thatched cottages before the uphill road bent to the right and disappeared. There was no one about, but then it was late afternoon and people probably had better things to do on a Saturday afternoon than stroll around the village.

Marc decided the shop looked a likely place to find someone to ask for directions. He wandered along to the junction and crossed the bridge towards the shop. It was then he could see it was a small Spar grocery store, post office and coffee shop. *Great. I'll text James and tell him I've arrived.*

As he crossed the bridge, he spotted a guy about his own age walking towards him, wearing jeans and a fleece with his hands pushed deep into the pockets. Marc had nearly reached the shop when the man looked up and said, 'Hi, are you Marcus?'

'Yes,' replied Marc and put out his hand to offer a handshake. 'You must be James.'

'Hi, yes, I'm James.' He shook Marc's hand firmly.

'Thanks for meeting me on a Saturday afternoon. I really appreciate it,' said Marc.

'No problem, I live here anyway, so it's no big deal. Shall we get a coffee and have a chat?'

'Yes, sure, I could do with a drink, it was rather a long drive from London, and I didn't stop. After you…' he indicated for James to lead him into the shop. On entering, they turned left into the extension, which he could now see was set up as a café, decorated in an attractive cottage style—a room with exposed beams, tables with gingham tablecloths and small vases of primroses.

He chose a table by the window bathed in sunshine and overlooking the sloping riverbank. He heard James greet the lady behind the counter and place an order before he joined him, sitting on the opposite side of the table.

James struck up the conversation. 'Pretty place, isn't it? I haven't lived here very long myself and I'm still doing-up my cottage. Well, I've progressed to the garden now and I need some help. I moved down here from Berkshire when I qualified and got my job with the firm in Greater Beliton. I've grown to love it here. Everyone is so welcoming and friendly.'

'It's certainly very quaint and very different from The Big Smoke. It looks quite laid back too—there's no one about. I've lived in London since I graduated and I'm getting rather tired of the constant noise and the crazy, busy lifestyle and so many people.'

'Joan might have handed you an opportunity then,' James smiled.

A lady approached their table carrying a tray with two cups of coffee, a jug of milk and a couple of toasted tea cakes on it. 'Thanks, Jan,' James said, as she placed the cups and plates in front of them. He turned to Marc, 'I figured you'd be hungry after your long drive.'

'Hi, thank you,' Marc said to Jan, and replied to James, 'Thanks, James, that's really kind.'

'No worries.' They started their snack and James continued, 'So Marcus, I have here Joan's Will,' as he retrieved some paperwork from an inside pocket of his fleece. 'Basically, Joan's left one cash bequest, which as Executor I've paid, and everything else is yours. There was another cash bequest to you, because originally everything else was left to your father, but since your father died per stirpes kicks in and now it's all yours. Including one beautiful house.' James handed Marc the document.

'Marc to friends.' He skim read it and soon he paused, looked up and said, 'Beliton Manor?'

'Oh yes. It's a beautiful house with land. The fields are leased out to local farmers, so it makes some income, and there's a small ancient woodland tucked away somewhere too.'

'Where is the house?'

'Just up the lane towards Beliton Tor and the land wraps around the back of that side of the village beneath the tor. It's the turning to the left at The Green. I'll take you there. She was a nice lady, Joan. Did you know her well?'

'No, I hadn't seen her since I was little. She was my grandad's sister and Grandma and Grandad used to take me to visit Auntie Joan and Uncle Simon when they lived near Brighton. She was nice. I remember sitting painting pictures with her at her dining room table once, for a whole afternoon. I think she inspired my hobby.'

'Good to have happy memories. Have you ever been down here before, to the south-west? Popular place for holidays.'

'No, the countryside wasn't my parents' idea of fun. I usually got dragged off to Marbella, or similar, in the school holidays. They were party animals and the lifestyle suited them. I'd wander off on my own trying to find a quiet place to read, or sketch, or something.'

'Shame you didn't come here to visit Joan and Simon. I've taken up surfing since I've moved down here. Not so much in the winter, I'm a bit averse to cold water even wearing a wetsuit, but now it's getting warmer I'll dust off the board and head to a beach soon. Devon and

Cornwall are a surfing paradise. There are loads of great beaches around without having to drive too far.'

'Sounds like fun.'

'In the winter, there are loads of places to go rambling over the moors to enjoy some peace and quiet. Or bike rides …'

'I'll have to build up my stamina to tackle the hills I've seen today! But it sounds ideal. By the way, is good broadband available in the village? I work remotely, and I need fast broadband.'

'Sure. Access to super-fast was put in a couple of years ago and Joan had it connected at her house. I work from home sometimes too. I think remote working is becoming very popular.'

'And today you're working, meeting me, and no internet is required. Cheers!'

'It came in really useful during the lockdowns - people still moved house, for example, and we needed to do the legal work.'

'Ah, yes. My employers switched to flexible, remote working with video conferencing meetings, and they found that actually more work got done. So, they've adopted it permanently and closed an office in the centre of London. Saved them a fortune in overheads and made a lot of employees very happy, with flexible working. While I don't have the childcare issues some of my colleagues have, I work much better in the peace and quiet of home where I can concentrate.'

'Yea, me too. Anyway, if you've finished, I'll take you to your new home. Let's go and get your car.' They got up and left, walking back over the bridge to the car park.

A few minutes later they were heading up the steep slope of the lane to the left, past the row of pretty cottages. This time the cottages were set back from the road and had lovely, long narrow front gardens. Then the lane became even steeper approaching a righthand bend in the road when a gorgeous house came into view tucked down to the left. The drive entrance had granite gateposts with stone balls on top. The tall iron gates were there, but obviously hadn't been closed for years as the grass, weeds, and ivy growing from the bank pinned the right one open. One of the gate posts had a slate plaque affixed reading, Beliton Manor.

'Your manor,' grinned James.

Marc drove through the gates and stopped on the driveway to take in the scene. The house appeared to be almost tucked into the hill. Half of it was two storeys with a thatched roof. The other half a single storey extension with a slate roof. There was a large garden sweeping down the slope of the valley and there were a few outbuildings dotted around. The driveway swept around descending to the left into a parking area at the front of the house. The background consisted of fields rising up the valley, which gave way to moorland and the tor in the distance.

'Beliton Tor, I presume? Wow, just wow! It's gorgeous. Such character,' gasped Marc.

'I picked up the vibe that you'd like it,' grinned James. 'Stunning, isn't it? Loads of potential, and a with bit of TLC, imagination, and future-proofing, it's perfect.'

'Yes. Definitely. I can see it needs a bit of renovating ... It's thatched too. Just ... Wow!'

'It's a Devon longhouse. Centuries old. I don't know exactly when it was built, but it's had improvements done over time, centuries possibly, updating it as the residents needed them. Originally longhouses were just one storey high with living accommodation on one side, and across a common entrance corridor to a barn —a shippon, originally for livestock on the other side. As you can see, the living accommodation side has been extended upwards, so there are two floors. There are several outbuildings dotted about too.'

Marc proceeded carefully down the drive, admiring the garden and the view as he went. He pulled up and parked next to a Mini in front of the house. It had its boot open. A beautiful young woman appeared from the front door of the house carrying a box.

Marc and James got out of the car. 'Hi Lucy,' said James, 'how are you doing?'

'I'm okay, thanks.'

'This is Joan's nephew, Marcus.'

'Marc—to friends. Hi Lucy,' said Marc, 'pleased to meet you.'

'Hi, Marc, I'd shake your hand but ...' carrying the box prevented it.

'What's going on?' said Marc.

'I'm moving out. It's your house now and you might want to sell it or move your wife and kids in—whatever.'

'You don't need to do that. You are the Lucy mentioned in Joan's will? She left you some money. You must have been a special person to her. I don't have a wife and kids and I don't have any plans right now, and you don't have to move out, it's your home.'

'Yes, I'm the Lucy. I was very lucky to be given a home here for a few years, with the lovely kind Joan. But I can't stay here, it's your house and anyway, we don't know each other.'

'No, we don't know each other, you're right, but the house seems quite big, so I'm sure we can live here amicably. Stay. Don't make any quick decisions. Have you got somewhere to go?'

'No, I don't have anywhere to go. Well, okay, thanks. We can talk about it and decide what to do after the funeral on Wednesday.'

James watched them closely before he interrupted the conversation and put out the sparks of attraction crackling between them. 'Well, you two seem to be hitting it off just fine,' he smiled. 'Give me that box, I'll take it back in for you, and close your boot. I need to show Marc around his new house.'

'Okay, thanks. I'll do that and go and put the kettle on. I'll make coffee. Enjoy your tour, Marc.'

James led Marc into the house from the doorway hidden in the corridor next to the barn extension. He entered the door and put the box down on the hall table. Marc looked around, with amazement. 'Wow! Amazing!' The walls were stone with beautiful, exposed beams, and a lovely wooden staircase leading to the first-floor level.

'Let's start down here.' James led the way through a door into a lovely large sunny lounge with a huge stone fireplace. Through the windows Marc admired the beautiful open view down the valley. At the back of the room was a doorway leading into the kitchen. Traditional style and rather dated, but quite large with plenty of cupboard space. Another doorway led from the kitchen into a spacious dining room, and another door led from the dining room back into the lounge. The lounge although large, felt cosy and inviting with its huge stone fireplace.

'It's all lovely. Loads of character, and the views are spectacular,' said Marc.

'Yes, it's nice isn't it? Spacious rooms with re-jigging possibilities. Let's look upstairs.' James led the way up the staircase with lovely balustrades. On the first floor there was a central corridor with doors leading off both sides. Four bedrooms and two bathrooms, and a large landing area, which included an office space area with a desk by the window and the same lovely views.

Lucy appeared. 'It's okay James, you can show him my room too. Marc's got to know what he's inherited.'

Marc opened the door and saw a pile of half-packed boxes and bags. He stepped in. It was a pretty room situated above the lounge and again had the same lovely views. 'Put your things away, Lucy. You really don't have to move out, it's your home. There are enough rooms for the two of us, and two bathrooms, we can both live here okay.'

'As we said, we'll talk about it, but thanks, I don't have anywhere organised to go to. I'll pay you rent and share the costs,' said Lucy.

'We'll chat and see how it goes,' Marc said thinking, *I don't need you paying rent.*

'Coffee is ready, downstairs in the lounge,' she said.

'Thanks.'

James and Marc went back downstairs while Lucy stayed in her room with the door closed. 'We'll look outside after coffee,' said James.

'Sure.'

They went back into the lounge again and chatted generally while having their drinks, then James showed him the shippon—the extension opposite the living accommodation. It was a spacious barn storage full of old, rather rusty garden items and tools strewn about. They continued outside and wandered around the garden glancing at some of the outbuildings. 'I see what you mean about potential,' Marc said. 'The shippon would make a lovely extension to the main living space, and as for the old barns ... I guess they could be converted into holiday lets, or something.'

'I thought that too. As I say, this is a great holiday area with moors and coasts nearby. There are a couple of cottages in the village, which are holiday lets, but I respect the villagers' feelings that they don't want too many more homes used for that purpose though. As they say, the soul would go out of the village if cottages spent months standing empty. It happens to so many places down here, some coastal villages feel utterly dead in the winter. However, a couple more here would probably be acceptable. It wouldn't change the dynamics of the village.'

'I've got a lot to think about. Thank you so much for all your help and the tour, I really appreciate it. And you've organised Joan's funeral too.'

'It's fine. Joan had a chat with me about it all a couple of months ago. She organised it all really. She had a funeral plan in place and told the funeral directors exactly what she wanted. They've done it all according to her wishes. The funeral will be in the church, and the Wake in the village hall. A good traditional Devonshire cream tea, of course. It will be a good chance for you to meet the villagers.'

Marc went quiet for a minute before he finally said, 'Yes, I'm sure. A good opportunity.'

'Don't worry, mostly they're a friendly bunch. They'll make you welcome.'

'It's the room full of people thing. And because I didn't really know her ... I'm almost a fraud.'

'Not at all. Simon's family have lived here for generations. The villagers all know that Joan had a mysterious nephew, they'll just be a bit curious about meeting you, but you're her family. All this is yours by right.'

'I suppose so.'

'Don't worry, honest.' James paused then said, 'I've got an idea, why don't we get the three of us a Chinese takeaway tonight. We can get to know each other.'

Lucy was still unloading her car and she came over to join them. 'Fancy a Chinese takeaway tonight, Lucy?' He turned to Marc, 'We have to drive over to Greater Beliton for it, but I can give you a whistle stop tour of the place to give you a sense of getting your bearings. If you want the big city vibe here, you're pretty much central to Exeter and Plymouth.'

'Chinese, that's a good idea,' said Lucy. 'I'll prepare the dining room while you're out and warm some plates. I'll put some wine in the fridge to chill too.'

'That sounds good,' said Marc. 'Can I give you a lift home and we'll meet up later? I'll settle in, unpack, and freshen up.'

'No, it's fine. It's not far back to the village, as you've seen, and my cottage isn't far from the shop, in the direction of the pub—The Fox on the Green. I'll come back about six thirty and pick you up.'

'Don't do that, I'll walk down to The Green, and we'll meet there. I could do with a stroll after the long drive today. A bit of fresh air would be good.'

'Sure. Great. See you in a while.' James turned and started walking up the drive.

'Bye,' said Marc and Lucy.

CHAPTER 2

The next day, Marc decided to stroll up onto the moors. He had noticed a bridle path signpost not far from the entrance to his driveway, where it looked as if the road ended on a flattish open area of the moors. He figured people might park there to go rambling.

It was a lovely sunny, spring day and he felt some fresh air would do him good. He didn't sleep particularly well the previous night, despite having pleasant company, nice food, and a couple of glasses of wine, but then again he hadn't slept particularly well for months. Too much going around in his mind, and too much agonising to make decisions to choose what was best for him to do. He had no one to turn to, to be a listening ear, or to bounce some ideas off.

Fortunately, he'd just completed an important project at work and it seemed to be going well. There was an interlude and easing back a bit before the next project, so work wasn't on top of his To-Do list of priorities. Making sense of the opportunities presented to him for a change of life direction and new responsibilities was his main concern.

Marc decided that some fresh air, new vistas, and chilling out a bit with his sketch book would take some pressure off. A review of ideas about his dilemmas he'd entered in his journal might be good too. He packed a drink and some snacks, his sketch book, journal, and some pencils in his backpack, put on his fleece and walking boots, which he kept permanently in the boot of his car.

He walked up to the top of the driveway out onto the road, turned left and headed up the steep lane to the bridle path signpost. From there he began walking along the track. The bridle way signpost indicated Beliton Tor and the path ran along the moor side of fields delineated by a Devon bank, which consists of a tall hedge planted on a stone walled earth bank the same as the ones he drove through to enter the village.

When he reached a gateway, he stopped to look in the field, which contained cattle—lovely, golden coloured Jersey cows with beautiful long eyelashes. The cow he was admiring stood still, staring back at him, before she put her head down and started grazing again.

Marc continued along the track, which was now leading up a gentle incline of open moor. There were a few rather shaggy sheep wandering about in the bracken. Some way away, he could see a couple of Dartmoor ponies—small, stocky ponies with chestnut coats and thick, long dark manes. The ponies have the freedom of the moor, "… and often wander across the roads …" Lucy told him, the previous evening. She also warned him of the 40 miles-per-hour speed limit on the moor. "So many animals are involved in traffic accidents, and some are killed. It's very sad," she'd said. Marc agreed and thanked her for the warning. He didn't ever like seeing animals hurt, maltreated, or hunted, believing everything has a right to life and to live its life without harm.

He stopped to catch his breath. The incline had become steeper as he reached the halfway point up towards the top of the tor. He stopped and turned to look at the view behind him. *Spectacular!* He could see far out across many miles of countryside and farmland to the south, and in the distance he could see what looked like the coast with the sea sparkling in the sunshine.

Oh, how absolutely stunning.

He retrieved his phone from his fleece pocket and took several photos, and a video sweeping around. Then he stood for a while, admiring the view. How peaceful, no noise whatsoever, except for a few birds twittering as they swooped about overhead, and the distant mooing of a cow. He took three deep, mindfulness breaths and continued walking up towards the tor.

A short while later, he was exploring the huge granite boulders on top of the tor and climbed onto the highest one. He stood quietly admiring the views again. He was surrounded by Dartmoor. To the north and west, in the far away distance he could see a few cars, which reminded him of the Minibox cars he played with as a child, whizzing them along a track. The cars he could see were silently travelling along a distant road, to somewhere tucked into the moor. He had no idea what was where yet. To the south, he could see a bit more of the coast from this elevation—towards the sparkling, blue sea. To the east he looked over Little Beliton, the fields and to the moors beyond. What a picturesque little village it was. It looked exactly like a model village his grandparents had taken him to for a day out when he was little, which he's sure inspired his love of building LEGO® houses ... still. And probably because he had had fun building them with his grandad, who had been a builder. He felt a warm, comfortable feeling recalling these memories.

Once again, he took photos and videos with his phone and figured he'd soon be back with his camera. He'd come often, he was sure. This place felt grounding—connecting him with the earth and nature.

Despite the sunshine, the breeze blowing across this high vantage point felt chilly, so he climbed down to find a sheltered sunny spot to sit awhile. He fancied his coffee and a snack, and to just rest quietly. Easily achieved—a large flat sheltered rock provided a seat and picnic table. Afterwards, he began losing himself in his thoughts while doing some sketching and reading his journal.

Time passed and the sun moved further west, indicating that it was approaching late afternoon. He glanced at his watch to check the time. Nearly four o'clock. He stowed everything back in his rucksack and walked around the tor back to the spot he arrived at, and began retracing his steps downhill towards the village. He felt relaxed. A couple of hours in a beautiful setting, with nothing to do except sketch and let his mind wander, wherever it wanted to go, had had a positive effect.

He passed the field where he'd watched the cows, which was now empty. *I guess they've gone for milking,* he thought. He continued along the path towards the top of the lane and home.

* * *

WEDNESDAY SOON CAME AROUND and the funeral. Marc was dreading it. The words "Joan's only living relative" circulated constantly in his head and he knew he'd be scrutinised, the centre of attention, and he hated that.

It was a sunny, spring day again, which somehow felt appropriate. James had offered moral support and would meet him on The Green. The funeral directors had organised everything, including the outside catering company to provide the cream tea. Marc learned that a cream tea was Joan's favourite and that's why she requested it. People could enjoy it while reminiscing about past teas with her maybe, as Joan organised many of them for charity and church events.

Marc and James stood outside awaiting the hearse. People meandered past towards the church porch, glancing in their direction, probably already speculating about the Mysterious Nephew. Some gave a polite smile, or nod of greeting, but did not stop to chat.

'The church will be full,' said James, 'just about the whole village will be here, but the church warden will have reserved seats for us, and Lucy, of course.' With that, the hearse appeared in the lane and pulled over stopping by the entrance gate.

Lucy appeared from the direction of the school. 'Hi James, hi Marc,' she said. 'Are you ready for this?'

'Hi Lucy, yes. I think it's time to go in,' James replied.

'Hi Lucy,' said Marc. They crossed to the church as the coffin was being carefully lifted out of the car.

The service proceeded, followed by the burial in the churchyard.

Joan had at last joined her beloved Simon. Then onto the Wake in the parish hall. 'Are you okay?' Lucy asked Marc.

'Yes, I guess so. You?'

'Yes thanks. It's sad. She was such a kind, caring lady, and it's a shame she got sick with this Covid thing. She'd had her jabs, but I guess always helping others she might have put herself at risk, especially if the protection started to wane, or if she had an underlying unknown health problem,' said Lucy.

'Yes, I understand it's happened to many people,' said Marc.

'They're leaving the doors open in the village hall for air flow as it's a nice day, and everyone will be seated while the tea is served. I guess people will drift outside into the garden to chat and mix afterwards. Luckily, it's a pleasant day,' said Lucy.

'Thank you for everything you've done with these arrangements,' said Marc.

Lucy smiled. 'If you thank me again, I'll scream. Joan put her plans in place. I would have helped her if she'd wanted me to, she's been like a second mother to me and perhaps I was company for her. It was an arrangement that benefitted both of us. And maybe, over the last few years, I got to know her best. It's wonderful to see that she got the send-off she wanted.'

'Uh-huh, tha...'

Lucy smiled, 'There you go again! Let's go and get this done.'

Marc stood to one side to allow Lucy to pass through the door first and he followed. James waved them over to join him at a table laden with a tier of plates loaded with scones and dishes of jam and clotted cream. They sat down and a waitress brought a tray with the tea.

'Just a tip,' James said, conspiratorially, 'you have to eat the scones with jam and cream. Traditionally Devonshire folk are supposed to spread the cream on and dollop the jam on top, but I'm a rebel and do it the other way round. That way you have more clotted cream. But, be prepared for scowls.' He grinned. 'Don't worry, it's just traditional banter with the Cornish—no one takes it seriously. I just thought I'd warn you.'

Marc chuckled, 'Thanks for the tip. As if I don't have enough to worry about.'

'Just laugh it off. People will be curious about you, but they're friendly,' said Lucy.

Lucy glanced around the room and Marc noticed she suddenly looked serious. 'What's the matter?' he asked.

'Nothing. ... My mum, Maggie, is over there. I haven't seen her for a few weeks, that's all. We occasionally meet for a coffee and a chat in the coffee shop, but Dick's with her.' Lucy continued looking around the room acknowledging greetings from people.

'So far, so good,' said James. The buzz of people chatting continued, and a few people started going outside. As people passed them, they'd offer their condolences and welcome Marc. 'Let's go outside and find a bench,' said James.

'I'll catch up with you,' said Lucy, 'I'm going to speak to mum. She's on her own right now.'

Outside was a pretty garden with picnic benches and raised flowerbeds, bursting with spring flowers. 'This is lovely,' said Marc.

'Yes. It started off as a community project to provide an outdoor meeting space supporting social distancing. It's become an often used social space. If the weather isn't great, they put up an awning. It was another project Joan supported and helped to organise.'

'I'm sure it will get plenty of use. It's really lovely.'

'It's the venue for events such as community barbecues, and music evenings with a local band providing entertainment. And of course, it's hired for private events—weddings, etc. People are coming up with great ideas for using it. Lucy brings children over from the school to plant seeds, and last summer they grew tomatoes here and sold them to raise money for the school. Joan was involved with that too, being a governor at the school.'

Busy lady, Marc thought, *was she ever at home?* He was in awe of everything Joan did and wondered if perhaps she had set a precedent for the next manor resident. He looked around the room and saw Lucy talking with a lady, who he presumed was her mum. He noticed a man sidling into the seat next to Lucy. Marc read Lucy's body language; she bristled and looked very uncomfortable. 'Who's that guy by Lucy?'

James looked across. 'Ah that's Maggie, Lucy's mum, and her partner Dick. He's the landlord of The Fox on the Green. I don't think Lucy likes him very much. She always refuses to go there.'

Lucy got up and returned to sitting with Marc and James. She sat down and closed her eyes for a few seconds, breathing deeply. 'Are you okay, Lucy?' Marc asked.

'Yes sure. I'll go back to school in about ten minutes. The supply teacher covering me might appreciate some help with the usual end of day chaos. I know the routine. In fact, I'll go now. I'll see you later.'

'Okay. See you later.'

'I think we can slip off now too,' said James. 'That wasn't so bad, was it? Lots of welcomes.'

They got up and left quietly, back through the hall where The Cream of the Crock catering team were clearing up and loading the van. 'Hi Debbie, this is Marc. Marc, Debbie.'

'Hi, Marc,' said Debbie. 'Sorry for your loss. It all seemed to go well, for you.'

'Hello Debbie. Yes, all fine and thank you for the lovely tea.'

'You're welcome.' Debbie carried on clearing up.

James and Marc continued outside. 'Thank you for everything James. You've done far more than most solicitors would do.'

'No worries, I'm a member of the village community and you and I seem to get on anyway. Are you staying around here for a bit? Perhaps we can go and check out one of my surfing venues at the weekend? Just a look, no cold water involved.'

'That sounds great, thanks.'

'I'll see you on Saturday morning, if not before.'

They parted company at the bridge. 'Bye,' said Marc.

* * *

LATER IN THE EARLY EVENING, Marc had prepared dinner for Lucy and himself. A lasagne ready to bake. He was getting concerned though, because Lucy hadn't arrived home when she said she'd be back. At first, he shrugged and thought, *Ah well, she's a free agent. We both said we'd do our own thing.* However, a quarter of an hour more passed, and he had second thoughts. *I'm going to walk to the school and make sure she's okay.* He put on a jacket and left.

When he reached the junction, near the bridge, he saw a man walking quickly up the opposite road away from him. *I'm sure that's Dick*, he thought as he turned right and walked up towards the school.

The school appeared to be locked up and empty, but he tried the door anyway as he could see a light on. Perhaps the caretaker was there? It was open, so he went in. He walked up the corridor towards a lit-up window. It was a window in an office door. He peeped in and saw Lucy sitting at a desk with her back towards him. It looked as if she was crying. He knocked softly on the door and cracked it open. Lucy swung around sharply, wiping her eyes. 'Marc.'

'Hi Lucy, are you alright?' Marc said, as he tentatively stepped into the room.

'Um, yes thanks. I was doing some marking and lost track of time, that's all,' said Lucy, sniffing.

'Marking is upsetting you?'

'No. I just had an argument with someone, that's all. I don't like conflict. It upsets me.'

'Yea, me too. Who upset you?'

'Someone who's been causing trouble for years, which is why Joan gave me a home.'

'Who?'

'It's awkward…' Lucy paused, 'it's my mum's partner, Dick.'

'Oh. Can I help?'

'No, thanks. It's something I've got to deal with.'

'That worries me if you feel you've got to deal with someone. I respect your privacy, but if you ever need support, or someone to listen, I'm here. Okay?'

'Thanks. Hey, I've finished this marking now. We'll go home. I need a glass of wine.'

'Sure, dinner's prepared. I'll wait while you do what you need to do.'

BACK AT HOME, with the lasagne in the oven, Marc opened a bottle of wine and poured two glasses while Lucy went to change. He was thinking about the day. The funeral had gone well, the Wake wasn't quite the ordeal been he'd expecting. People had been welcoming: Are you moving to the village? Are you selling? What are your plans? If you need any building work done, or whatever, let me know. He put the little pile of business cards on the worktop as he mused. *What bothers me most though, is what upset Lucy. She was quite happy with James and me until she went to talk with her mum. I wonder what's wrong.*

Lucy breezed back into the room. 'Wine—you read my mind.' Marc passed a glass to her. 'Cheers!'

Marc replied, 'Cheers! Garlic bread and salad with the lasagne, okay?'

'Lovely. Nice to come home to a cooked meal again.'

Marc laughed. 'You haven't tasted it yet. You might change your mind.'

'Smells scrummy, I'm looking forward to it.'

'Let's relax while it cooks. About twenty minutes left.'

They flopped onto the sofas in the lounge. 'What a day. It all went well, didn't it?' said Lucy.

'It did. Many people told me about their memories of Joan and how much she helped people. I'm worried she's blazed a trail I can't follow.'

'Don't worry. Just get to know the community and they'll tell you what goes on.'

'Yes, sure. I'm certain I can help supporting some community things … I'm quite handy with a barbecue,' Marc grinned. 'I just need some time to sort my head out, I've a lot of personal stuff I'm working through right now. I don't want to rush making decisions I'll regret later.'

'Definitely. Take your time. If you need someone to listen, or bounce ideas off, I'm here.'

'Cheers.' They paused sipping their wine.

'I'll go and check the lasagne and put the garlic bread in. Go and sit at the table in a few minutes and your dinner will be served.' Marc left the room.

Lucy watched him, thinking, *he's a really nice guy. Quiet. Good looking and friendly. I feel comfortable with him.* She went into the dining room and found the table laid including a small vase of primroses. She smiled and sat down.

Marc came in carrying a bowl of salad. He grinned. 'Like them?'

'Sure.'

'Home grown… I found them in the garden.'

'It's the thought that counts.'

Marc left the room and returned with the lasagne bubbling in the dish. He placed it on the table mat and went to fetch the basket of bread, while Lucy helped herself to some food.

Marc returned and offered the bread. 'Bon appetite, enjoy.'

CHAPTER 3

One afternoon, after Marc finished working, he decided he'd take a look in the filing cabinet near the desk. He would see what he could learn about the running of the house. It was meticulously organised, with paperwork going way back to the time when Simon's parents were alive. It was interesting to skim read as he began to flip through it.

Part of his inheritance included the business of the leasing of fields and that was all filed and entered manually in a ledger. James was still working through the legal work of the estate to calculate the dreaded inheritance tax, so he didn't really know exactly how much the estate was worth yet. But he could tell it would be a reasonable amount.

Already he was coming up with development ideas, such as converting two of the barns, and he would also like to do something with the attached shippon. Extend it upwards perhaps, to match the accommodation side. At the moment it was a dump for the load of old garden implements, many of them appeared beyond use. It needed properly assessing and clearing out.

In one folder he found some sketches of the house with the proposed conversion. *Simon must have done them*, he thought, *after all he was an architect, I wonder why he never did it?*

Later that evening, while having dinner, Lucy asked, 'Have you any thoughts about what you want to do yet?'

'I think my heart has. I love it here. It's so peaceful. I sit at a desk to do my work and glance up out of the window to beautiful views. I really think it makes sense to live here and take over running this place. I'll have a chat with my team leader at work and make sure remote working isn't likely to change before I finally make up my mind though.'

'What about your flat?' asked Lucy.

'I rent it, so that's easy, I don't have the worry of selling. I guess it depends on the outcome of my chat with work. I'll have to go and organise packing up and moving my things here. That's straightforward enough. Finding temporary storage space for it might be a bit tricky, particularly as I have a few more belongings that I need to remove from my parents' place too, now that sale is hopefully going through.'

'Crikey, you have got a lot to deal with right now.'

'I had been considering renting a storage unit, but now I have a free alternative here. I could clear out the shippon, it looks dry.'

'Good luck with that,' said Lucy. 'It's crammed full of old stuff and probably infested with creepy crawlies.'

'Probably, but it's a job that needs to be done.'

'Talk to Bertie, the gardener. He'd be able to tell you what's of any use and what can be scrapped. He'll be here next week. Joan had an arrangement with him to come once a fortnight, to keep on top of what she couldn't manage.'

'Ah, thanks. I'll have a chat with him. I started looking through the filing cabinet earlier. Did you know that at one time Simon and Joan were planning an extension? A roof lift of the shippon.'

'No, I didn't. Joan never talked about plans like that. She never really stopped grieving for Simon, I think. She was a capable, intelligent lady but rather than worry about what might have been, she just got more and more involved with village life in the present. I guess it kept her busy, her mind occupied, and motivated. It gave her a reason to keep getting up in the morning, and meeting people she knew stopped her feeling quite so lonely.'

'Yes, I suppose so,' Marc agreed.

'Would improvements be something you might consider doing?'

'Possibly. The house is spacious and comfortable, if a bit tired and in need of updating, and with the way the world is going, I wonder perhaps if modern eco technologies could be incorporated. I know roof solar panels would definitely not be possible, aesthetically or practically on a thatched roof and certainly wouldn't get planning approval,' Marc laughed, 'But maybe other strategies could be explored.'

'Interesting. I hadn't marked you out as an eco-warrior. Yes, I think you're right. I know climate issues bothered Joan, but she was past doing much here at her age. Anyway, wasn't your dad something to do with building? I think she thought he'd come up with some ideas when he inherited the place.'

'Yes, he started out working for his dad, Joan's brother, and learning the building trade. But he followed his own interests building up a rental property portfolio business in partnership with my mum. I guess Joan thought leaving it to people who know the business was sensible.'

'What happened to them?'

'They were both killed in a car accident back in January. A drunk driver caused the accident. The police report stated that their car was pushed off the road and it rolled down an embankment.'

'I'm so sorry. That's very sad. To lose them both so suddenly and young?'

'Yeah, mid-fifties and living life to the full.' He paused. 'Life cut short.'

They finished their meal and cleared up. 'I have marking to do,' said Lucy. 'I'll go to my room and work, then have an early night.'

'Sure, night night.'

Marc retreated to the lounge to relax in front of the television. Perhaps there was something mildly entertaining on for a means of escape for his brain for a while.

Text message: Bleep, Bleep.

From James: Still up for exploring a surfing beach this weekend? Weather forecast good. Nice bit of bracing sea air and a walk?

Marc's reply: Yes, sounds good.

James: Pick you up at nine on Saturday.

Marc: Great.

He settled down to watch a film.

* * *

SATURDAY ARRIVED, and James and Marc were walking along the beach at Polzeath. 'I love this beach,' said James. 'It's a good place to forget about everything and just watch the waves for a while. Especially when you're waiting to catch one.'

There were a surprising number of hardy surfers in the water. It was a lovely sunny day again with a clear blue sky, but there was also a chilly onshore breeze. They stood watching, enjoying the fresh air and James explained a few basics of surfing. Marc had always enjoyed watching big breaking waves and saw them as connecting with nature. Surfing them must be exciting. Challenging.

Eventually, they strolled back up the beach towards the road. 'There's a cafe just up here. They do tasty bacon rolls,' said James.

'That sounds good. My shout,' said Marc.

They sat at an outside table enjoying their brunch. 'Do you fancy a go at surfing sometime then?' asked James.

'Yes, I do. I'll have to get kitted out. I'm not brave when it comes to cold water.'

'Me neither. Yes, get a wet suit, but you'll be too busy learning to catch waves and getting to stand up on the board to worry about the temperature too much.'

Marc laughed. 'Yes, it looks tricky and needs a good level of fitness.'

James said, 'Done? We'll go for a drive down the coast a bit and I'll show you the area. It's lovely round here, especially this time of year when it's quiet. Have you any thoughts about what you want to do?'

'I've got some ideas, but nothing final yet. There's so much going round in my mind and I'm feeling quite lost. I don't want to make any quick decisions if I'm not sure what to do, and I've no family left to consult. No guidance. Whilst I realise that sets me free to do whatever I feel is right, it's also a bit scary that I might make the wrong decisions. It's my future.'

'I don't envy you. Obviously, I know some of it as I originally tracked you down through the solicitor dealing with your parents' estate. If you want to talk, you can bounce ideas off me. I'm a good listener ... so I've been told.'

'Thanks. Yes, I picked up on that. My parents were good businesspeople and built up a portfolio of rental properties, as property developers. Dad was good at project managing—organising teams of builders and he had some practical skills himself. Mum was more focussed on interior design and doing the paperwork. They were an efficient team. They had contacts with tradesmen who worked for them, and a rental agency business that deals with the clients. There are still two houses currently undergoing work, which I could either add to the portfolio and rent them out when they're complete, or just flip them and sell them on the open market. So, I don't know what to do with all that and I don't know the business. And now, I seem to have been given the responsibility of following a trail Joan has blazed. I don't think I can be anything like as good as she was. And then there's my career, which I love, and my flat in London. Many big dilemmas and deciding what to do.'

'Heck, you have had a rush of problems to manage in a short space of time. Want to talk about it?' said James.

'Please. Maybe you have different perspectives that I haven't considered?'

'You say you don't really know the building trade well enough to carry on your parents' business. I think, if it was me, I'd probably sell the properties currently being worked on, to reduce my responsibilities. How good is your letting agent for managing the rental portfolio? Have you seen what services they cover? It's not just about finding tenants and collecting rent, it's also about managing property, inspections, maintenance, and repairs.'

'Yes, I figured that. I guess I need to go and have a meeting with the agent to discuss it all. The good thing is that I've just received an offer for my parents' house, if it completes this time. The first sale fell through. So, I must get cracking with sorting out and emptying the house and collect the last of my belongings they kept for me. I was considering renting a storage unit, but now I'm thinking of clearing out and cleaning up the shippon for storage for the time being.'

'That's a great idea. I've seen some of what's in there and I can put you in touch with someone who loves antique farm machinery and old garden tools,' said James.

'That's useful, thanks. Lucy suggested chatting with Bertie too, the guy who helps with the garden.'

'Good one! He's a great guy and he'll be able to help you a lot.'

'I'll arrange a meeting with my manager at work and make sure they're keeping the remote working, and not returning to office-based work now lockdowns are phasing out. If so, there's no reason to keep the flat on. It's rented, so depending on the outcome of that meeting, I can follow what my heart's telling me and move down here. This week it's felt good to feel ... grounded. And, if I can sort out the shippon for storage, for the time being, it will be great.'

'I think you're doing better than you give yourself credit for. You've only been down here for a week, sussing everything out, and you've fallen in love with the place. I get that, the same thing happened for me. You have got a lot of things not entirely within your control until the legal work is done and it's finally all yours, so it's hard to make decisions. Go on a fact-finding mission and talk to people. See what the letting agent thinks of the two incomplete properties too. He wants commission for letting them and extra income always comes in handy, eh?'

'Yes. I've got a well-paid job, which I really enjoy. I've inherited my parents' business once that is finally sorted, and now I've inherited Joan's estate and we've already discussed potential development ideas there. I've definitely been offered some different opportunities for my life direction recently. I just need to make sure I choose the right path. I found some interesting paperwork this week,' Marc said.

'Oh yes, go on.'

'Sketches and drawings of home improvements Simon must have done. He was an architect, which is how he met Joan. My grandad was a builder and Joan was his sister. Grandad must have known Simon or worked with him sometimes. Perhaps they socialised?'

'Heh, heh, being involved with property is in your genes then. It's your destiny. I understand how you must feel though. It's a lot to take in if you've never been involved with the business.'

'No, I wasn't. I left school and went to uni, then got the IT job with the bank in London and settled there renting my flat. I'm not entirely clear about the processes of buying and selling property.' Marc paused. 'And that's another decision. My flat. Luckily, I rent it so that's more straightforward. I'll do the house clearing first and then, I think, the first thing I need to do is make sure remote working is remaining for the future and then the flat decision is an easy one to make.'

'I agree. How is it working out with you and Lucy?'

'We're fine. Compatible, amicable house-sharing friends. She's an easy person to get along with, but I am worried about her. There's something troubling her. She doesn't want to talk about it, but I have offered to help, if I can.' Marc said.

'Lucy is a very strong, independent person. I don't know her backstory, but I think Joan offered her a solution to a problem by giving her a home. Plus, I think Joan was lonely and Lucy was … good company. A companion.'

'I agree, from what I've learned so far. Thanks for listening, James. Let's just enjoy exploring Cornwall for the rest of the day. I'll let my brain mull it all over.'

'Yes, we've come quite a way down the coast. Let's explore Padstow. We can drive back up the dual carriageway over Bodmin Moor and find a pub nearer home for dinner.'

* * *

LATER THAT EVENING Marc sat in front of the TV doodling ideas in his journal considering his options. He made a list of all the things he needed to do and people he needed to talk with. Chatting with James had helped calm his brain loops a bit and the one thing he knew was that no quick decisions had to be made, except for clearing his parents' house, and the most urgent priority to enable that, was to clear out the shippon.

He felt quite chuffed for making one decision, at last. He'd do that task this week and have a chat with Bertie.

CHAPTER 4

A man arrived early on Monday morning and Marc went out to the garden to meet him. 'Hello, are you Bertie?'

'Hello, Marcus. Yes. I saw you at your auntie's funeral. You have my condolences.'

'Marc—to my friends. Thank you. I've been hoping to have a chat with you.'

'Ok-a-y,' Bertie said hesitantly.

'I really don't know anything about gardening, let alone the country ways. I'm happy to offer you more hours, or days of work. I don't know exactly what you arranged with Joan, but can we negotiate?'

'Yes, mate. I was worried that you were going to sell up or didn't want my services anymore. I'm more than pleased to do more work for you,' Bertie smiled, clearly relieved.

'Wonderful. We can talk about that, and wages. As I say, I know nothing about gardening and how it works, but I'm willing to learn. Can we discuss some ideas and things like that?'

'Yes, of course. Sometimes I suggested ideas for the garden to Joan, but she knew what she wanted. It's a lovely garden and there's lots more it could do for you. There's a lovely hidden vegetable plot, to grow-your-own. It just needs some clearing and organising.'

'Well, that's something I hadn't considered, or I've even seen yet. Great idea! And I understand you're the guy to talk to about all that clutter in the shippon too. What are all those rusty items? Are they of any use, or can we just clear it out?'

'I've not been in there for a long time. Let's have a look. It's probably just as well to do that today, I think it's going to rain anyway.'

Marc looked up at the grey sky and swore he felt a raindrop on his nose. 'What I've got in mind, for the time being, is to sort it out and give it a clean-up. I need to store some personal belongings in there.'

They walked up the garden towards the house. Bertie said, 'Hey, that's good. People have been wondering if you were going to stay or sell up. You're going to move here then?'

'Yes, I think so. This last week or so, I feel ... connected with the area, I love it here. The house is pretty too, and there's a lot of potential for improvements. I realise I have a lot to learn about the country ways, the village, and how to manage an old house—a listed building, and the land.'

'I can help you with the gardens and guide you. Anything you want to know, just ask.'

'Thanks. I've been thinking about those two larger barns—they might be suitable for converting? And the smaller building, at the end of the garden ... perhaps that can be turned into a shed and greenhouse space? The building is all open down one side at the moment and I thought reroof it and put windows between the timber supports and the stone area behind, create some storage for garden tools and machinery, maybe?' They reached the covered passageway between the house and the shippon and continued talking.

'Ah, the linhay, the old stables. Yes, I reckon that's quite likely possible. Linhays are converted into many different types of buildings. Stables. Garages. Hay barns. The cafe area of the village shop, for example, that was a linhay. It would be good to see the old stables put to a practical use again. These old buildings are an important part of our heritage,' Bertie said.

'Ah, yes, I like that and it's what inspired my thinking.'

Bertie added, 'There's a spring that starts up on the moor that runs through that area too, in a gulley. 'Twas handy for the horses originally, I expect. If that area was cleared of the years of accumulated debris, we can see how it is. Eventually the spring goes underground and comes out in the village and empties into the river.'

Marc's brain was ticking away. 'Don't people use streams and rivers for generating electricity?'

'Sometimes, yes, they install a water turbine. Sometimes springs provide water for household use too,' said Bertie. 'The water has to be tested regularly.'

'I'll have a think about all this and find someone who knows about these things and see what we can do. In the meantime, let's sort this out.'

'You could try talking to Harry Barker, in the village, about buildings—he's an expert. Let's see what's here. I think there are a few antique items that might be salvaged. A lot of it is junk though, and beyond use. We might need a skip to get rid of that.'

'We'll pile it up in the corner of the parking area outside for the time being and I'll look into hiring a skip.'

They worked hard all morning, stopping only briefly for a coffee, and braving the rain to take items outside ready to dump. The implements Bertie thought would be of interest to a restorer were put to one side. They stopped for a quick bite to eat for lunch and carried on working all afternoon. Marc enjoyed Bertie's interesting company. They chatted as they worked and he learned a quite a bit about farming and gardening.

By the end of the afternoon, there was a clean dry area to store boxes, which was the primary goal. In addition, there were quite a few items stacked to one side of the shippon and a big pile of junk outside ready for a skip.

'Proper job!' Bertie exclaimed, joking in an exaggerated local accent.

Marc laughed. 'I get that one—Great work! Thank you.'

'Okay, Marc, I'll come back on Wednesday to do the gardening I planned to do today. Glad we found something else useful to do.'

'Yes, as I said, I need more help. Wednesday's fine. Thank you for today, it's been really good.'

The rain had stopped, and Bertie climbed onto his bike. 'No problem,' he called. 'Bye.'

'Bye.'

Marc watched him leave thinking; *I understand the advantage of working in the village where you live. No commuting involved. Just a nice walk, or cycle, and you've reached your destination. Exercise done in the process and no polluting the planet. Heck, I do sound like an eco-warrior!*

WHEN LUCY GOT BACK from school, Marc was preparing dinner again. 'I could get used to this, thanks,' she smiled warmly at Marc as he passed her a glass of wine.

'Had a good day?' he asked.

'Yes thanks. You?'

'Sure. A really good day. Come and see.' Marc led the way to the shippon and opened the door.

Lucy stepped in, 'Gosh, just look at the amount of space you've created. I wondered what you'd been doing when I walked past that huge pile of junk outside.'

'I can't take all the credit for it, Bertie helped me. He knew what most of the stuff was used for and whether it was likely to be scrap or salvageable.'

'Yes, he's good. He's the village's own Alan Titchmarsh when it comes to gardening. He's always willing to help and offer advice. He helps with the school activities and over at the village hall too. The children think he's great fun. I'm glad you've met him.'

'Yes, he's a hard worker and I learned a lot today. I think he was worried his job had ended here and visibly cheered up when I offered him more hours.'

'I'm sure he was happy. I have a feeling he and his wife are struggling a bit financially. His wife has health issues, not sure what, and they have two young children at the school.'

'Ah, that would explain it. I told him I'm going to investigate converting the old stables into a shed-come-greenhouse unit. He thought it was a great idea and sounded keen to help. And, you'll laugh at this, he told me about a stream that flows down from the moor through that area of the garden and we chatted briefly about water turbines.'

Lucy laughed. 'Love it! Another eco idea. I'm sure a bit of research will give you plenty to think about to do here. Anyway, I'm impressed with the clear out.'

'Let's have dinner,' said Marc, leading Lucy out and back to the kitchen.

As Marc hadn't looked at his work all day, after dinner he sat at the desk and logged in and started working. Lucy had marking to do and retreated to the dining room table to spread it out.

It occurred to Marc that he was really enjoying this change of lifestyle. His work was very satisfying as he really enjoys getting stuck into new projects and systems, and designing them to work well. Today, he'd really enjoyed doing some manual work and learning about country living. He realised he was convincing himself, more and more, that he was ready for this change, this opportunity to do something good. He really hoped that he could choose this new path into the future, if there aren't any hitches.

* * *

THE NEXT WEEK, he'd taken leave from work to go to his parents' house. He had to empty it. It made him sad to go there, because of the memories of his mum and dad's antics at their parties and barbecues. Every time he'd been recently, he visualised them there. Now his enduring memories would be of clearing the house and boxing up belongings: to donate some to charities, some to keep—framed photos and items with specific memories.

When he got as far as the loft, there were his belongings, such as his lovely LEGO® kits he remembered working on with his grandad. More memories. Some kits were still made up. He went out to buy several lidded crates from the local DIY store to ensure he could move them without losing any pieces.

He found a box full of his old favourite books that he'd wanted to keep. And his tennis racket, which brought back memories of winning the tennis tournament at school one year, and he found the trophy he was awarded for it too.

Next, he discovered a box of baby items and a photo album. *Well, I never*, he thought, *Mum was more sentimental than I gave her credit for. She kept all this.*

He glanced through the photo album and was surprised to see more photos of him with his grandma and grandad than with his parents. When he thought about it though, perhaps he shouldn't have been surprised. He remembered he did spend a lot of time with his grandparents, especially before he started school. That was when he spent time with Joan too. Once again, he recalled the afternoons he spent painting with Joan, and building the houses with his grandad. He felt mellow.

I wish I could remember activities with my parents. What were they so busy doing? Building up the business, I suppose. How else would they have afforded to send me to boarding school?

Box by box the loft was emptied and taken downstairs and sorted into piles for their final destinations. Luckily, he'd emptied clothes from wardrobes and drawers on a previous visit. He had bagged it all up and taken the bags to a charity shop. His old bedroom had long since been reutilised as a guest bedroom, so it was fairly empty already, as were the other two bedrooms. Just the furniture to be removed.

It was when he went downstairs to the office, he had more things to sort out. The laptop had already been removed. He'd needed it to find office documents, mail, and spreadsheets a couple of months ago. Tim, the solicitor, needed information off it to do the legal work. Marc wanted to keep in touch with their business contacts and those details were stored on it too.

He pulled out the desk drawers and bundled up paperwork and folders into boxes. He'd go through it later. He cleared bookshelves, racks of CDs and even found a carrying case of LPs. There was a pile of holiday brochures, which he didn't find surprising. His parents were always off somewhere. A week here, a weekend away there. He smiled when he thought about their excitement at going away again. They had certainly lived life to the full. He chucked the brochures into the recycling box.

Next, he opened the safe. Jewellery in boxes. Documents and certificates. A small amount of cash in envelopes—pounds and euros. And a small bundle of notebooks parcelled up with rubber bands. He piled it all into a crate. Most of the documents, including their Will and the house deeds, had been retrieved before and given to Tim for the legal work. Once empty, he left the safe door ajar with the keys in the lock ready for the next owner.

When it came to the kitchen and dining room, there was a massive amount of things to pack up. A complete dinner service, glasses—loads of glasses, kitchen equipment, pots and pans, and electrical items. So much. His mum had enjoyed cooking and usually did the catering for their parties, so the kitchen was well-equipped. He wrapped it all in bubble wrap and boxed it, then cleaned the cupboards.

He was so relieved to have had the foresight to hire a decent size van to move all the crates. He really didn't want to come back to the house again. He'd ask the estate agent to let house-clearance people in to move furniture out. He was donating it to charity.

He had a meeting with Tim, the solicitor, for a progress report on the legal work. The house sale was going through, and a completion date agreed. But the complete estate could not be finalised yet until Marc decided what to do about the property business portfolio. Marc admitted he still wasn't sure what to do and advised Tim that he was meeting the letting agent and the accountant for information and guidance before making a decision.

Marc had a meeting with, Claire, the letting agent. He wasn't entirely sure exactly what she managed, and he wanted clarity. He knew being a landlord had seemed lucrative once, but he got the feeling times had changed somewhat since his parents started up the business and gradually built it up over the years. He knew his parents' long-term plan was to build it up to maintain a decent income to retire early and have a good standard of living. Claire, it seemed, worked on their behalf for keeping the properties occupied and maintained, looked after the tenants' needs, collected rent, and so on, for her fees. However, he had no idea if the commission was fair or competitive. He promised he'd let Claire know his decision as soon as possible.

He organised a meeting with his dad's friend, Barry, who was in the same business, to see if he would give him some advice. He had so many questions: Should he keep the portfolio and let it tick over for an income? Should he add the two latest acquisitions once they're completed, or just sell them? Should he just sell up the whole lot and not have the worry?

Marc also met the accountant to discuss the business finances in order to work out what to do.

Everything constantly circulated in his mind, day and night. He felt overwhelmed and way out of his depth. He knew he had to make decisions to break the pressure.

He drove the van back to Devon loaded with his belongings and with a heavy heart.

*　*　*

A FEW DAYS LATER, everything had been stacked neatly in the shippon, and the rental van returned. Marc had tossed and turned every night and was not sleeping. He was feeling very down. Lucy was concerned.

'Is there anything I can do?'

'I'm afraid not. I must make decisions. The right decisions. And live by them.'

'What's the worst thing that can happen?'

'It seems I can either keep the business running as it has been, but I have no good understanding of it or whether my ignorance is being exploited, or whether it's a good opportunity to provide a passive income. Alternatively I can sell it all and have a complete break and stop worrying about it.'

'What does your heart feel? What's your intuition telling you?'

'To sell it all. I don't know enough about it, and the inheritance tax must be paid anyway.'

'I think, if it was me, I'd follow my heart. You have come up with ideas you want to do here that have fired your interest. You want to learn about and focus on them. This will be your main project and you'll develop your ideas as you go. At the time your parents died you had no idea you would be offered this alternative opportunity. I think to run both and do your job that you really enjoy is too much. Something has to give.'

'Yes, I think you're right. There's just one of me trying to take on two businesses that three or four people with the right skills, knowledge, and understanding used to run. I've always just lived an easy life of working for someone else and switching off when I'm not working. I have no one to think about but myself.' He paused, 'And the world has changed somewhat too.'

'If you'd really been interested in your parents' business, you would have picked that for a career and learned what you needed to from them. Or maybe chosen a career in the building trade, or trained to be an architect, or surveying, to be hands-on and learn project management, or the financial side and accountancy. But you didn't. You chose a completely different career path. Maybe it was a subconscious choice to avoid joining the business. So do you want a career change to it now?'

'Not really. I already think I can develop the manor, my new home, and maybe take on some community projects, like Joan used to do, and I can do my work, which I enjoy.

'So, what are you going to do then? I think, in your heart of hearts, you've actually made up your mind. It's committing to it is your problem,' said Lucy.

'You could well be right. Selling up means I have available finances I can invest here.'

'Exactly. Look, don't just do it because I said so, you must make up your own mind. I just hope I gave you a different perspective to think about. Why don't you talk to James too. See what he thinks.'

'Yes, I have. I will. Thank you,' said Marc. He knew it was a personality trait of his that his brain would keep on thinking.

CHAPTER 5

On Wednesday Marc met James in his office. James had good news for him; Joan's estate was at the point of being wound up and just needed his signature on various documents. Marc was pleased. This was one worry off his mind, and it had been straightforward. Beliton Manor was his.

'If only mum and dad's estate was so simple.' He sighed. 'Thanks for all your work, James.'

'No problem. How's it all going?'

Marc rolled his eyes. 'Apart from keeping me awake at night?'

'What's wrong? Can I help?'

'I would really appreciate having another chat with you, James. I'd value a different opinion … from a friend. You might give me another way of thinking about it.'

'Yes, no problem. When?'

'Are you free on Saturday? Come in the afternoon and stay for dinner. Do you like Indian food? I'm not a bad chef and can produce something tasty. I haven't poisoned Lucy yet, anyway.'

James smiled. 'Sounds great. Thanks. Yes, I saw her walking to school this morning, she looks fit and healthy. In fact, I'd say positively glowing.'

'Well, there you go then, my food is edible.'
'I look forward to it.'

MARC PREPARED the meal in advance, so the flavour could marinade and develop. He wanted to be free to talk. James arrived and brought some beers and wine. 'Hi Marc, dinner smells delicious. How's it going?'

'Hello, good thanks.'

James handed him the bag of drinks. 'Thought these would be welcome.'

'Cool, thanks.' Marc got out two beers and put the rest in the fridge.

'As it's a nice day, shall we go into the garden?'

'Yep, lead the way.'

They went down to the sunny decking patio where there were two rattan garden sofas. 'They're new,' said James. 'Very nice.' They sat down. 'So, how can I help?'

Marc told James about the information he'd gathered regarding his parents' business. 'My dilemma now is whether to sell some of it, or all of it. I can either learn the business and manage it and have an income, or sell it and let it go and stop worrying about it. I did as you suggested and talked to the various agents.'

'Do you know anything about property letting?'

'No. Apart from being a tenant in my flat in London. I don't know how it works from the landlord's point of view. How do you learn it if you don't know the right people well enough?'

'Is the property development business something that interests you?'

'Not really. I remember dad had problem tenants in the past. One didn't pay rent and when he was evicted, he had seriously damaged the property. I remember dad was fuming, but he was determined to deal with it and get it back into good liveable condition to rent out again. I couldn't cope with that kind of aggravation.'

'And what about the two houses that are still a work in progress?'

'Dad's friend Barry has taken over finishing the project for me. I'm grateful to him. He knows the business and they're both nearly done. Just the kitchen to be fitted in one, and a bathroom in the other. Final tweaks with colour schemes and paint, and they're ready to go. Then I must decide whether to add them to the rental portfolio and Claire will find tenants, and so on. Or I could just flip them. Sell them on the open market as renovated.'

'Okay. Here's my thinking. Do you really have the time, and do you want the hassle of running the business? Do you know how it all works? Yes, you've got a letting agent and an accountant who both know how your mum and dad ran it, but it still takes time and commitment. Living down here you're not available to pop round to sort out any problems for tenants. You don't know teams of reliable tradesmen there to help you and you've even handed over the project management to finish the two properties. You haven't got time for it, have you? It doesn't interest you either. You've got your work that you enjoy. You're inspired by this place and its potential, and who wouldn't be? You're not motivated to run the rental business, are you? You think you "should" out of loyalty to your parents, maybe?'

'It's pretty much what Lucy said.'

'I get that initially, once you dealt with the shock of your parents' deaths, you felt you should continue what they started. But why? Your heart isn't in it. It was their dream, not yours. You're not driven to do it, which is why you're agonising now, and you wouldn't have chosen to go to university pursuing a completely different career. If it really interested and energised you, you would have worked with your parents and learned the business with a view to taking over when they retired, or when they wanted to take more of a back seat, but they would still be available as mentors for you to consult for guidance. As it is, you feel as though you're stuck up a creek without a paddle.'

'Uh-huh, that just about sums up how I feel.'

'If it was me … I'd concentrate on what makes me want to get up in the morning to do it. You get immense job satisfaction from your work. You had a complete surprise of inheriting this place, you've got great ideas for it and you get really animated talking about them. It fires your enthusiasm. Focus on here. A couple of months ago, you were only thinking about your parents' business, and you had no idea that fate would present this opportunity to you and offer a different path for you to follow.'

'So, are you suggesting that I have to stop procrastinating and sell it all?'

'If it was me, yep, I'd sell it and invest the money. You never know, some other interesting opportunities might come your way around here that you might like to pursue. And you'd be able to. If you want to get into renting out homes you might even choose to acquire some Buy To Lets in the village, for instance. If properties are on your doorstep and you build the right connections, it would be easier to do. You're even thinking along those lines already talking about possibly converting the two barns here for a couple of holiday lets. Make your life simple. You haven't got enough hours in the day to keep commuting up there whenever you're summoned. Life's too short.'

'I was coming to that conclusion. Another beer?'

'Yes, thanks.'

Marc strolled back to the kitchen, thinking. *Yes, decision made. James has confirmed what my heart was telling me. Sell it and focus on developing my interests here in Little Beliton.*

The next thing to clarify is my London life.

* * *

MARC'S BOSS requested a meeting at the office, so he planned a few days away and would stay in his flat.

The meeting went well. Marc was promoted to team leader to manage a new project coming up, and there was no intention of ending the remote working. There would only be occasional meetings to attend face-to-face in the office and everything else would be conducted over video conferencing. Brilliant. Marc was pleased, it was the answer he hoped for.

He returned to his flat. Although nice, spacious, light, and airy, he hadn't missed it. He'd long been feeling being confined in a flat and rather claustrophobic. It didn't suit his nature. It felt wrong. But it was all he could afford when he graduated and secured a new job. Now it was time to move on.

He went through his belongings packing them up. There wasn't that much there really. Clothing he no longer wanted was welcomed by a local charity shop. The furniture came with the flat. All he needed to do was pack up any personal bits and pieces, and he was quite happy to leave some items for the next tenant. He contacted his landlord's agent and made arrangements to end the tenancy and loaded his belongings into his car.

A few days there was all he could stand now. The noise was getting to him, he'd got used to peace and quiet, and bird song. He was happy to be driving westbound. He got a warm fuzzy feeling as he thought *Home*.

'Thank you, Auntie Joan. I'm grateful and I will do you proud,' he said.

Nearing the end of his journey, he drove cautiously along the narrow lane into the village. Around a bend, the farmer he'd greeted on the first day he arrived was chugging down the lane driving his tractor. Marc crawled along behind him until Brian, the farmer, turned and they exchanged waves. Brian pulled into the lane where Marc had noticed the rustic farmhouse that first day. He grinned when he considered how very extra-cautious, he'd felt those few weeks ago. Now he was waving at someone in the village and knew his name. What a difference! It added to his sense of connectedness, of belonging. He entered the village and turned left at The Green into the lane leading home.

He turned into the driveway and hesitated, as he often did, to look at the scene in front of him. A beautiful house, the garden sweeping down the valley looking spectacular with colourful flower borders and mowed lawn. *Bertie has worked wonders. It looks lovely.*

Once he moved the new boxes into the shippon, adding them to the neatly stacked pile, he went on into the kitchen where Lucy was cooking. 'Hi Marc, good trip?'

'Yes, thanks. I made a decision too.'

'Let me guess ... you've moved out of your flat.'

'Yes, how did you guess?'

'I knew you weren't happy in London. And I saw you moving boxes in from your car. Big giveaway that one!' She passed him a glass of wine.

'I'm that transparent, am I? Thanks.' He took a sip and put it on the worktop. 'I've just got a few things to sort out and I'll have a quick shower and I'm ready to relax. Does that fit in with dinner plans?'

'Wonderful, see you in a bit.'

The clothes Marc brought home he sorted out between hanging them in his wardrobe and putting them in the laundry basket. He put his laptop on his desk ready to work and went for his shower. Back in his bedroom he opened the window and took a few deep breaths of the fresh country air. And the peace—all he could hear was a few birds twittering.

Home.

He felt calmer. He was feeling better about making a few decisions. More relaxed. Settled. He could now get on with his new life path and focus on here. He stood a few minutes longer enjoying the view, then turned and went downstairs, back to the kitchen. He retrieved his wine and asked, 'Do you want any help?'

'No, it's all under control,' said Lucy.

'How's your week been?'

'Okay, thanks. I took groups of children over to the village hall garden to plant some flowers Bertie helped them to propagate. That was fun.'

'Bertie's been and had a lovely session here too. Mowed lawns and trimmed hedges. And he managed the skip hire,' said Lucy.

'It's great to see that pile of junk we cleared out of the shippon has finally gone,' said Marc.

'Yes, the skip people came a couple of days ago and now it's looking lovely. Are you ready for dinner?'

'I certainly am. I'll pay Bertie a bonus for doing that horrid job.'

They went into the dining room.

* * *

AFTER DINNER, Marc checked his emails. Good news from Tim. The sale of his parents' house was completed.

Barry mailed to say the two houses were now finished and ready to go on the market. He had organised valuations with a couple of estate agents.

Just the portfolio to go and an auctioneer estate agent working with Claire to gain access to write up the details and take photos. Two of the tenants asked if they could put in offers to buy their homes. Claire was working with him for those valuations too.

Marc thought, *Well I never, this is going too straightforwardly. What problem will arise? Something will, I'm sure. The good thing is, Lucy and James were right—making decisions and following my heart is the right thing to do. I hope I can soon sleep soundly again.*

* * *

MARC DID SLEEP SOUNDLY. He got up early the next day to review his new work project and begin planning the teamwork. By early afternoon, he was ready for something different and he decided to walk up to the tor again and take his sketchbook. Some chill-out time would be good.

He gathered the items together in his backpack—including a drink and snacks and set off up the lane to the bridle path. The cows were in the field again, lazily munching the luscious green grass while they watched Marc looking over the gate admiring their lovely golden coats and beautiful brown eyes.

Marc turned and continued up to his new favourite place on the tor. He wandered around to it and sat on the rock. He retrieved his pencils from his backpack and settled down to work.

After a while he took a break and stopped for his drink and an apple. He noticed a couple walking towards him, but still some way off. They hadn't looked up to see where he was sitting and were mucking about having fun as they walked. Then they must have reached a gulley; the man jumped across it but the lady hesitated. The man leaned forward and held out his hand towards the lady to encourage her to jump across. She took some persuading until eventually she took his hand and as she jumped, he supported her across and steadied her. He pulled her into a cuddle, and they kissed.

Marc felt envious. It must be lovely to have a special lady to share your life with and to love. He thought about Lucy. He liked her a lot and felt they got on really well, as friends and compatible housemates. No wonder Joan had offered her a home because there was no doubt she was great company, kind and thoughtful, and Joan must have been lonely after Simon died.

Marc still wondered about the circumstances of Lucy moving in with Joan. He'd noticed that Lucy didn't see her mum very often, even though they both lived in the village. Just occasional meetings in the coffee shop, and that was about it. He wondered why Lucy didn't go to The Fox on the Green to visit her. But then again, he hadn't gone there yet, not even for a drink with James. Pubs weren't really his thing. Perhaps it was the same for Lucy.

The couple disappeared out of sight and they were obviously heading up the path to the top of the tor, as he had. He could hear them laughing. Next time he saw them they were standing on the big boulder at the highest point of the tor that he had enjoyed. He heard several "Wows" and then silence. He understood that. They were admiring the amazing views.

Today it was easy to see the sea, which shimmered under a cerulean sky. A few skylarks swooped overhead twittering to each other. Apart from that, silence. Peace. Marc turned his attention back to his art, getting lost in the scene he was trying to create. He was feeling quite pleased with his progress. He'd brought his paintbox this time, to wash some colours over his sketch.

The next thing he heard was footsteps on the nearby rocks. 'Oh hello,' said the lady. 'We didn't see you there.'

'Hello. No problem. It's a fabulous place with gorgeous views and it would be selfish to keep it all to myself. Made for sharing.'

'Do you live round here?' she asked.

'Yes, I do.'

'You lucky thing! We're just visiting … on holiday.'

'Ah-ha, good. I hope you're enjoying yourselves.'

The man replied this time. 'Oh yes. We love it.'

Marc finished the conversation, 'Have a good time.' He gathered his belongings into his backpack. 'I'll leave you to enjoy it, bye.'

'Bye,' they said, settling into the spot Marc vacated as he started walking around the tor.

He back down the tor, along the bridle path past the field of cows, and along to the top of the lane towards home. It had been nice just to let his mind wander where it wanted to go, and the words, "You lucky thing" echoed in his brain.

CHAPTER 6

Walking home from school, Lucy was thinking about Marc. *I really admire how he's been coping with everything that has come his way recently. I'm happy to listen and offer a different perspective of looking at his dilemmas. It was good that James did too and now Marc seems more able to relax a bit having made some decisions—in his head, at least. It can't have been easy grieving at the same time, especially for his parents. He's beginning to adjust to his new lifestyle here, which might be just what he needs. A new start.*

On the other hand, Lucy was feeling uptight after Dick had cornered her in school that evening after the funeral, when Marc went looking for her. She was scared; he was up to his old tricks of making salacious threats. Luckily the caretaker had been around that evening and Dick hastily left. *Why has he started again?*

She carried on thinking. *Despite my toxic relationship with Dick, Mum seems happy with him. He gives Marty attention and occasionally takes him to activities, so they seem to get on okay. Marty is doing alright at school, I think. He's not in my class, thank goodness—teaching my half-brother wouldn't be good. Dick left me alone when Joan gave me a home. I think she warned him off, somehow. So, I suppose now she's died, he thinks he has a clear path again. Mum doesn't believe me when I tell her what he's like and she won't defend me. She just tells me not to cause trouble. When I do meet her lately, she's too busy trying to tell me to "get in there" with Marc—hint, hint. She says, "You'll be alright with him. Good looking wealthy man." How dare she try to control my life! Marc and I are getting on fine as friends and I don't want to screw that up. Anyway, where would I go?*

As she turned the bend in the road near the driveway, she saw Marc walking towards her from the direction of the moors. 'Hi Marc. Been for a nice walk?'

'Yes, I needed some peace to reconnect. I spoke to a couple of holidaymakers on the tor.'

'Ah, they start appearing this time of year.' They walked down the drive together. 'I'll cook tonight. Hungry?' Lucy said.

'It's all done. I made the bolognese sauce before I left, so it won't take long.' They arrived at the house. Marc asked, 'Do you know where the spring is that runs down to here from the tor?'

'Yes, I think so. I'll take you there and we'll walk down beside it.'

'Great. I've got some ideas.'

'Yes, Mr Eco Warrior!' She winked at him.

'I've got a few ideas in mind I want to explore, that's all.'

'Okay, I'm only teasing. Climate change and the environment is something I'm interested in learning about too, especially with projects for the children. It's becoming part of the curriculum. Lucy's phone rang and Marc stepped indoors to leave her some privacy.

'Hi Bertie. Everything okay?'

She listened.

'I'm so sorry. I hope Emily will be alright. How can I help you?'

She listened.

'Yes, of course. No problem. Would you like the children to come and stay here with me? You will probably be with Emily until late. The children will be able to get some sleep without being disturbed.'

She listened again.

'Give me five minutes and I'll call you back. Bye'

Lucy went indoors and found Marc in the kitchen. 'Marc, it was Bertie. Emily has been taken poorly again and he has to go and take her to hospital—I mentioned to you that she's not very well.'

'Yes, I remember.'

'It seems she's quite poorly. Would you mind if their two children come to stay tonight? They're good kids and won't misbehave.'

'Of course, no problem. I love kids.'

'I'll make up the beds for them and ask Bertie to drop them up. Thank you.'

'If they haven't had their evening meal, there's plenty of pasta bol to share.'

'Oh lovely, thank you. I'll call Bertie back.'

Lucy left the room and went upstairs to the spare bedroom with twin beds while calling Bertie back. Marc followed her a few minutes later. 'Do you need some help?'

'Thanks.'

THEY'D JUST FINISHED MAKING beds and returned to the kitchen, where Marc was boiling water for pasta when Bertie arrived with Oscar and Gemma. Bertie looked worried. 'Hello Marc, thank you so much for this. Emily's not feeling very well at all.'

'No problem, it will be fun. You told me about the children when we were clearing out. I'm happy to meet them.' He smiled at the children, 'Hello.'

'Hello, I'm Oscar and I'm in Miss Trethewey's class. I'm five.'

'Hello Oscar. I'm Marc. High five!'

'Hello, I'm Gemma and I'm seven.'

'Hello Gemma. I'm Marc. High five!'

Lucy said, 'I think here, at home, you can call me Lucy. At school though, I must be Miss Trethewey. Is that okay?'

'Yes,' replied the children.

'I'll take you upstairs and show you to your bedroom and the bathroom and you can settle in.' Lucy picked up Oscar's bag, while Gemma put her backpack on her shoulder and started up the stairs.

'You get off and focus on Emily, Bertie. Oscar and Gemma will be fine. We'll look after them and get them to school tomorrow morning,' said Marc.

'I really appreciate this ...,' said Bertie.

'Glad to help. Bye.'

'Bye.'

Lucy, Oscar, and Gemma returned downstairs a short while later. 'All settled in? Dinner's nearly ready,' said Marc. Lucy took the children through to the dining room and settled them down. Marc brought in the bowls of pasta bolognese and they began tucking into their tasty meal.

After they cleared up, they had a session of board games from Marc's new stash. He thought, *I knew these would come in handy one day!*

Once again, Lucy was impressed with Marc and his willingness to help. She saw a fun side of his character, playing the games and interacting with the children. While Lucy went and supervised the bedtime shower, Marc made mugs of hot chocolate sprinkled with marshmallows, and he dug out a book of bedtime stories he used to enjoy as a child. While the children sipped their drinks, Marc read a story. He put on funny voices for each of the characters and asked the children to find things in the illustrations. Once the teeth cleaning routine was done, the children snuggled up under the duvets ready to sleep.

'Thank you very much Marc,' said Gemma.

'You're welcome,' said Marc, 'thank you for your company.'

'Night night.' She gave him a friendly hug.

'Night night,' said a sleepy Oscar.

Marc ruffled his hair. 'Sweet dreams.'

Lucy and Marc retreated downstairs leaving them to sleep. 'That was good fun,' said Marc.

'You were amazing,' said Lucy. 'I can tell they loved your acting abilities with the stories, they were having fun.'

'I figured they needed some light-hearted entertainment to give them a distraction from worrying too much about their mum.'

'Your goal was achieved, I think. I've told them to talk to us if they're worried. Is that okay? I think Oscar clicks with you. He trusts you.'

'Of course. I'm happy to listen and help where I can. I'm going to login to work for an hour.'

'I have some preparations to do for tomorrow. Catch you later for a spot of TV.'

* * *

THE NEXT MORNING Marc walked to school with Lucy and the children. They played I Spy as they walked, and peered over the bridge wall to see if they could spot some fish in the river. When they arrived at the school gate Marc wished them a fun day and carried on up the lane past the school to explore further.

He hadn't been up this lane yet. Lucy told him he could carry on up to where his fields ended, and eventually it meets the bridle path to take a circular route home. The lane climbed steeply in the direction of the tor, then bent around to the left and the tarmac fizzled out to a dirt track, with grass growing in the middle, leading to a farm.

Marc continued up towards the moors, climbed over a stile onto the moor, and carried on uphill next to a stream that ran down alongside a Devon bank. He saw the cattle in the field grazing. Eventually he reached the corner where he turned right and found the now familiar bridle path. He turned to walk past the empty field, where the cows had been before, and carried along towards the lane and home.

When he arrived home, he made a mug of coffee and settled down to work at his nice sunny desk. He thought, *what a great way to start the day*.

* * *

A FEW HOURS LATER, with a short break for lunch, he closed down his laptop, put on his walking shoes and went outside. He wanted to have a good look around the garden and take a proper look at the vegetable plot and the old stable to see if he could find the stream.

The lawn and flower garden ended at a tall conifer hedge, which contained a gateway. He went through it to discover a big square plot, surrounded by more tall hedging. It reminded him of the walled vegetable gardens he'd seen visiting National Trust stately homes. It was badly overgrown, despite being laid out in planting beds with gravel paths, but he felt it had the potential to be renovated and reused. He also noticed a few apple trees forming a small orchard.

A path ran along beside the garden hedge and through another gap, which opened out into a paddock, again overgrown. He carried on walking along the hedge path until he reached the rear of the old stables, which he'd only seen from the garden side. There was an empty doorway into the building. He cautiously went in looking around carefully and wondering if it was completely safe.

As he knew from his view from the garden side the front of the building was open, with vertical wooden beams supporting cross beams for the roof, as he'd seen. He'd researched the internet about old Dartmoor buildings and this was indeed a linhay. He'd seen photos showing how they could be converted for many different uses as James and Bertie had said.

After a good look around, and taking photos with his phone, he went back through the rear doorway and walked up to the top end of the paddock to look at the barn. This time, there was a leat and an old waterwheel, ceased up and thick with rust. The water ran along the old leat, through the broken wheel and gushed into the stream below. Where it went then, he couldn't see, it was overgrown with weeds. *Interesting. I wonder if this is the spring.*

He went through the rickety doorway into the barn to see what the wheel used to drive and was surprised to see two large grindstones. *It must have been a mill.* He looked around the building, which was rather dilapidated. It had signs of a few roof leaks—there were giveaway marks on the muddy floor and a few broken roof slates lying around. There was a broken beam, which clung on to the beam it was nailed to and hung there, dangling through from the floor above. Most of the floor above had gone, except for the cross beams. *I don't think that looks very safe.*

He decided not to go up but took a series of photos again. He retreated outside, assessed the paddock area, and stood looking at the lovely view over a few cottage rooftops in the village, and up towards the moor where the main road was. He was considering various possibilities for the building. There's no doubt he needed professional advice, but he was getting some ideas.

He went back towards the flower garden and through the gateway and turned down along the garden side of the hedge to the front of the old stables. He wasn't convinced it had been used as stables because it opened into the garden and not the paddock, but perhaps the garden had been planned and the hedge planted after it ceased to be used as stables. It would make an interesting feature greenhouse and garden store, whilst retaining the rustic look of the building. It still had sun shining on the broken slate roof, even though it was quite late in the afternoon. He made a mental note.

He walked back towards the house and went to look at the other barn that stood in a field behind the house. This one seemed in slightly better condition. It was a single storey building constructed with wooden shiplap walls and a thatched roof. Once again, he took photos and assessed the lay of the land, the orientation of the building, and the view—up to the tor.

Hmm, more ideas sprang into his mind. He turned and went back to the house. Enough exploring for one day.

* * *

WHEN LUCY ARRIVED HOME ALONE, Marc greeted her, 'Hello, Bertie's collected the children? How's Emily?'

'Hiya, she's still in hospital, but feeling a bit better. She'll need a few days rest. Bertie has taken the children home but has asked if they can come again tomorrow. Oscar was telling him about your storytelling skills and Bertie says now he'll have to up his game.' Lucy smiled. 'And Gemma said you cooked a yummy bolognese. She was very impressed. Bertie is really grateful.'

'No problem, it was fun. I enjoyed their company. They're lovely children and very well-mannered. We'll have to think of something to do with them tomorrow,' said Marc.

'I was thinking about tomorrow too. What if we go up to the tor for a walk and I can show you where the spring is. We can take a frisbee with us and have a bit of fun.'

'That sounds great. We'll pack a picnic too. In the meantime, I've got our dinner in the oven. It's nearly ready. I made a lasagne with what was left of yesterday's bol sauce.'

'Oh lovely. I'll prep the salad. What have you done today?'

'Worked. Then I went for a look around the old barns, it's given me some ideas. I reckon the old stables would convert into a lovely garden storage shed and greenhouse. It's a big building with potential. It's central to the garden because I sussed out the old vegetable plot too,' said Marc.

'There are a few apple trees in there that sometimes produce a nice crop later in the year. The rest needs a good deal of digging.'

'Yes, and hedge restoration. It must be very sheltered in there though.'

Marc took the lasagne and garlic bread out of the oven and through to the dining room and Lucy carried the salad. They began their meal and continued chatting.

Marc said, 'And I reckon there are possibilities for the two barns. I see one has millstones inside with a leat and a rusted-up waterwheel, which has given me something to think about. Both barns have nice views and the areas around them are pleasant, and quite sunny for most of the day.'

'Uh-huh and sheltered. You knew about the stream. What are you thinking?'

'They'd make unusual holiday lets, if sympathetically converted. Or as the top field is fairly level, it might be suitable for setting up glamping.'

'You've been doing some research.'

'Yes, I have, and with all the talk of climate change and energy conservation and all that, I think there might be possibilities.'

'I know I tease you about being an eco-warrior, but I think you have some seriously good ideas. Why don't I introduce you to Robbie in the village. You'll find he's interesting to talk to and you could run some ideas past him. He designs and advises people on sustainable buildings.'

'He sounds interesting. Bertie told me about Harry Barker too, an architect?'

'Great idea. Robbie and Harry work together.'

'And when Emily is feeling better, I'm going to have a conversation with Bertie about restoring and using the vegetable garden. I think, judging by the size of it, it would produce more than we could use, and we could share the produce with Bertie and his family. I thought that might help them out a bit.'

'Great idea. I'm sure Jan, in the shop, might sell spare fresh produce too. You could talk to her.'

'That's a thought. We'll see how it works out. It will be a big project. I'll enjoy learning all about it and I'll value your input too,' Marc smiled.

'I'd love to help,' said Lucy. 'It all sounds very exciting. Let's clear up and chill out. There's a good film on TV tonight.'

'Sounds like a plan.'

CHAPTER 7

The next morning, Marc was up early and walked to the shop to buy some goodies and snacks to put together a picnic. He was just returning home, back up the lane, when Bertie saw him. 'Morning, hop in. Those bags look heavy.'

'Morning. Not really, more bulky than anything, but thanks.' He climbed into the passenger seat. 'Good morning, Oscar and Gemma, are you ready for some fun? Did Lucy call you and mention a moor walk?'

'Yes, we've brought our wellies,' said Oscar excitedly.

Bertie pulled up in the parking area and everyone got out. 'Thank you again, Marc, I really appreciate your help,' he said. 'The kids had a load of fun the other evening and asked if they could visit again.'

'Absolutely no problem. I hope Emily is feeling much better today.'

'Cheers. Hey kids, here are your backpacks. Be good and have fun,' Bertie said.

'Yes Dad,' they said taking their backpacks and running over to Lucy, who'd just appeared at the end of the passageway. 'Morning Bertie, I hope Emily is feeling better today.'

'Thanks. I'll be off. See you later.'

'Sure.'

Marc carried the shopping into the kitchen, while Lucy went into the lounge with the children and Marc joined them. 'Let's swap. I'll make the picnic,' said Lucy. 'It looks like you have a building session in mind.'

'Yes, I thought the children might enjoy building a village. We can start now and do more when we get back.'

'Brilliant!' Both children cheered.

Lucy left the three of them rifling through a crate of loose bricks.

***

A SHORT WHILE LATER, up on the moor, they climbed the tor and played King of the Castle. Then Marc took them down to his favourite spot for the picnic and a sketching session, for which he'd packed some sketch pads, pencils, and the box of watercolour paints. The children enjoyed having a go with Marc's gentle guidance. At the end of the session, Oscar's picture was a recognisable depiction of the scene, for one so young, and he was chuffed to receive praise for it. Gemma had focussed on a shaggy Dartmoor pony grazing in the ferns. Again, it was very good.

They packed everything up and walked around the tor and Lucy showed Marc the area close to the source of the stream. He recognised it as being the spot where he saw the holidaymakers and their romantic crossing.

The children, wearing their wellies, had fun paddling and splashing in the stream. Just for a moment, Marc had a fleeting thought that he'd like to cross the stream romantically with Lucy, who had actually promptly and confidently crossed on some stepping-stones. He felt slightly disappointed as he followed behind thinking, *Lucy's such an independent lady. Ah well...* He sighed.

They walked downhill following the stream, the children were enjoying their wellie-paddling and racing sticks downstream in the water. Marc and Lucy chatted as they walked beside them. 'I think this is a natural spring that starts underground, then it surfaces not far from where we joined it. As you can see, the stream is quite quick flowing,' said Lucy.

'Is it the same one that runs down by the fields towards the school?'

'I'm not sure.'

'I wonder where the stream originates that runs to the barn where I found the millstones, or to the old stables? That will be interesting to find out. To drive millstones, it must have quite a flow, I imagine, and I suppose it might carry on down to the old stables. I'll have to check it out.'

'There's another stream that runs around the tor too. From the far side,' said Lucy.

'Hmm, we'll have to explore,' Mark said, then called, 'Right, Oscar, can you catch a frisbee?' Marc tossed it gently towards him and it landed at his feet. Oscar picked it up and tried to throw it back. Gemma intercepted and threw it to Lucy. 'Hey Oscar, we can't let the girls beat us,' said Marc.

They had fun tossing it between them all the way back along the bridle path and home.

Back to the village waiting to be built.

* * *

AFTER DINNER BERTIE arrived to collect the children to take them home. 'Hello Bertie, how's Emily doing?' said Lucy as she opened the front door.

'She's much better thanks. She'll probably be discharged tomorrow, but I won't tell the children in case it doesn't happen.'

'That's great news, the children will be pleased. They've been talking a bit and they're worried,' Lucy said.

'Yes, I know. They sense when Emily isn't well and do their best to help. She's missing them too. I'll take them with me to visit tomorrow and they might get a nice surprise. And Emily will feel upbeat for seeing them.'

'It's difficult when they're so young.' Lucy led him through to where Marc and the children were busy building.

'Hi Bertie, how are you doing?' said Marc.

'Me? Okay, I guess. Worried I suppose...' Bertie shrugged his shoulders. 'You just cope ... don't you? Hi kids, having fun?'

'Yes! Look at what we've done,' said Oscar, showing him some of the houses they'd built.

'Wow, they look good to live in.' He turned to Marc, 'I'll try to catch up with the garden this week.'

'Don't worry if you're looking after Emily,' said Marc.

'No, I'll do my best to do some work,' said Bertie. 'I can't let my clients down, especially you. You've been so kind.'

'Sure, okay. That'll be great. But if you can't, that's fine too.' Marc knew that Bertie was probably needing to work financially.

'Children, have you packed your bags? Your wellies are clean and dry now,' said Lucy.

'Yes, thank you, Lucy. And thanks for a fun day,' said Gemma.

'We did some painting too, Dad,' said Oscar.

'They are talented,' said Marc.

'We'll show you later, Dad,' said Oscar.

'Thank you very much,' said Bertie to Lucy and Marc.

'Our pleasure, they're great kids. Anytime,' Marc said.

'Definitely,' said Lucy.

Bertie left the room to help the children and Lucy and Marc followed to see them out. 'Bye children, thank you for visiting us.'

They waved them off then turned and went indoors. 'Bertie said that Emily will probably be allowed home tomorrow,' said Lucy.

'That's good. I'm worried about him trying to do too much next week though, especially if he's looking after them all. How can I let him have some pay, without hurting his pride? Up to now, he invoices me for the hours he does.'

'What about some cash in an envelope and call it sick pay or holiday pay?' said Lucy.

'Good idea, I'll do that. Wine?' said Marc.

'You're a mind reader, thanks. I think we've earned a chill-out evening.'

Marc fetched the bottle of wine and two glasses and joined Lucy on the sofa. She was scrolling for something to watch on the TV. Marc poured the wine and handed Lucy a glass. 'You're great with children,' Lucy said.

'I love kids. I hope they find me an okay adult and a bit of fun,' said Marc.

'Objective achieved, especially for Oscar. He was really enjoying the painting session with you. It was lovely to see him really listening and learning. And then building houses ... he was thoroughly enjoying that.'

'He's a smart little chap. I was enjoying letting him lead the activities. It's what Grandad used to do with me. It helps with learning problem-solving which is an important life skill—looking from different angles to choose the best option.'

'I totally agree,' said Lucy.

'Oscar was focussing on where the stairs should go and where people would sleep. I let him decide how it would work. Passive learning through play, eh?'

'Brilliant. You should have been a teacher.'

'Really? I just treat children as an equal and pay attention to what they say. It's what Grandad and Auntie Joan did. They didn't lecture me, or talk down to me, but listened to me and credited me with having valid opinions. We'd say, "What if ..." and we'd come up with different permutations.'

'I heard you talking with the children like that. Seriously though, did you ever consider teaching as a career?'

'No, a roomful of people all day would drain me, even though it could be fun. When it comes to getting stuck into something it's best to give me the work with any special instructions and deadlines, leave a line of communication open, and leave me to get on with it.'

'Ah, a bit like me then—an introvert.'

'Yes, I think so. I don't go in for parties, or the pub culture. I don't thrive in contexts of banter, bragging and shallow talk. I need interesting, deep meaningful discussions.'

'Like we're having now?' Lucy smiled. 'I know exactly what you mean. I had to work at overcoming shyness, especially that thing of having to stand up and talk in front of people. But I wanted to be a teacher, so I learned strategies to cope with various situations I find difficult. And my people are little people and I don't find them threatening.'

'I would never have known you find anything difficult. You appear so confident and outgoing,' said Marc.

'Years of practice and some great advice from Joan. She was an enabler and motivator.'

'A great team leader too?'

'Yes, exactly right. She was a central figure in the village, as you've learned. On the board of governors at school, a member of the parish council, a charity fund raiser, a coordinator of projects that benefit the community.'

'I don't know how she found time for all the things she did, I'm truly amazed. I think she blazed a trail that will be hard for me to follow.'

'Believe me, no one in the village expects you to. Just join in with projects that interest you, that are within your capability and interests, and others will support you. It's an amazing community here where just about everyone joins in. There aren't many that don't,' said Lucy.

'I expect with all the difficulties of the lockdowns, communities like this did what they could to support each other?'

'Yes. Anyone who was struggling, feeling ill, or needed something, we all tried to help. Delivered some groceries, for instance, left carrier bags on the doorsteps. I think it did a lot to enhance community spirit.'

'I can understand that it would help to build up trust. And of course, as the lockdowns and social distancing carried on, the community came up with the idea of the village hall garden. It will be a facility that is used a lot.'

'Well, apart from Dick who scowls a lot at me,' said Marc, 'everyone, so far, has been friendly and welcoming.'

'Yes, Dick is a problem and I can't deal with him either, but I don't want to talk about him and spoil a nice evening.'

'We'll drop the subject, except to say, if you ever want to talk—I'm here, okay?'

'Yes, thanks.' Lucy paused then said, 'Shall we find a film?'

'Yes, you choose and I'll get another bottle of wine.'

'Pretty Woman suit you?'

'I haven't watched that for ages, yes sure.' Marc refilled their glasses.

'Okay. What's your favourite bit?'

'It has to be the ending, when he overcomes his fear ... because he loves her.'

'My favourite bit too. I've found it. Ready to begin?'

A couple of hours later, Lucy cried at the end of the film. 'I've watched this film so many times and still I cry—every time. Sorry.'

'No problem, it gets to me too,' said Marc. Lucy glanced at him as he wiped his eyes. 'It must be so wonderful to find true love.'

'Yes,' Lucy sniffed. 'Does it reflect real life? Or a is it a well-constructed story?'

'Of course, it reflects real life. Joan and Simon were deeply in love. They were sad that they weren't blessed with children, but they always had each other until death parted them.'

'How do you know this?' asked Lucy.

'I found Joan's journals. I felt a bit uncomfortable reading them at first, but then I realised that as she planned everything else for her death, if she didn't want anyone to read them, she'd have burned them, or something. Simon left drawings, sketches, and notes, she left her journals crammed full of pondering. It's as if they were deliberately passing on their ideas or showing that they wouldn't disapprove of progress.'

'Hmm, that's one way of looking at it. Perhaps she wanted you to get to know them? You hadn't seen them since you were small.'

'Possibly. This house had been in Simon's family for several generations and the bloodline had finally fizzled out. Simon was the last one. But, of course, they thought they were leaving the house to dad, who'd have probably put it on the market by now. I can't see my parents would choose a quiet life.' Marc looked wistful.

'Well, there you go. Anyway, the house is yours and maybe exploring the family history in the context of the house would be interesting. Write it, maybe? The house has obviously been adapted over time. I wonder how old it actually is?'

'Not sure. I'd need to research. Pretty old though. And the other reason I think Joan left the journals on purpose is because they were carefully bundled up in date order, tied up with a ribbon. No note though. But Simon's drawings were with them, so I think it was deliberate to present the full picture. Dad might have known some of it, but since he died, she had to do something to let me know. Do you reckon?' Marc said, looking at Lucy. 'Did she do it for me?'

'Yes, I see what you mean. She must have recognised your dilemma if anything happened to her and she left you a research project as a sales pitch to choose here. Choose this project! Do it for Simon and see his vision, and his dreams fulfilled.' Lucy smiled.

'That's a romantic idea. Keep it going down the generations, even if it is just related by marriage. Hmm, sounds like I have another responsibility—one day.'

'Indeed. Right, I'm off to bed,' said Lucy picking up the empty glasses and the wine bottle. 'I'll see you in the morning, night night,'

'Night night, thank you for a lovely day. One to remember.'

Lucy smiled at Marc, 'Sweet dreams.' She left the room.

Marc looked at the door a while longer visualising Lucy standing there smiling at him. It was emblazoned in his memory. He looked away and got up off the sofa and went around the room turning off the table lamps and then looked out of the window at the moon shining brightly in the starlit sky. They rarely drew the curtains. *I wonder...,* he thought, *I wonder if I've fallen in love with Lucy. How can I tell her without spoiling our friendship? Should I? Or just wait and see. We're happy and we haven't known each other for very long.*

He left the room and went upstairs to bed.

. . .

AT THE SAME TIME, Lucy was lying in bed looking out of her window, also with the curtains back. She thought the moon looked particularly beautiful in the sky full of stars and she was thinking about Marc. *I think I've fallen in love with him. He's so kind, polite, and courteous, gentlemanly, sensitive, and fun. I trust him completely. Do I say anything? But I don't want to spoil the friendship we've been building. What do I do? Keep it to myself, I think. Wait and see what happens? Settle for friendship?*

She closed her eyes and visualised Marc playing frisbee with the children. *I think I've definitely fallen in love with him,* she thought as she drifted off to sleep.

CHAPTER 8

Lucy woke early feeling mellow. Her final thought about falling in love with Marc had played on her mind through the night. She remembered dreaming that Marc romantically swept her off her feet and she submitted to his passion reciprocating.

Then she'd had a nightmare. Dick attacked Marc—beating him up, threatening more if he didn't leave Lucy alone, saying "How dare you take advantage of my stepdaughter." Lucy remembered feeling furious hissing back at Dick, "I am NOT your stepdaughter, you feel angry because I'm a challenge you will never have. You're my mother's man and you will not have me".

"Oh, won't I…" Dick taunted menacingly.

She recalled the real-life nightmare experience, which happened before she ran away from home as a teenager. Dick had tried to assault her in her bedroom one day after school, while she was changing out of her school uniform. Luckily, he heard Maggie arrive home, which had prevented the full assault. He quietly hissed at Lucy that if she screamed, or told her mum, he'd "get her" and he skulked off out of her bedroom and disappeared into the bathroom.

Lucy had tried to tell her mum so many times about Dick's

behaviour towards her, but her mum always said, "don't be ridiculous, he's not interested in you, he's a nice man—he's my man and Marty's dad. What's your problem?"

Lucy felt sad that her mum always defended him and would never listen to her, or show she really cared about her—her daughter. What's the point of trying to talk to her? Lucy also thought her mum probably felt she had to show Dick loyalty and defend him, or where would she live, or work and have money? And Marty needed his dad.

Lucy thought. *Huh! I don't even know who my father is and look at what I put up with as a child, especially since mum moved us in with Dick. He's a lecherous, dirty old man who thinks he's God's gift to the world—especially women. Conceited narcissist!* It was then that Lucy packed her rucksack and quietly left home intending to run away. But as she walked up the lane, Joan rescued her. It was a nightmare that frequently circled in her mind.

Lucy's thoughts continued. *Now I am scared. My subconscious detects trouble ahead. Dick already sneaked into school the other week when I was doing marking. I won't work late at school again and I'm very grateful to Marc for coming to make sure I was alright. He's such a kind, caring, gentle guy. I care so much about him and I don't want to put him in danger defending me, if Dick does attempt to carry out his threat, and I don't put it past him.*

On the other hand, I can't live my life in constant fear and ruin any chance of happiness that comes my way. Maybe I should apply for a job elsewhere? Emigrate even. I don't need to stay here now Joan's gone. Mum wouldn't care. Anyway, this is Marc's home and he might meet someone he falls in love with. I can't stay here.

Lucy sighed and continued thinking, *But I get the feeling that Marc would like a relationship with me and he'd be a great guy to spend the rest of my life with. On the other hand, maybe I'm wrong and he doesn't feel like that, but I honestly don't pick up a bad vibe. Marc's good company and we've become good friends. Why shouldn't I be happy? I've done nothing wrong.*

Lucy decided she'd been lying there thinking long enough and got out of bed. On the way to the bathroom, she could hear Marc singing along to some music playing downstairs in the kitchen. Then she got a whiff of coffee. She smiled and stepped into the bathroom.

Marc was happily preparing breakfast in the kitchen. Coffee machine hissing, porridge simmering, toaster prepared ready with slices of bread. He was cheerful.

He'd gone to bed happy thinking about Lucy. His reservation about asking her for a closer relationship was that he didn't want to spoil their friendship. He felt they were very compatible housemates and he valued her opinions as a friend. He was convinced he'd fallen in love with her, but he had absolutely no idea how Lucy felt about him. She seemed keen to remain distant, but he had the feeling she was warming to him. He was thinking, *She's kind, intelligent, interesting, and very pretty. I'll just have to wait for a sign she feels the same.*

Lucy breezed into the kitchen with a cheerful, 'Good morning.'

'You smelt the coffee?' said Marc.

Lucy said, 'Of course. You must make time to smell the coffee. No point constantly rushing around, is there?' They continued chatting over breakfast. She said, 'What are your plans today?'

'I've got some work to do.'

'Really? On Sunday?' Lucy tutted.

'There's someone, not a million miles away from here, who always sits reading through a pile of work on Sunday morning, pen in hand. I might be wrong, but isn't that working?'

'Hmm, okay, yes but I enjoy doing it so it doesn't feel like work.'

'Well, I enjoy my work too. I'm planning allocating tasks for a new project across the team. I love it when a project goes well. It gives me a buzz.'

'You're right, of course, and it's a bit cloudy this morning anyway. No outdoor distractions until later maybe.'

They cleared up. 'Retreat to our work corners with another coffee?' said Mark.

'Yes please,' said Lucy as she hung a tea towel over the oven door handle to dry.

Marc passed her a fresh mug of coffee, 'See you later.' He set the machine going for his.

'Thanks,' said Lucy. 'See you later.' She left the kitchen heading for the dining room and the pile of the work waiting on the table.

Marc picked up his coffee and headed upstairs to his desk on the landing. He put his coffee down, took a seat, lifted the lid of his laptop, and looked out of the window while it booted up. He was thinking, *perfect, what could be better than the serenity of this beautiful view, even if the sun isn't shining today.* He settled down to work.

An hour later, his phone rang. 'Hello, Barry. How are you?'

Barry: 'Fine thanks. How are you doing? Have you settled into your new life?'

Marc: 'I'm doing okay thanks. I feel a bit less stressed having decided to make the move down here. It's wonderful.'

Barry: 'I think you're making a good decision to sell up here. Your heart isn't in it, you just thought you should continue with the business because it was your parents".

Marc: 'I think you're right. I'm interested in property, but I'm not sure about managing a portfolio of rentals miles away.'

Barry: 'When we met, you were telling me about your house there and it sounds an interesting project—a heritage building. It won't be plain sailing, but a really satisfying thing to do.'

Marc: 'Yes, I figured that, and I'm doing it for me to live in, my home, so I can put my ideas into it and there's no hurry because it's liveable. It's giving me time to get a feel for it.'

Barry: 'Sounds great and just right for you. You've always been creative since you were a little boy. That's what I meant about your heart wouldn't be into managing quick turnarounds or rentals. Anyway, I've got some valuations for the two houses, they're all ready to go. I asked three estate agents and they're all similar. I'll email them to you.'

Marc: 'Thank you, Barry, I really appreciate everything you've done. We'll have to discuss some finances.'

Barry: 'No, it's fine. I've been happy to help my old friend's son. I've watched you grow up and I wouldn't let John and Mary down by not helping you. John and I often worked together and shared problems and ideas, to me it's repaying the help he's given to me over the years.'

Marc: 'Cheers Barry, I'm very grateful. Let me know if ever you're down this way. You'd be most welcome.'

Barry: 'Thanks lad. Anyway, I'll send you the valuations and if you want to chat, please call me. They didn't come in quite as much as I hoped, but who knows what interest the market will generate. You've only got to have two people wanting it, or bidding against each other for it—if you choose to go to auction, and the price will rise. Has John's house sale gone through alright?'

Marc: 'Yes, it completed this week. Then Tim needs to work with the accountant about the tax. Thank goodness. It was getting a bit stressful when the first buyer backed out. Anyway, Tim's the executor, so he'll be signing paperwork. I was only a teenager when mum and dad wrote their Will and they hadn't updated it.'

Barry: 'Ah, right. They had dreams they wanted to live, before considering any amendments, I think. And John thought there was no hurry. So sad they didn't get chance to make their dreams come true. Anyway, they've taken good care of you.'

Marc: 'Yes, indeed. I'll carefully read the valuations. Would you go to auction or just normal sale?'

Barry: 'I'm around the auction rooms a lot when I'm buying, so I'd probably go for auction. But do whatever you feel comfortable with. You can always come and visit us and I'll go with you to the auction for moral support, if that's what you choose to do.'

Marc: 'Thanks, Barry. I'll call you soon.'

Barry: 'Bye, Marc.'

Marc: 'Bye, Barry.'

Marc went back to his work, while he waited for the email.

Ping! It arrived, with the six attachments.

Marc read the message and opened the attachments. He decided that just for once he'd print them to study them carefully to be able to make his decision. He thought he might have a chat with James again. From the photos, he could see the houses had been finished nicely. They looked clean and comfortable with nice modern neutral interiors. They'd be good homes, for someone. He saw that the valuations were a bit less than they estimated, as Barry said. However, with the current economic climate and the news headlines every day talking about rising energy costs, mortgage rates and food prices, he supposed it was understandable. Time will tell.

Marc closed down his computer and gathered up the paperwork and went downstairs. *Time for lunch.*

Lucy was busy in the kitchen. 'Ah, there you are. Hungry?'

'Yes, I am. I hadn't noticed until you asked, or maybe it's the aroma. What are you cooking?'

'No pastry quiches and salad, with warm bread rolls.'

'It smells delicious.'

'Do you want to eat outside? The sun is out now and it's warming up nicely,' said Lucy.

'Yes, lovely. What can I do?'

'Organise plates and cutlery. Oh, and wine. We must have wine!'

Marc organised the items and went outside. He was about to cross the parking area to the patio when he saw James walking down the drive.

'Hi James, how are you? Have you had lunch yet?' said Marc.

'Hi Marc, no I haven't.'

'Then join us. I'll let Lucy know and pick up more items. Beer or wine?'

'Wine's good. Thanks. Here give me those and I'll take them to the table.'

'Cheers.' Marc handed him the plates, glasses, and cutlery he was carrying and returned to the kitchen to talk to Lucy. 'James has just arrived. Can we stretch the food a bit?'

'Yes, no problem, I've made plenty.'

Marc picked up another place setting and took a bottle of wine from the fridge. 'Can I help? Take the salad bowl?'

'Thanks. I'll bring the rest when they're ready.'

Marc left the kitchen to join James. He laid the place setting on the table, poured a couple of glasses of wine, and joined James on the sofas. 'How are you doing? I haven't seen you for a couple of weeks.'

'I've been down to Cornwall surfing,' said James.

'Did you have fun?'

'Yes, I met a nice girl there too. We get on well.'

'Brilliant.'

'We're meeting again next weekend. She's living there and recently started working as a beach lifeguard for the season. She's just finished uni and decided to have the summer in Cornwall instead of taking the traditional year out.'

'Makes sense. Good for you, James.'

'Yes, I hope so. She's a surfer too.'

'Match made in heaven.'

'Yes, we'll see how it goes. How are things with you?'

'Good thanks. My work project has started well, so that's been keeping me busy with all the planning. We had Bertie's kids for the day yesterday, that was fun. And today I learned that the two properties have been finished and dad's friend Barry, who's helping me, has got the valuations. I'd value your opinion.'

'Sure, I'll take a look and help if I can.'

Lucy appeared carrying the food, which she placed on the table. 'Come on guys, grub's up.'

'Hi Lucy, thanks,' said James. They got up from the sofas and joined Lucy at the table. Marc poured her a glass of wine and topped up their glasses.

After enjoying a leisurely lunch, Lucy cleared up and Marc produced the valuations. 'I'll leave you guys to chat. I've a few things to do then I'll join you with some coffee.'

Marc and James returned to sitting in the sunshine on the sofas. 'What do you think of these?' Marc handed him the paperwork.

They sat in silence while James read them. Eventually he said, 'They're nice-looking houses, good family homes. I'm sure they'll sell quickly because they are in a popular price range.'

'They're a little under what we originally thought they're worth, but then again, I'd like to move them on. Would you go for auction or general sale?'

'If they were mine, I think I'd try general sale. I might be wrong, but often people go to auction to buy a project. Something that needs some work and updating. If you go for general sale, you could maybe ask a little bit more and be open to offers. They'll soon sell, but if they didn't you could try auction later.'

Marc thought for a few minutes. 'Pretty much what I was thinking. I thought offers in excess of a price I choose and then take sealed bids, perhaps? I'm not so sure about auction.'

'I think you know what to do. You're learning to follow your heart and it makes good sense. Whichever you choose they'll soon sell. Despite everything, and the speculations about the economy ... people still need homes.'

Lucy returned carrying a tray of coffees. She passed the mugs and sat down next to Marc, leaned back on the sofa, and turned her face to the sun and closed her eyes. 'Ah, lovely,' she smiled.

'Thanks for the chat, James, I'll have another chat with Barry too and we'll see what happens,' said Marc.

'Good luck!' said James.

CHAPTER 9

Later that evening, after James had left, Lucy and Marc were talking. Marc said, 'Is there something bothering you, Lucy?'

Lucy hesitated. 'No, not really.'

'So, there is then. Can I help?'

'No, it's my problem. You've got enough on your mind with all you've been dealing with recently and I don't want to add to it.'

'That's ambiguous. I've made decisions for my general direction to a new goal unless anything goes wrong. Something will, for sure. I'd really like you to be free to travel forward with me, so as they say, a problem shared is a problem halved—share it.'

'I can't. I really don't want to put you in danger.'

'Danger? From what? Who?'

Lucy paused and took a deep breath. 'I think I'm going to have to move out, or away, and find a job somewhere else.'

Marc was shocked. 'Why? You love it here, you love your job, you're part of the village community, and this is your home. And I'd really like us to …'

'That's the problem. We've become good friends, close, and I don't want you to get hurt.'

'Right, now you're getting me really worried. Who's troubling you? It's Dick, isn't it?'

'Um … yes.'

'Tell me what's wrong. It was Dick who upset you when I came to walk you home after the funeral the other week, wasn't it? I saw him scurrying away towards the pub on my way to the school. What did he do?'

'He reopened old wounds making salacious threats.'

'Right, tell me. We'll deal with this together.'

'Well, I'm really embarrassed about it, but if you're sure…'

'Yes.'

'Dick used to abuse me when I was a kid. He used to … touch me, inappropriately, let's say, when mum wasn't around. One day when I got in from school and I was changing out of my uniform, he burst into my bedroom making his usual threats, except this time he attacked me. Threw me down on the bed. He groped me and tried to rip off my underwear, I know he had every intention of raping me. Luckily, he heard mum coming in downstairs. He pinned me down on the bed with his hand over my mouth and hissed that if I told her, or anyone, about what happened, he'd deny it and say I'd been trying to seduce him. Who would they believe? A smart, popular guy like him in a happy relationship, or a right little slut like me. He sidled out of my room and went to the bathroom. I was so scared I closed the bedroom door, wedged it shut with a chair and sobbed. I felt dirty.

'I decided I had to run away. I'd tried telling mum, many times, about what he was doing but I gave up, she wouldn't listen. She was, and is, besotted with him. Completely taken in by his narcissistic control. I had no idea where I was going to go, but I had to go. I packed my backpack and when they were busy doing … whatever, I slipped out and got away. The trouble with living in a remote, pretty village is it's a long walk to anywhere and I started to walk up the lane towards the main road. I thought that by walking purposefully and wearing a backpack, anyone who saw me might think I was doing something constructive, like hiking, but no. That's when Joan found me, in the lane, and rescued me. She brought me here and kept me safe. Protected me.'

'Uh-huh.'

'She asked me why I didn't tell my mum. I told her that Mum wouldn't listen. She was too grateful to Dick for taking her in, with her baggage—me. She had a job with him, financial security, and a place to call home and they had Marty, so she was busy with a baby too. At long last she had a steady relationship and a kid with a dad around, and not all the trouble I'd caused her. She was happy. She was fifteen when she had me and I've no idea who my father is. So, I'm blamed for ending her fun teenage life, partying like her friends enjoyed. She was made to be "responsible" and I'd ruined her life. She resented me, I suppose.'

'That's really sad.'

'Anyway, Joan rescued me and treated me as though I was her daughter, and I will be forever grateful. She helped me through college, and uni, and getting my job, but most of all for giving me a safe home and affection. I could never thank her enough.'

'So why has Dick started troubling you again?'

'I don't know what hold Joan had over Dick to stay away, but he did, all the time Joan looked after me. And now she's died, he's starting again. And I'm scared. He told me that if he can't have me, no one can—especially you. He thinks that's what we're doing here. And that's why I must get away.'

'You can't let him win and control your life. You have a right to be here and live your life as you want to. And have a relationship with someone your heart chooses ... and I really hope that one day, we can date ... and not just as friends. But I won't put any pressure on you ...'

'So, what can I do about Dick?'

'Ignore him. I won't let anything happen to you. I'll walk you to school and meet you to come home...'

'Marc, that's really kind, but I can't impose on your life like that. It's almost like giving in to him and having him control my life ... and yours.'

'We'll work something out, but for the time being ...'

'For the time being, we'll carry on as normal and not living under a threat. It spoils it.' Lucy had tears in her eyes and she looked utterly miserable.

Marc longed to spontaneously take her in his arms. Instead, he asked, 'Can I give you a hug? As a friend, no strings.'

'I'd like that,' said Lucy. Marc moved to Lucy's sofa and gently put his arms around her and pulled her close and held her for a few minutes.

'I don't know what we're going to do,' he said softly, 'but he won't win.'

'Thanks.' Lucy blew out her breath to change the subject, flapping her hands in front of her face to compose herself. 'Anyway, I've told you my biggest secret, haven't you got a story? You're such a nice guy, girls must have been beating a path to your door.' Lucy pulled away and Marc put his hands in his lap and looked thoughtful.

'No, not really. I went on a few dates when I was at uni, but as I'm not a party animal and don't enjoy the pub culture, I didn't meet many girls. My parents tried to do a kind of arranged marriage thing, a couple of years ago ... they tried to pair me off with one of their friends' daughter. She's a pretty girl and nice enough, but like her parents and mine, went for the mad social life extrovert thing. Not my type at all. We went on a couple of dates, but I knew we weren't going to hit it off romantically and we agreed just to be friends. She was soon whisked off her feet and got married last year. I guess I've always been happier with privacy and being alone.'

'A bit like me. I thought my problem was living in the flat above a pub. Constant noise and too many people. But since Joan gave me a home here, I've realised 'peaceful' is my true nature. I'm a bit reclusive and quiet with just the companionship of a nice person nearby, is enough for me.'

'We're okay then?' Marc looked in her eyes.

'Yes, Marc, we can deal with whatever happens, but I'll still think about moving out or away. Maybe having a new start.' Lucy sighed.

'I understand how you feel. I've moved here and chosen a new start to get on with my life and, since I met you, it's been a great decision being here with you and we've become good friends.'

'Yeah, let's not risk spoiling that. Hot chocolate?'

'Thanks.'

Lucy got up and went to the kitchen. Marc respected that she needed some privacy to compose herself. He sat back on the sofa trying to work out what they could do. He knew he didn't want Lucy to leave, he loved her company even if it was only ever as housemates. What could they do? What hold did Joan have over Dick to make him keep away? He wished he could find out.

He closed his eyes thinking. Then after a few minutes it occurred to him that there might be a clue in Joan's journals. He'd have to read them properly. After all, he'd figured Joan kept them for that reason, so he knew why she made certain decisions and hoping that Marc would read them after she died.

Lucy came back into the room carrying two steaming mugs, she placed them on the coffee table. 'Thanks for the chat, Marc. I feel better for telling you about it, but as I say I don't want to cause you any trouble, or for you to get hurt, because I'm sure he'll take his frustrations out on you. Take care, please.'

'It's fine and you take care too. It's not an easy situation to deal with and despite that I'd already noticed you're not close to your mum, now I know why.'

'Hmm, because she was so young when she had me. Now she's too busy thinking we're mates, not mother and daughter. "Mates" is never going to happen. She's shown me exactly how little I mean to her. Anyway, you've had some good news you were chatting about with James?'

'Yeah, the two houses being done up are finished and ready to put on the market. There's a bit of a market slump, right now, in view of the economic problems regarding their likely value, but they're ready to go.'

'That's positive. Good luck.'

'Thanks.'

'And the rental properties?'

'That's still being discussed and decided, but hopefully soon. It would be good to get it all wound up and I'll know where I am financially, to decide where I'm going with Project Beliton,' said Marc.

'I know you're keen to explore some of your ideas, and I understand your hesitance.'

'We'll get there, one step at a time. Finished your drink? I'll go and wash the cups.'

'Yes thanks. I'm off to bed. It's been a nice weekend. Different, anyway.'

'Yes, it has. Night night.'

* * *

THE NEXT FRIDAY AFTERNOON, Marc's phone rang, he answered: 'Hello James, how are you?'

'Good thanks and you?'

'Fine. What can I do for you?'

'Actually, I'm calling to invite you and Lucy to dinner tomorrow. Steph's coming to stay this weekend and I thought we could meet up and have a takeaway. Indian?'

'It sounds good to me. I'll ask Lucy if she's got any plans when she gets home and let you know.'

Marc carried on working until Lucy arrived. He went downstairs to meet her and make a coffee. 'Hi Lucy, how was your day?'

'It was good, thanks.'

'James has invited us to dinner tomorrow—to meet Steph. She's staying with him this weekend.'

'Sounds good. It will be nice to meet her.'

'Tomorrow, okay?'

'Sure.'

'I'll call James back.'

'I saw Emily today,' said Lucy. 'She walked to school to pick up the children.'

'She must be feeling better.'

'Yes, I think so. She said Bertie will be coming here next week. He's been trying to catch up with his backlog of work.'

'That's great. I was going to mow the lawns this weekend.'

'Perhaps you don't need to. I think if Emily's mentioned it, it's her subtle way of saying Bertie wants the work. I've mentioned before that I think they struggle a bit, financially.'

'Yes. I can give Bertie plenty more work. I think we should start work on the kitchen garden. It's a bit late in the season for summer planting, but planning what we can do and preparing for the autumn will be a positive step forward. I don't know anything about seasonal planting, but Bertie does. We'll discuss more about converting the stable barn too. When I went to look, I didn't realise how big it is, or could be with a roof lift. I think it could be multifunctional, including living accommodation on the first floor. I went to meet Harry Barker this week to talk over some of my ideas—to see how workable they are. He's coming to meet me here and we'll survey it and discuss some ideas to see what's possible.'

'That will be the beginning of Project Beliton,' said Lucy.

'Yes, and I'd value your opinions. I'm sure you have some great ideas.'

'I'd be happy to help. It will be interesting. By the way, would you be interested in getting involved with the school? The board of governors hasn't filled Joan's vacancy yet. A few of them have mentioned it to me and wonder if you'd be interested? We've been discussing some ideas to develop the school and keeping it the thriving heart of the community. The village hall gardening project is a successful community project and we've been offered a small gardening plot, next to the school, to develop too. I think it lends itself to growing food, like your kitchen garden project. It would help the children develop some useful life skills. We're also interested in doing an eco-assessment and making it a development project, especially the way energy prices are rising so rapidly. We're keen on keeping the village school thriving and we're even considering running evening classes for adult education.'

I'd be interested to find out more, especially as it relates to the projects I'd like to do here too,' said Marc. 'It makes sense to expand ideas and pool learning and resources. I think the value of such projects will be working together as a community.'

Lucy nodded her head. 'I couldn't agree with you more. The world has changed since all the lockdowns. Communities seem to be working better together. Remote working is becoming more popular. Buying local and cutting back on air miles. All kinds of changes. So, anyway, you'd be interested in meeting the governors?'

'Yes.'

'I'll organise a meeting with the Chair, Maureen. She's keen to show you around the school and have a chat before the next meeting. You can meet the staff and see how the school operates.'

'Cool, it will be interesting to see Joan's blazed trail.'

'As I've said before, don't see it as taking up the reins of the projects that interested her. Just see what projects interest you. It will give you a chance to really get to know kindred spirits in the village. Anyway, I'll go and prepare dinner. You can call James back.'

'And then I'll find us some wine.'

CHAPTER 10

Marc and Lucy were lazing in the sunshine on the garden sofas reading when they heard voices. They looked up the drive to see James with a pretty girl walking towards them. 'Hello,' called James, and as he neared them, 'we thought we'd surprise you. This is Steph.'

'Hi Steph, welcome,' said Lucy, 'I'll get some more glasses and another bottle of wine.'

'Hi Lucy, lovely thanks,' said Steph.

'Nice to meet you, Steph,' said Marc, 'come and join us.' He indicated the garden sofas on the decking.

'It's such a lovely day,' said James, 'we decided to go walking on the moors and thought we'd pop in and say hello as we were on the way home.'

Lucy returned, poured wine, and handed them around. 'James tells us you're a beach lifeguard,' Lucy said to Steph.

'Yes, for the summer. I start my job in September so as I've nowhere else to be, and Cornwall is lovely especially this time of year, it seemed a nice thing to do to earn a bit of money for a few months.'

'And what will you be doing in September?'

'Teaching.'

'Ah, me too, in the village school. What ages will you teach?'

'English at secondary level. And what do you do Marc?' asked Steph turning to him.

'I'm a software developer for a bank in London and I work remotely—from home.'

'Great, it's a lovely place, I wouldn't want to leave it either.'

'Yes, it is. I'm very lucky.'

'Does working remotely work for you? Don't you miss the office buzz?'

'Not at all. I have to go to London for occasional meetings, but we work well as a team using video conferencing meetings, messaging, and phone calls. Each of us has specialisms and work on our own specific areas of projects and collaborate as it progresses.'

'That's good,' said Steph. 'You certainly have a beautiful home, you lucky pair.'

Lucy went quiet and looked at the ground. Marc said, 'Yes we're very lucky.'

James said to Steph, 'Marc's up for learning to surf. A few weekends ago I showed him Polzeath.'

'Oh, that's great, you must join us one weekend and we can get you started. What about you, Lucy? Are you up for it? If so, the two of you can come and stay with me for a weekend, I've a spare bedroom,' said Steph.

'It's kind of you to offer, Steph, but I'm not sure it's my thing,' said Lucy. She visibly squirmed a bit in her seat.

'It's kind of you, Steph, but I think if we come down, we'll come for a day, we're a bit busy at the moment,' said Marc.

James recognised the conversation was getting a little awkward. 'I haven't told you yet that Little Beliton is a busy little community. Lucy does a lot of projects linked with the school and now summer has arrived there are quite a few events.'

'Oh right,' said Steph.

'And you'll understand the summer term work of tests, reports, planning sports days, and all those sorts of tasks,' said Lucy.

'You should see the piles of work Lucy gets through. She saves it for Sunday mornings,' said Marc, winking at Lucy.

'When you log in and work too,' said Lucy, smiling back.

'Yes, of course,' said Steph. 'Well, maybe later, in the school holidays.'

'We'll come down for a day and meet you. That will be fun,' said Marc.

'And you never know, I might give it a go too,' said Lucy.

'Definitely.'

James changed the subject and they chatted more generally. Lucy left them to fetch another bottle of wine and snacks. Marc recognised that she needed to have a break from the conversation. Clearly Steph thought they were a couple and James hadn't told her they were house-sharing friends. James had said before he thought they would make a great couple and were very compatible. He could see they obviously cared about each other and he wondered why they hadn't progressed beyond friendship, after all he watched their instant sparks of attraction when they met.

Steph relaxed back on the sofa enjoying the warmth of the sunshine. She picked up the magazine Lucy had been reading. Marc wanted to make sure Lucy was alright. He stood up and topped up the wine glasses and taking the empty bottle said, 'I'll give Lucy a hand. Just chill, we'll be back soon.' He walked up to the house.

He found Lucy in the kitchen, putting some snacks in dishes. 'Steph seems friendly,' he said pausing, 'she didn't mean to say the wrong thing.'

'I know, it just felt awkward. I suppose everyone assumes we're a couple now. I expect the village is waiting for a sign to qualify any assumptions too.'

'It's no one's business but ours how we live,' said Marc, 'and I appreciate you don't want to discuss your problems with people, most of all strangers. I did think though, maybe we could talk to James and see if there is something legal we can do about Dick. I don't know, a restraining order or something, until we find out what hold Joan had over Dick. If we can find out, that is.'

'You're probably right,' Lucy sighed, 'but you can see why I don't want to admit to being abused, stalked, threatened, whatever. It looks like vulnerability, or I'm encouraging him in some way?'

'As I said, I understand. It's not at all your fault and not a nice thing to talk about.'

'We'll talk about it later. I don't want to cause trouble for mum for not defending me, however little she thinks of me ... Let's get past this weekend. Steph seems nice and if she and James become a permanent relationship, I'm sure we'll be great friends.'

'Yes, we'll talk to James when he's on his own. Right, what can I carry out to the decking?'

Lucy passed him the tray of snacks she'd put in dishes. 'I'll catch up with you.'

The rest of the afternoon ran into the evening with everyone chatting comfortably and ordering an Indian meal to be delivered, since the wine had flowed with the conversation. Steph admitted to nurturing a dream of writing fantasy fiction books, which drove an interesting topic of discussing books and films.

By the time James and Steph were about to leave, the four of them agreed they'd got on well. Lucy apologised to Steph for the initial awkwardness. 'It's just that I have a problem I don't want to talk about until I can find a solution and I don't want to involve anyone else.'

'It's okay,' said Steph. 'I don't judge. You never know what anyone is dealing with or working through. If you need a friendly ear, I'm available.'

'Thanks,' said Lucy. 'Likewise. I'll always help anyone if I can.'

Marc and James, standing a little apart from the ladies, finished their conversation too. They all exchanged Goodnights and James and Steph walked up the driveway.

'That ended up going well,' said Marc as they headed back to the garden sofas. 'It's a lovely evening to enjoy the stars.'

'Yes, it did,' agreed Lucy. 'I'm sure we'll have plenty more pleasant evenings with them.'

They flopped down onto a sofa and snuggled under the blankets they'd all been using. 'I'd like to go and have a surfing session with

James, the weekend after next. Fancy coming too? We might need wet suits, or we can hire them initially. I don't know about you, but I've got an aversion to cold water,' said Marc.

'Me too. Yes, that would be nice. On the Sunday? It's the summer fair on Saturday.'

'Fine. We'll be glad of a day off after a long busy day. Maureen roped me in to help when she showed me round the school last week.'

Lucy laughed, 'She obviously picked up the vibe you would be interested in giving the board of school governors a go. She's very enthusiastic, isn't she?'

'To be fair, I suppose I was an easy target. She said it would be an informal way of meeting people while helping out by selling raffle tickets.'

'Brilliant idea, Maureen! The raffle tickets.'

'Just don't give me the microphone for any announcements.'

'That won't happen. It's Baz's territory. He won't hand that job over to anyone. He loves the sound of his own voice.'

'Fine. Some of us aren't cut out for public speaking.'

Lucy laughed again. 'Nor me.'

'And you stand up in front of a load of children!'

'Well, that's the whole point—they're children. They won't ask awkward embarrassing questions, or put forward political points of view, or harass. They are just little open books who joyfully absorb learning and ask pertinent questions for everyone to discuss. Not scary at all.'

Marc considered her answer. 'I hadn't thought of it that way. If the audience is really interested in the topic, it makes a difference.'

'Talking of interesting topics, how did your chat with Robbie and Harry go? What did they think?'

'Interesting guys. We talked for ages about various projects, not just my ideas for here, which they think are great. But also, other ideas for projects in the village, such as the school.'

'Ah, yes, more solar panels on the roof,' said Lucy, 'It's what the main fund raising is for, right now. It began when environmental issues became widely considered and now with the energy costs ... well, it's become very important.'

'I suggested maybe we could explore some community projects and get the whole village working together and supporting each other.'

'That's a good idea.'

'So, we found plenty to talk about. At least I'll have two familiar faces at the summer fair,' said Marc.

'Robbie's daughter is in my class, she's a smart girl. I know you feel you have had a lot of decisions to make recently, but I think by getting involved with some of these village projects you'll have some fun and make new friends. Especially as you've chosen your future path is here, it will help you make it successful.'

'I'm happy enough with my decision. This was an opportunity that I was lucky to be given. I love it here—it's so quiet and beautiful, even when it's pouring with rain. And most of all, I've made some good friends, especially you ... James and Bertie. I don't want anything, or anyone, to spoil that and you know what I mean.'

'Yes, I do and I'm glad you've come into my life. And yes, we'll ask James if there's anything we can do.' Lucy paused then continued, 'let's just admire the scenery for a bit ... count the stars, and then go in.'

An owl hooted nearby: T'wit, T'woo, T'wit, T'woo.

* * *

BY THE TIME Marc snuggled under his duvet, he was feeling tired but sleep eluded him. He turned on his bedside light and picked up the top few journals from the pile Joan had left tied with a ribbon. He'd put them on the bedside cabinet ready to read. They were still in date order, just minus the ribbon. He had flipped through a few of them first, to get a feel for what Joan wrote and he put them back into date order.

The first one he chose from the stack was 1996, when Simon and Joan began their new life in Little Beliton. Joan journaled in the same way as he did, noting down special events with thoughts and ideas to muse over, especially ideas for developing the house that Simon and Joan had come up with. Many more ideas than they got round to implementing. It seemed Simon was taken ill in 2002 and struggled on for another three years before he died.

At times tears welled in Marc's eyes as he read. He thought, *Joan was absolutely devastated to be left on her own. Even though she'd gradually been taking over the running of the estate, she was sad and lost.*

Graham, Marc's grandad, used to come and visit sometimes, as by then he was on his own too, but he died in 2009 and Joan had no one else to talk to. Marc's parents, John and Mary visited once, one weekend, but didn't really connect with the place. "It's too quiet here for them," Joan observed. She agonised for a while about who to leave it to when she died, but finally decided that with no other living relatives on Simon's side of the family and "John and Mary with young Marcus ... by now a teenager", she had her Will updated to leave it to them. "They'll probably sell it though ..." she noted.

Marc saved his place with a bookmark thinking, *I wonder what she thought this year when mum and dad died. I wonder if she thought about me becoming 30 and that I am an adult now. I should have tried harder to keep in touch with her, especially when Grandad died, while I was at university, but sadly I didn't think about it. If I had, I could maybe have reconnected with her and had a quiet place to come and learn all about it. But I didn't.*

Marc put the journals carefully back in the pile and turned off the light. He snuggled down. He felt sure he would sleep now; his eyes were too tired to stay open. If he could only keep his brain loops quiet.

CHAPTER 11

Sunday morning began as usual with a breakfast chat and withdrawing to their respective workspaces. Marc logged into work for a few hours, then as the sky cleared and the sun appeared, he picked up another couple of journals and went outside to the garden sofa, taking a coffee with him.

He began with October 5th, 2005: Will I ever get used to the big empty void I live in? The silence. The aching loneliness. I miss Simon so much, Joan wrote.

Marc empathised, feeling her pain. He carried on reading: Today I met Rita. She noticed me sitting on the bench on The Green when she went into the shop, and noted I hadn't moved at all when she came out. I was still staring into the river. I don't know how long I'd been there; I lose track of time lately. Nothing matters anymore. I'm constantly surrounded with silence and loneliness. Emptiness. Home doesn't feel right and yet, it's all I want.

Rita crossed the bridge, walked over to me, and sat on the bench beside me. She didn't say anything for a few minutes. It felt comfortable just to have someone sitting nearby and not having to engage in a superficial conversation. I know people mean well, but I don't feel like talking. No one really wants to know how I feel. No one understands.

Joan had transcribed the gist of the conversation that followed:

JOAN'S JOURNAL

"You look troubled. Can I help?" she said. We introduced ourselves. She was Rita.

When I said I was Joan, she said, "Ah, now I understand. You recently lost your husband, Simon?"

"I did."

"I heard some villagers talking in the bar. They said Simon was a nice man and they were sorry he'd died and felt sorry for you."

"You're from The Fox on the Green?"

"Yes."

"Simon used to meet people there sometimes. Before he was ill."

"I maybe met him then. I can't imagine the pain you're feeling right now knowing you'll never see him again. The man you love. I'm so sorry."

I paused to choke back yet more tears and compose myself. "Thank you. I wonder if the ache ever stops and if the tears ever dry up." I sighed.

Rita said, "I don't know what it's like to feel love like that."

"You and your husband are the landlords, aren't you?"

"Yes."

"Oh, I see. Not so happy. I'm sorry."

We chatted for a little while and I felt a bit better. She had distracted me from focussing on my problems. Instead, I sensed she had problems she might like to share, but she suddenly ended the conversation saying she had to get back, or she'd be in trouble. She scurried back across The Green, crossed over the bridge and disappeared up the lane towards the pub.

The next time I bumped into her we were both in the shop. I saw her climb out of a car, which rushed off up the lane. *Great*, I thought, *he leaves her to carry the shopping back. Charming man!*

Rita walked into the shop looking very agitated. I noticed a bruise on her cheek, near her eye. There were a few people in the shop and

Jan was busy. I went over to Rita and steered her towards a table at the far end of the cafe area. Figuring discretion was needed, I sat her in the chair with her back to the shop, and I sat opposite her. I asked her what had happened. Rita had tears rolling down her cheeks as she told me what a bully Dick was. I asked her why she didn't leave him? She told me she'd nowhere to go and no money of her own, and no one to help her. Then she said, "He's not like it all the time ... he just has a short fuse, that's all." I recognised she was making excuses for his behaviour, but let it go and told her that she could always confide in me.

Jan cleared the shop queue and came over bringing coffee. I got the feeling she'd seen something like this before. Rita thanked us saying, "I can't stay long, he'll go berserk if I don't get back and cook the lunches." Jan fetched a clean flannel, a bowl of water and some ice cubes, and told her to sit there for a bit.

We mopped her up and gave her the cold compress to put on the bruise. Eventually, Jan took the bowl of water and the flannel away, and returned to distract and serve another customer who just came into the shop.

We talked for a while and I listened. Dick bullies her often. He manipulates her using emotional blackmail and sometimes violence. When it suits him, and to achieve some objective or other, he would be nice and treat her well, and then without any warning totally change. It seemed their marriage had started off okay and then over the years he changed. Rita told me, "It's okay if I'm doing all the work and he can sit drinking with people in the bar. He puts on a great facade of being Mr Nice Guy, but if he's got to do any work ... well, he's ... obnoxious. Lazy. Drunk a lot of the time. He doesn't let me have much personal money and therefore he totally controls me. There's nothing much I can do. I can't leave and he knows it."

Joan wrote, I asked her if she wanted to leave. Even if it takes a while. She replied that she'd like to have the choice, so if she needed to she could choose freedom and leave to feel safe. I assured her that we'll think of something. So, I'm here, writing a précis of our conversations, while pondering in my journal.

I suppose if Simon's gone and I'm still here, it must be for a reason. There must be something for me to do. Perhaps it's helping Rita?

2022

Marc continued reading the journal entries. Joan continued discussing meetings with Rita, where they worked out that Rita needed to make reports of events and they took photos of her injuries with solid evidence of the date, holding up a newspaper—to prove what she wrote was accurate.

When Dick was being amenable and gave her some money, she took care to save it safely. Initially, she gave cash to Joan, which progressed to a secret savings account. Rita was terrified Dick would find out and pleaded with the bank not to have correspondence sent to her at the pub and sent to Joan's address instead.

As Marc read on, it was clear Joan and Rita became the best of friends. Rita came up with the suggestion that the two of them join in with the village fundraising events and she encouraged Joan to run projects with her help. Joan wrote, I think she considered it is good therapy for me. Dick complained she was skiving off work, but she argued that it was a way of getting to know the villagers better and quietly promote some extra business for them, so he let her go.

We met often in the coffee shop when Rita was on a shopping errand. She was careful not to do anything to provoke Dick's temper though. Occasionally he did lose it and lashed out, we'd take more photos and keep a record in a journal created for the purpose. I wished Rita would report him to the police, but Rita thought that revenge would be better. She could make him suffer by limiting his freedom to move on when she left him. She planned to disappear as soon as she has what she considers is enough money saved to start a new life alone. She plans to go abroad and try something new and Dick wouldn't be able to trace her.

. . .

MARC CONTINUED READING: It took five years to save enough money. There were a few good times when Dick would be nice, take her on holidays, and buy her nice things, which is when she'd doubt her overall goal, thinking he'd reverted to loving her and being nice. Then out of the blue he'd start again. Sometimes in public, in the bar, he'd belittle her. Often there were marks on her, which some people noticed and she'd make flippant excuses and got pretty good at disguising them with makeup.

In January 2011, with a file of evidence compiled and legal papers to change her name, organised by Joan's solicitors, the time came for Rita to leave. She had had enough. She finally realised that nothing would ever change and she wanted control of her life.

Joan wrote that Rita packed a small case and rucksack and gave them to her when Dick had gone somewhere, one day. Then early one morning, Rita walked out of the pub, leaving Dick asleep in bed. If anyone had seen her, they'd think she was going to the shop, walking purposefully down the road without a backward glance.

Joan met her in the church car park, as arranged, and they drove unseen out of the village.

JOAN'S JOURNAL

The next entry read: Dick, being his usual self-centred self, didn't report her missing for nearly a week. He thought she was just being stupid and she'd soon be back. That had actually made Rita's getaway simple. When he did get around to going to the police to report Rita missing, door-to-door enquiries revealed that many villagers weren't surprised, some mentioned Rita often had injuries, or they'd heard when she had been yelled at. Dick was taken in for questioning under suspicion of her murder, but as no body was found and there wasn't any evidence to suggest murder, he was released. However, a few nights in custody while they investigated, with time to reflect on his attitude towards her and his misogynistic, narcissistic behaviour, mellowed him for a while.

Eventually, Dick accepted that Rita had left him and he has no idea where she could have gone. He decided he needed help to run the pub. Someone to take her place.

2022

Marc carried on reading, noting that he soon employed Maggie as a barmaid and general help and to justify not paying her, he allowed her to move in with her ten-year-old daughter, Lucy, using the excuse that her wages are board and living expenses. He was "providing them a home".

Joan admitted she never went to the pub herself; she didn't like the pub atmosphere. That resonated with Marc. But she heard from village friends that Maggie apparently idolises Dick and he, of course, is flattered—a young woman falling at his feet boosts his ego. It doesn't take too long before she's expecting his child.

As Joan had written, *Hmm, leopards don't change their spots. There will be trouble ahead.*

MARC CLOSED the journals and put them on the seat beside him. He relaxed back and closed his eyes to enjoy the sun on his face while reflecting for a while on what he'd read.

'I'm shattering your peace. Here you are,' said Lucy. Marc opened his eyes and saw that she was holding out a glass of fresh lemonade to him.

'Thank you,' he said as Lucy seated herself beside him.

'Interesting reading?' she said, nodding towards the journals.

'Yes,' said Marc. 'I think it explains the hold Joan had over Dick.'

'Really?'

'Yes. And I think James is the person to ask. His firm are holding some papers for a lady called Rita.'

'Um ... Rita.' Lucy paused to think, 'I think I remember ... from when mum first moved us into the pub when I was a kid. That was Dick's wife's name.'

'Yes, indeed. I think you should read these too.' Marc handed her the two journals he'd been reading. 'Then tell me what you think.'

Lucy hesitantly took the journals. 'Are you sure? She was your aunt.'

'You were her friend. Of course, I'm sure.'

'Okay.'

* * *

LATER OVER DINNER, Lucy said, 'I learned a lot from reading the journals.'

'Interesting aren't they? Do you reckon Dick's had a go at your mum?'

'Verbally, yes at times, I've heard him. He controls her pretty much the way he controlled Rita. No money of her own, so no independence. He repeats the "be grateful I give you a home" line constantly. She has to do most of the work in the pub. Yes. Physically? I don't know. Maybe he's learned not to do that.'

'Or learned not to leave visible marks. He's been rough with you, hasn't he?'

'Verbally threatening mostly. Emotional blackmail. And yes, he did try to rape me that day. I know that was his intention.'

Marc asked, 'And what did he say that day I came to the school ... after the funeral?'

'He threatened me again, saying, "now that old busybody is out of the way...". Of course, I didn't know what he meant, but we know now. Joan had something over him.'

'And don't you think that the file, lodged for safekeeping with the solicitors is the evidence she controlled him with, to protect you?' said Marc.

'Do you reckon?'

'Of course. Hand that over to the police and together with their investigation when Rita left ... don't you think Joan told him that if he carried on doing that, she would give the police something they needed.'

'Really? An elderly lady controlling the village bully ...' Lucy couldn't quite believe it.

Marc seemed very animated. 'Precisely. On the surface it seems pretty unlikely, but obviously he thought she had something because he left you alone. He knew Joan and Rita had been friends.'

'Well ... yes,' said Lucy, 'he left me alone. He also knew that my mum doesn't like me much, so he's been playing happy families with just Mum and Marty and I was out of the way.'

'How did that work? I mean, your Mum didn't mind you moving in with Joan?'

'No, not at all. I was the thorn removed from her side. She was willing to hand over responsibility for me. After all, it didn't cost her anything and she couldn't give me anything, like other mums do. So, I don't know if she did it for herself, or for me. Joan looked after me and set me up for a better future than I ever would have had in prospect with Mum. She was too busy delegating the pub washing up and cleaning, and work like that to me, rather than me studying for my GCSEs.

'You see, she and I have completely different personalities. When she was at school, it seems, she was a rebel. She'd sooner be partying, trying drugs and spending time with boyfriends than reading books, handing in homework, and setting herself up for a future. But that is my nature, quiet and I love learning. Allegedly she was always truanting from school too. As I said, she was fifteen when she had me and she says she's no idea who my father is.'

'That's sad ... for you. My parents just didn't understand me, I was far too quiet and studious for them, but my life was never that bad. How was your relationship with your grandparents?'

'They were at their wits end, I think, trying to bring Mum up. They didn't know she was pregnant, until she was past the abortion limit. And as she was just fifteen, they were utterly ashamed and devastated. They made her face up to her "responsibilities" and look after me. It's no wonder she resents me. I was the reason she didn't enjoy her teens with her mates.'

'It was hardly your fault. So, when Joan offered you a home to keep you safe…'

'Mum jumped at the chance. After all, with Marty she has his father around, even if Dick isn't particularly nice to her. And with Joan I got the chance… no, I was encouraged to live a decent life … study, supported, and treated with genuine affection. It was in time for me to pass my exams, go on to A levels and higher education. I would never have done that if I stayed with Mum.'

'Gosh.' Marc paused to think about what Lucy had told him. 'Reading the journals has brought out a lot of the past. Thank you for sharing that with me.'

'I trust you. It's not something I'm proud of, but it makes me very aware that many children have issues they might need to talk about with someone they can trust. I had no one. My grandparents had decided to follow their dreams and sold up and cleared off to Spain to run a bar, and that's why mum moved us in with Dick. They left her to live her own life the way she wanted to. They email me occasionally, to make sure I'm okay, and they've said I can go and visit for a holiday, if I want to. I've never been though.'

'Given all this, how do you feel about talking to James? He must be able to find out about the file.'

'I'm sure Joan probably talked about meeting me and her thoughts of the situation, in her journals. But yes, I think I don't have a choice—I need to find out about the file,' said Lucy.

'I won't read any more of the journals, if you like, you've told me your side of events and that's all that matters to us,' said Marc.

'No, read them. I'm sure she passes on more wisdom.'

'Okay, but the file … it's not anything to do with Joan really. James would have said if he'd come across it when dealing with her estate. It's Rita's business.'

'Hmm, you're right. We'll ask him.'

CHAPTER 12

Marc and Lucy arranged a meeting with James and told him about the problem and what they had read in the journals.

'Lucy, it's an awful situation you've had to deal with,' he said, sympathetically. 'I've always known you won't meet anyone in the pub. Now I understand why. I'll do some research at work about any documents, although they probably weren't for Joan to access, in view of what you've said, and despite that she helped to collate evidence. This all happened before I joined the firm, so I'll have to find out. I'll consult my colleagues to see if they remember anything. As for Dick threatening you, we'll explore that too. You don't have any physical evidence, or witnesses to support applying for an injunction, do you?'

'No, I don't,' replied Lucy, 'Clearly the evidence Joan and Rita collated was enough to worry Dick for a few years, and the threat that it might surface and be released has been sufficient to keep him at bay. Maybe it's still enough? I don't want to cause trouble for mum, despite that she won't ever defend me.'

'I understand. Try not to worry too much. Whenever I've been in the pub and heard him, I get the impression Dick has a huge ego and is full of himself, but I think that's the sign of a bullying coward. Don't you?'

'Yes, I agree, James,' said Marc, 'and he's trying to exert control over Lucy and stop her living her life, her way. Maybe it's linked, in some way, to the way he controls her mum, but he's got no right to do it to Lucy.'

'I've been very wary since the funeral,' said Lucy, 'because later that same evening, was when he threatened me again—he won't win. I won't let him.' Lucy sounded feisty.

'As I said, I'll look after you Lucy,' said Marc.

'You shouldn't have to, Marc, but thanks,' said Lucy.

'Leave it with me,' said James, 'And don't worry, this is a confidential conversation. I'll check the office document vault and get back to you.'

'Thank you,' said Marc. 'It's very much appreciated.'

'It is,' said Lucy, 'very much.'

* * *

THE FRIDAY EVENING, before the summer fair, they spent helping a group of parents decorating the school with bunting and pop-up awnings, setting up entertainment and stalls. Marc was given his pile of raffle tickets and was relieved to find some had already been sold—the stubs needed separating and folding, and putting into the tombola. Lucy helped him. 'Oscar has asked if he can help you tomorrow,' she said. 'He'll love being given some tasks to do, whether it's handling some money, or filling out the stubs. All good learning for him.'

'Of course,' said Marc, 'I'm sure he will charm people into parting with their cash with his cheeky smile. It will be fun.' They finished folding the tickets and joined in helping others until the preparations were complete for the evening.

Marc and Lucy started walking home together and as they approached the junction of school lane with the main village road, Dick appeared in front of them. 'Oh no,' whispered Lucy to Marc.

'Hello Lucy,' said Dick smarmily. 'What a cosy pair you appear to be. I warned you about having a relationship with him,' Dick tossed his head towards Marc.

'Whether or not, we're having a relationship is none of your business,' said Marc, 'Lucy can choose who she wants to be with.'

Dick stepped forward closer to Marc and glared at him. 'Are you screwing my stepdaughter?'

Lucy hissed, 'I've told you before, you are not, NOT, my stepfather and whether or not we're in a relationship is none of your business. Leave us alone.'

Dick slowly turned his head to look at her and scowled, then turned back to look at Marc again. 'Are you using MY Lucy to get your end away?' Dick aimed a punch at Marc, which he deflected and sent Dick staggering off balance.

'You are a nasty bully and you're at it again,' said Marc.

Dick looked at them both. 'You don't know anything,' he snarled.

'Oh, don't we,' said Lucy. 'We will not hesitate to release what we know if you don't leave us alone. And don't you ever treat my mum the way you treated Rita.'

Dick just stared back at them with a look of fear and his jaw dropped. 'You don't know anything' he snarled again.

'Do you want to risk it?' said Lucy. 'We know exactly what you got up to—you've been warned. You keep away from me and don't you dare start on my mum,' said Lucy. With that Lucy tucked her arm firmly into the crook of Marc's elbow and they turned and walked on towards the main road and around the corner to go home.

Dick stood still, gawping, watching them walk away.

'I thought he'd follow us,' said Lucy quietly to Marc as they turned the corner.

'I don't think he'll dare. All the same, take care. I don't trust him not to try again, especially if you're on your own,' said Marc, 'but you've shown him, you're not giving him an inch and I'm with you.'

'I dreamed that he might have a go at you. Sorry about that.'

'Hey, I might be quiet but I did Tae Kwan Do at school. I needed to, to keep some bullies at bay. If I had to, I'd make mincemeat of him!

Well, perhaps I'm a bit rusty—it's a while since I've done it, but I'm definitely not a pushover.' Marc grinned.

Lucy gave a little laugh. 'You have totally surprised me, yet again.'

'I told you I'd look after you,' said Marc. 'Now whose turn is it to cook supper?'

'Hmm, do we have a rota? Or we could work as a team,' said Lucy.

'Good idea.'

They turned to walk up the lane in silence. Marc felt happy that Lucy was walking closely beside him, her arm still tucked around his. He smiled quietly to himself as a feeling of warmth ran through his body. As they reached the top of the drive, Marc broke the silence. 'On Sunday, do you still fancy the day out in Cornwall? Go and meet James and Steph, as we said. Maybe get kitted out with some surfing gear.'

'Yes, great. It would be fun to relax. Yes, message James and organise it.'

'I will.' Another warm feeling rushed through Marc.

***

THE SUMMER FAIR seemed to be going well. Everyone appeared to be prepared to have fun, spend money, and support the school. The children enjoyed the games and some, like Oscar, enjoyed helping. Oscar had fun handling the money and learning to give change, and with some guidance with spellings, he wrote some of the draw ticket stubs in his neatest handwriting. He was very sweet thanking people for buying the books of tickets and wishing them luck. So much so, that some people bought another book of tickets.

Lucy relaxed when she saw her mum attended the fair with Marty and without Dick. They sat and had a cup of coffee together, while Marty had a couple of goes at the coconut shy and was chuffed to win a prize. Lucy wanted to check everything was okay with her mum, after her altercation with Dick, the previous evening. She gave Marty some money for an ice cream. He ran off happily to get it.

'Everything good at home, Mum?'

'Yes, why do you ask?' said Maggie, then continued, 'Dick seemed placid today, he's clearly got something on his mind. He even gave me a generous amount of cash to spend this afternoon and said to make sure Marty had fun.'

'Good,' said Lucy. 'Marty is obviously enjoying himself.'

A friend of Maggie's appeared, so Lucy left them to it and went to see how the raffle tickets were selling. As she approached the table, she was pleased to see Marc engaged in a conversation with Harry, at the same time helping Oscar with some writing. Lucy hung back watching them. Marc looked so natural at his task, and part of the community. Oscar looked up at him when he needed help and Marc responded immediately. He'd be a lovely, kind attentive dad, thought Lucy. She smiled and continued towards them. 'Hi guys,' she said to them, 'how's it going?'

Oscar answered, 'There are only three books of tickets left,' he said excitedly.

'Well, I'll tell you what,' said Marc, 'here's the money for them and you can write your name on the tickets and anything you might win— is yours. Thank you for all your hard work.'

'Thanks,' said Oscar with a big grin on his little face. He'd had his eye on a huge bar of chocolate all afternoon. He told Marc it was "big enough to share with the whole family." He finished off folding the tickets and put them in the drum of the tombola. Bertie joined them. 'Have you had fun, little man?'

'Oh yes, Dad,' said Oscar.

'He's been a great help. Thank you very much, Oscar,' said Marc.

They left to join Emily and Gemma, who were working serving tea and cakes. Later, Oscar returned to Marc for his reward … spinning the tombola and drawing the winning tickets, which he passed to Baz on the public address system to announce the winners. It was lovely to see him feeling important, and even nicer when one of his tickets was drawn and he could choose the bar of chocolate. He grinned from ear to ear.

Once the fair ended, everyone was happy to pitch in and help to clear up and put everything away, and the school was returned to normal ready for Monday morning.

Marc and Lucy walked home, chatting. 'I reckon that's the best fund-raising event yet,' said Lucy, 'and I've been to quite a few over the years. There was such a positive buzz.'

'I think everyone sees the benefit of installing solar panels on the school roof. Harry was chatting to me about it,' said Marc.

'Definitely. The overheads are so expensive these days, let alone with the rising energy costs. We're lucky here, the community is very supportive of the PTA and we all pull together, which is why we try to pay back to the community when the children grow food items and propagate plants for the parish hall garden. It's especially important to help families who are struggling a bit.'

'It's a lovely ethos,' said Marc.

'Come to think of it, that small triangular field—over there,' said Lucy pointing, 'people think it belongs to the manor. It's just standing unused.'

'I'll check the deeds. Why? What are you thinking?'

'Well ...' said Lucy, 'I wondered if the school could use it, so we can expand our growing activities. We've started on the new little plot next to the school, but with the long summer holidays coming up, we could run holiday club sessions to clear and prepare the field to use it. I'm sure we'd soon rally up some assistance.'

'Yes, brilliant idea. Bertie has mentioned he'd like to help the children learn more horticultural skills, arguing they are life skills, which indeed they are. I'll check the deeds and see if it does belong to the manor. Looking at it, the fields where I've seen the cows ... the last field, runs next to it so you might be right. It's only small and being triangular it's probably not useful for much. I'll have a look.'

'Thanks,' said Lucy. 'Are you feeling settled and happy here?'

'Yes, I do. It feels like home. I've never lived anywhere so beautiful, and quiet, and to be quite honest—friendly. I feel like I'm part of the community already and it's only been a few months.'

'You looked settled this afternoon. Relaxed.' Lucy smiled.

'You were watching me?'

'No, not all afternoon. Just before I came over, while you were chatting with Harry. You looked as if you were enjoying yourself.'

'I was, Harry is interesting to chat with and little Oscar is a ray of sunshine. He's funny and good company.'

'Yes, they're a nice family.'

'Fancy a takeaway tonight? Or we could have a meal out in Greater Beliton. I've seen a couple of nice-looking restaurants when I've been with James,' said Marc.

'I reckon we should get a takeaway delivered today. First, I think a glass of wine would hit the right spot to relax, so no driving. And two, we're leaving early tomorrow and a late night at a restaurant ... wouldn't do a nice experience justice. Another time?' Lucy smiled.

'Sure. Whatever you'd like. Good idea.' Marc got the warm fuzzy feeling again as Lucy tucked her arm through the crook of his elbow again. They walked up the lane towards home in silence, both lost in their own thoughts and enjoying the moment.

CHAPTER 13

The next morning, Marc and Lucy were up early and headed for Cornwall to meet James. Steph was on duty, but she urged the friends to meet and she'd catch up with them later.

They started the day with coffee and bacon rolls for breakfast at the beach cafe. 'I've got some news for you,' said James. 'The file you mentioned exists, and I'm currently reading through it. Joan and Rita collated a lot of evidence, notes, and photographs, as you told me. But, as I thought, Joan didn't have the authority to release the information, it's kept for Rita if she ever needs access to it. What we don't know, is where Rita is. Clearly there was once a suspicion that she'd been murdered, but you have shown that is not so.'

'Right, and there's nothing to indicate where Rita is?' asked Marc.

'No, but ... you might be able to help,' said James, 'because there are copies of the Deed Poll and some other papers.'

'And ...?' said Lucy.

'Her new name is Ann Smith, but that's all we know. We have no idea where she went and no way to contact her. I wondered if you had found anything in Joan's papers, or on her computer, to show that Joan kept in contact. Of course, Joan would have been very careful about not letting anything slip to anyone about where Rita/Ann had gone, or even if she's moved on from her original destination to her present whereabouts.'

'Ah, okay, we need to do some detective work then. I've not looked at any more of the journals since we found the information we needed, so there might be something in a later one. Neither have I done anything with her computer lately. She didn't do much on the computer, but she did have an email address, so maybe they kept in touch by email. When I briefly looked through it even if I'd seen Ann Smith, I wouldn't have had a clue about any of this,' said Marc. 'I'd have just thought she was an old friend, maybe.'

'Exactly what I thought, if you weren't looking for anyone in particular,' said James. 'So, can you have a look and see what you can find? I suggest that you don't contact her if you find anything, just let me know and we'll contact her officially. For one thing, if you did email her, she might not see it anyway. New email contacts often go to SPAM, don't they?'

'But not if I send it from Joan's mailbox, if they'd been keeping in touch. Is it illegal to use a deceased person's email address?' said Marc. 'I could send an email just to inform her of who I am and tell her the news ....'

'That's a reasonable approach, surely?' said Lucy.

'Yes, okay. Keep it simple. We don't want to frighten her that we're going to break any confidences,' said James. 'Let me know what you find out. Right guys, let's go for a wet suit search on the other side of the beach in the surf shop.'

They chatted as they walked. 'How did the summer fair go?'

'Great thanks,' said Lucy, 'you missed a fun event.'

'Yes, but I would have missed seeing Steph,' said James.

'Fair enough,' said Marc.

'I'll give the PTA a donation,' said James.

'You don't have to do that,' Lucy said. 'You don't have any children at the school.'

James laughed, 'I might, one day, you never know. And so might you guys... Don't panic, I'm not insinuating anything.'

'James, Marc and I really like each other, and we care about each other, it's just that with all the troubles I've had with Dick I don't want to draw Marc into it and put him at risk of Dick picking on or harming him, so we've agreed to be friends. We're just good, close friends who get on well,' said Lucy.

James patted them both on their shoulders as he walked between them. 'It's no one else's business, you must do what's right for you. But from what I've seen ... you guys are made for each other and I hope we solve the problem soon.'

'It's okay James,' said Marc, 'I respect Lucy's need for boundaries.'

'Actually,' said Lucy, 'we've got it under control, right now.' They went on to tell James what happened on the Friday evening and Dick's reactions.

'That's good, he's obviously worried now. He doesn't know what you've got, but he's not going to chance anything. Hopefully he'll back off from harassing you again. If he's got any sense he will. It will give us time to do our research.'

'Thanks, James,' said Lucy, 'and one day, we might surprise you and you'll be the first to know.'

Marc listened smiling to himself with that warm fuzzy feeling rising again thinking, *I really hope that's soon.*

ONCE KITTED out with wet suits, they hired surfboards and headed for the waves. James suggested they learn to bodyboard first and catch the waves to ride into shore. Neither of them felt confident enough to swim too far out, but they spent a couple of hours having fun learning to get the hang of it.

When Steph finished work, she joined them for a fish and chip supper and an evening stroll on the beach. There was no doubt that Lucy and Steph got on well together, apart from having similar jobs, they had similar hobbies and interests too.

Eventually the time came for Marc and Lucy to leave and drive home. They had had a fun relaxing day learning some new skills with pleasant company.

Later, in bed, Marc began reading another of Joan's journals. Joan had indeed kept in touch with Rita, now Ann, and was pleased to note that she was having a good start and meeting some new people. She travelled around France until she found a small pretty town where she felt comfortable, and she got herself a job in a coffee shop. She found an affordable apartment and was learning French, and it was going quite well, although her boss was pleased that because she was English, so she could make the British visitors feel welcome.

Ann invited Joan to visit her as she had a spare bedroom. Joan was initially reluctant. She'd only ever been on holiday with Simon and hadn't even been anywhere in England alone. Going to France was a very scary prospect. However, exchanging emails regularly, Ann persuaded her to give it a try. Ann would meet her at the airport, so apart from the flight, Joan wouldn't be alone, and staying with Ann meant she didn't have to deal with being amongst a lot of strangers and feeling very odd and lonely being single.

Joan wrote about the fun they had visiting local places and she was enjoying time to read and paint, particularly while Ann was working, and a couple of weeks quickly passed. She'd be happy to visit again now the ice had been broken with the first trip.

Ann asked for updates on people she knew in Little Beliton and what Dick was getting up to. She thought it was amusing that he'd been taken in for questioning regarding her disappearance and had spent a couple of nights in gaol. Joan recorded Ann's words, "I'm sure it did him good to have time off the whisky and contemplate his attitude and behaviour, but I can't imagine he really changed much."

Joan recorded an outline of their conversation. I agreed with Ann and I told her about the young single mother with a little girl living-in and working for him. From what I understand she's mostly working in exchange for board and rent for the two of them and is receiving little more than pocket money. Ann remarked that it was typical of him to take advantage of someone who actually needs proper constructive support. I told Ann that I heard she idolises him though, and that really boosts his ego. Ann agreed, but she said she was concerned for the little girl's safety. He used to drool over the dirty mags he had.

Reading this reported exchange worried Marc. He thought, It was obvious Ann knew what he was like. Had she really done the right thing just running away? If she'd reported him, maybe the police could have searched the place for the evidence. But then again, Marc supposed she thought he'd do his time and be back to make her life even more of a misery. Hard one.

He carried on reading: Joan wrote she was happy to see the confidence growing in her friend. Ann was enjoying being herself and making her own decisions and being with her new friends. She projected an aura of being relaxed and happy.

At this point tiredness overcame Marc. He put a bookmark in the journal, switched off the light and snuggled down to sleep.

* * *

THE NEXT MORNING, Marc switched on Joan's laptop. It hadn't been hard to guess her password to access it when he originally checked it for any information for settling the estate. He'd then set a new password.

He opened her email and signed in—same as the original laptop password, Simon1965. The year of their wedding. The Inbox needed looking at and clearing sometime. He checked the folders to see if there was one for Ann, or any permutations of her name. There was nothing obvious. He used Create, New and started typing A to see what the computer suggested for a recipient and sure enough, a.smith ... completed the To box, then he entered a subject line, "Sad News", and started writing ...

Dear Ann

I am Marc and I'm Joan's great nephew. My Grandad was Joan's brother, Graham, and my dad was his son John.

I am writing to tell you some sad news. I'm very sorry to say that Joan died at the end of March. I know that was over three months ago, but until recently I didn't know about you, and have only just found out and how you both kept in touch.

Only three of us know about you; me, Joan's solicitor, and Joan's friend, housemate and companion, Lucy. Your secret is safe with us. However, we hope you can help us solve a problem, so I hope you will reply and we can discuss it.

If it feels strange to you using Joan's email address, contact me on mine. Here's the link ...

With all good wishes, Marc

Marc checked what he'd written before pressing Send. He was quite pleased he'd thought of the option to reply to the message, or to his own email address. He pondered, if, or how long it might take to get a reply. He closed Joan's computer and fired up his own. Time for work.

A couple of hours later Marc's computer pinged, notifying him of new mail. He clicked it to open it. a.smith@...

Dear Marc,

Just a quick reply to thank you for letting me know about Joan. I'm sorry to hear the news and send my condolences to you. I know your father was Joan's heir, so I was surprised to get a message from you.

Joan told me about happy memories of time spent with you. I hope you still enjoy art. She was very proud of you and what you have achieved.

Joan was a kind and caring lady and I am proud and grateful she was my friend. I hope you'll understand that I need some time to come to terms that she's gone. To grieve for her. Give me a few days and I'll message you again.

Kind regards, Ann

Marc leaned back in his chair thinking. That's a nice reply. They must have been good friends and the news was a bit of a shock for her. He finished closing down his computer before going downstairs for some lunch. He glanced out of the window and saw Bertie busy mowing the lawn. He made two sandwiches and mugs of coffee and took them outside to the decking. 'Hi Bertie.'

Bertie came over. 'Thanks, Marc, that's kind.' They sat at the table. 'Oscar had a great time with you on Saturday. He felt he'd done something really useful to help the school get its solar panels.'

'I think it's a project that's fired up the whole community, especially with the way energy prices are rising and the school budget is stretched. I know Lucy personally buys some resources for the children to use,' said Marc, 'she shouldn't have to though. Austere times.'

'Yes,' agreed Bertie. 'That's the value of the community garden projects we have too. That way the school kitchen ensures all the children get nutritious lunches, especially important for the families that struggle. It's why we'd like to grow more. The kids have fun learning about it too.'

'Ah, that's something I was going to talk to you about. Lucy told me about the idea to use the triangular field,' said Marc. 'She told me people think it could be put to good use.'

'Yes,' said Bertie.

'I've checked the deeds for here and the field is part of the land. I'm going to hand it over to the school to use. I think it would make a great community project, right in the middle of the village. I can see it needs a lot of work and coordination. The school can run it and the community can join in so it benefits everyone, and the children learn valuable life skills.'

'That's great. What with the little plot the school was recently given and supplying the parish hall garden, we can do even more. We can get people with different skills to help such as getting some machinery in to clear it. Lucy will be pleased, especially with the school holidays coming up. Talking of which, I'm borrowing a rotavator and I'll make a start on the kitchen garden here tomorrow.'

'I'll plan my work so I can help. Are you sure we can manage on our own? We could always hire some extra help.'

'We'll make a start and see how it goes. I'll be up when I've dropped the children to school. Thanks for the sandwich and coffee, I'll finish the lawns and tidy the borders.'

'Thanks, Bertie. I must get back to my work today, especially if I'm busy tomorrow.' Marc gathered up the plates and mugs and stood up.

'No problem. See you later.' Bertie returned to the lawn mower.

CHAPTER 14

Lucy was pleased that Marc had received a reply from Ann so quickly. 'I bet she's wondering why we're asking for her help,' said Lucy, 'she's probably presumed that Dick's been causing trouble. What other help would we ask for? She'll be trying to decide whether she wants to get involved and open old wounds by helping us, or keep out of it because she's moved on. It's not her problem.'

'Totally agree,' said Marc, 'James is aware of that too, which is why he suggested if we found any contact details he would write. But anyway, she's replied and said she'll be in touch again soon. She could have just deleted the email. We'll give her some time and wait and see what she says, and then give her the option of discussing it with James.'

'It's positive that she replied immediately,' said Lucy. 'By the way, changing the subject, the summer fair raised the highest amount of funds ever. Everyone is buzzing about it. It was a good event. The PTA still needs to raise more money, but the fair was a huge boost to the funds. So far, they've saved enough to get the rest of the solar panels fitted to get the project going and add more later.'

'That's great,' said Marc, 'It's a shame they haven't got enough to have the full number of panels and batteries fitted at the outset. I really hope they can get them all done soon. We need to think up some more fundraising ideas and events.'

'I agree,' said Lucy.

'Oh, and while we're changing subjects, I checked the deeds,' said Marc, 'the field does belong with here and I'm happy to let the school use it. In fact, when Bertie was here today, we talked about it. He said people are keen to take part in the project. He can organise a clearance team and a rotavator and get going. I'll check with James to make sure there is no legal problem with the school using it, but I can't think anyone would object to it being used for horticulture, and it's better than it standing idle gathering weeds.'

'Fantastic!' Lucy grinned. 'I don't know about seasonal crops and planting, but there must be something useful we can start propagating for the winter. I'm learning with the children. And, as you know, Bertie is keen to pass on his knowledge.'

'And an almost related topic … Bertie and I are going to start on the kitchen garden here tomorrow morning. So, I'm going to focus on my work this evening, and tomorrow evening, to make time for it.'

'Just as well that we've had dinner early then. I've end of year reports to start writing, so I'm busy too. We'll clear up and meet later.'

'Looking forward to it,' smiled Marc.

So am I, thought Lucy.

***

THE NEXT FEW days were busy for Marc and Lucy. Bertie and Marc had several sessions working on the kitchen garden and Bertie organised a team of people to work on the school field. Despite aching from doing his own garden project, Marc volunteered to help with the school project too. *Nothing a soak in a hot bath won't solve, and doing something useful is a much more interesting way of exercising. And I'm building more social connections. And Lucy is involved, so I'll make sure we're there together.*

Lucy began planning the holiday sessions to involve the children propagating seedlings to plant when the time was right. A few other parents volunteered to help and Lucy was grateful. She needed people with the right knowledge.

The field proved to be very suitable. The stream Marc had seen running by the upper fields where the cows grazed, ran through it on its onward journey to join the river. Surely it must be possible to use some water from it for the produce. Maybe, in future, build a pond to reserve water to use in droughts, without impeding the flow too much? Another project that required professional assessment.

Announcing the field project fired up the enthusiasm of the entire community. Regular fund-raising barbecues were planned for many weekends throughout the summer in the parish hall garden—social events after the field working sessions, and planning meetings for future work in the field.

Robbie and Harry invited some experts to visit the village and appraise the potential for organising various community eco-projects to go beyond the needs of the school.

* * *

MARC RECEIVED AN EMAIL FROM ANN. It read...
Dear Marc
Thank you for your patience awaiting my reply.
I knew about you—as I said, Joan was very proud of you and your achievements. I think I also know a little about Lucy. Is she the young lady who Joan had given a home to? You cannot possibly know how much pleasure she got from Lucy's company. It was as if she finally got what she and Simon had always hoped for—a family. She treated Lucy like a daughter, I think, but I don't know the circumstances of Lucy's arrival in her life.

What a good mum Joan would have been and I'm very sad a family never happened for them. Joan told me all about Simon. It wasn't long after his death that I met her. She was sitting on the bench by the river on The Green looking terribly lost and sad, so I went over to sit with her. When we talked, she told me her story and it tugged my heart-strings. Eternal love! It turned out that she needed a friend, and so did I. Neither of us were in a good place in our lives, for different reasons, and we formed a very close bond helping and supporting each other.

I've been wondering about why you might need to talk to me. I'm thinking that, as you mentioned Joan's solicitor, it's something to do with some papers I lodged with her firm of solicitors for safekeeping, and Dick has been causing trouble for someone?

As you can appreciate, it's hard for me to consider stirring up old troubles. It's easier to let sleeping dogs lie, as I've moved on and have a new love in my life. But I also think there is a reason you have looked for me and you have reassured me you will keep my contact details confidential. There is obviously someone who needs some help before something tragic happens.

Joan did tell me Dick had employed a young woman with a small child, to live in and help him run the pub doing what I used to do. It must have boosted his ego to have a young woman with him and I hope, for her sake, the novelty hasn't worn off.

Perhaps we could arrange a video call? Or maybe Joan's solicitor can talk with me?'

It's not that I won't help, if you really need me to, but it's more *how* I can help, without undoing the good I've done for my life by leaving.

I do have to say though, leaving was hard. I love Little Beliton. It was nice when Joan came to visit me here for holidays and keep me up to date with the news, and I think a change of scene occasionally was good for her too. I know only too well how hard it is to travel alone when everyone around you appears to be a couple. I wanted a new life, so for me it was about freedom and an adventure. But for Joan it was lonely, reminding her of Simon and how much she missed him and how alone she was.

Please let me know how I can help you.

My very best wishes, Ann

Marc considered his reply and completely understood Ann's reluctance. It was exactly what he'd expected.

Dear Ann,

Thank you very much for your reply. I emailed you, not dad,

because my parents died just a couple of months before Joan, in January. It's been a very difficult time for me. I'm very grateful that Joan has given me the chance to live here and create a new life and move on.

I've copied James into this reply, as you can see from his email address. He is Joan's solicitor, and he sorted out her estate very efficiently. You are correct about Lucy's identity. We are house sharing very amicably, and the three of us, with James, have become very good friends over these last few months.

To chat and meet you with a video call sometime would be lovely. I respect that you'd like to know what is going on and how you might be able to help us. James is the best person to discuss it with.

All I will say is, yes, it's Dick. But you can rest assured we won't compromise your anonymity or do anything you're not in agreement with.

Very best wishes, Marc

Marc carried on working for a while before closing down his computer. He then went downstairs to chill out and relax for a while. He could hear Lucy was watching the TV and went to make their hot chocolate.

Lucy smiled when he entered the room carrying two steaming mugs. She didn't like to admit to herself that it was her favourite time of the day. 'Thank you,' she said, as he put the mugs down on the coasters on the coffee table.

'You're welcome,' Marc said. 'I've had a reply from Ann. Pretty much what we thought, so I've replied and copied James in so they can discuss it.'

'Good idea.'

'She also suggested perhaps we can organise a video call meeting sometime and have a chat.'

'That would be nice. I'd like to meet her.'

'Anyway, I've left it for James and Ann to work something out.' They fell into companionable silence and settled down to quietly relax, watching a TV programme.

* * *

THE NEXT NEWS Marc received was about the sale of the portfolio properties. The two newly refurbished properties had both received decent offers and would be completing soon, as long as no further economic troubles created problems preventing the sales going through.

The sale of the two of the rental portfolio properties that the sitting tenants wanted to buy had gone through and completed. The rest of the portfolio was with the estate agents and generating interest, but in view of the state of the economy, rising mortgage rates and properties not selling quite as hoped, it was slow.

Marc was reluctant to endorse the suggestion of evicting tenants just to sell the properties. Some had been tenants for years. Some had young families. A couple of apartments were rented by elderly people and he knew they'd be particularly distressed if forced to vacate their homes just to sell them. By far the best choice would be if someone bought the complete portfolio.

Marc was given some advice that there were considerations of the situation: properties occupied by tenants often have selling prices reduced by a substantial amount. On the other hand, the way Marc saw it, good tenants paying their rent means a buyer wouldn't have to find tenants. But then again, he supposed, it prevented the buyer reassessing the rent he wanted to charge. Marc realised how little he understood about the matter and it confirmed to him he'd made the right decision to sell it.

Marc worried about how to make the right decision to resolve his problem. It kept him awake at night again, tossing and turning. He felt as though the weight of the world was on his shoulders. He felt sad that he was the last one left in the family, and he had to decide what to do. Despite that he knew he was lucky to have such decisions to make, he was also very aware that his parents would know what to do. It was their dream.

To him it was a nightmare. He also knew what they'd say—he heard them in his head. "You're too soft to be a businessman." "Sometimes you just have to get on with it." "You overthink things too much." This did nothing to help.

Finally, he thought of consulting Barry, again. Marc knew he desperately needed reassurance and he hoped that, in the meantime, some miracle would present the right answer.

Lucy was worried about the change in Marc's demeanour. He wasn't any less kind and thoughtful, but he was very quiet and distracted, and he looked troubled. She offered to listen to his problems, but she knew she didn't know anything about it to help.

The one thing she was relieved about was that Dick had gone quiet again and left her alone. She'd only seen him once since their exchange. He went to the parents' evening at school with her mum. Fortunately, his attention was focussed on Marty whilst chatting to his teacher. Lucy focussed on talking to her students' parents.

Lucy had noticed that Marc was always with her, walking to and from events to do with the field project. He always said he was free to help with the project at the same times she went. She was grateful for his support, but also felt guilty she was stealing his time, especially work time.

She thought, *Tricky. We both have our problems to solve to be able to move on. I did think of running away, pretty much like Rita did. But now, I know, it's not the right thing for me to do. Why should one bully destroy someone's right to choose their own path? It will be interesting to hear Rita's story in full, one day, and hear how it's worked out for her. The more I think about it now, the less I'd ever want to go. I'm too introverted for one thing, and I'd miss Marc.*

CHAPTER 15

Marc was often quiet. Lost in his thoughts and just recently he felt he had plenty to think about again. His solution was journaling it to try and stop the brain loops.

MARC'S JOURNAL

I think I'm slipping into depression. This year, so far, has been a huge challenge—the shock and grief of my parents' deaths, and then Joan's death, sorting out both the estates, and so many decisions to make. I've always been a calm, rational thinker, but the situation now is keeping me awake at night. I know I'm prone to overthinking, it's a character trait of an introvert, and this is so hard.

I've never been one to discuss my problems with just anyone, and I've no relative to consult, and I feel ... responsible for various people. I know the decisions I make don't really matter to anyone else, it's just choosing my future path, and if it all goes wrong, or I change my mind, I can just sell up, go elsewhere, and do something different, it doesn't really affect anyone else.

Except that it does ... If no one else ... Lucy.

The village community has welcomed me and I feel morally

responsible to the people who have befriended and helped me. I'm building positive relationships. Simon and Joan have been a positive influence, blazing the trail for me, and now I'm doing my part. Or at least I'm trying.

My emotions are in turmoil, especially about mum and dad, and memories of my childhood. I never said thank you to them for the start they gave me in life. For my education. I feel guilty that I never took an interest in their business, and maybe I should have. I should have learned about managing it. They might have needed my help one day, let alone this situation, now.

Yes, it's the right thing to do, sell up and let it go, but how are the tenants feeling? I've got mum and dad's solicitor, accountant and the rental agency helping, but they are acting on whatever I decide. Ultimately, I'm their client now. And I worry.

The world is a difficult place now - getting over the effects of coronavirus, influence of an unexpected war, the threat of recession, the world economy has slowed down, and everybody is struggling financially. Is it the right time to sell a string of properties with a probable downturn in the market? What would Mum and Dad do? Probably nothing, except manage any difficulties that arise. They'd probably rest on their laurels and clear off to the sunshine.

Hey-Ho! Not my style.

I need security. Lucy needs security too; with everything she's been through. Joan treated her like a daughter and I care about her ... a lot. I'm not kicking her out of her home. She deserves security and happiness. Hopefully James can come up with a solution to help her permanently.

I've settled down here and I'm getting to know people. I've good, loyal friends especially James and Lucy. So, why do I feel so uncertain, worried and ... depressed?

I'll phone Barry and arrange a meeting. I need some reassurance and guidance. When I wind it all up, at least I can move on. If Lucy's problem is solved as well, hopefully we can move on together. I really hope so.

Right now, I respect Lucy's boundaries. I understand her problems and I can't help thinking she has many more problems and issues from the past to come to terms with than she's told me about. We've both had difficulties to put behind us to move on. I'm sure we'll get there.

2022

Marc picked up his phone. Right ... Barry...

* * *

THE NEXT MORNING at breakfast Marc told Lucy he had to go away for a few days. 'There are two ways we can do this, Lucy. Do you have a friend who would come and stay with you?' he asked.

'No. I'll be fine. I'm not being controlled by anyone. At least, not that creep.'

'Or the other option is ... come with me. I'll book a second room.'

'No. I won't do that. I won't argue that a change of scene, for a few days wouldn't be nice and being with you lovely, but to me it's giving in to the control,' argued Lucy.

'Why not contact Steph? She offered a spare room, go and visit her.'

'No, same reason. I'll be fine.'

'Please Lucy, I'll worry. I just have to go and sort my head out, once and for all, and I have a work meeting, then I'll be back.'

'Exactly. You'll only be away two or three days. I won't be intimidated. He's kept out of my way recently and it's all gone quiet.'

'Please, Lucy. I'll worry,' Marc repeated.

'This is exactly what I don't want to happen. I can't let you take responsibility for me. I must look after myself.'

Marc sighed. 'It's not a case of taking responsibility. I just want to keep you safe ... from being harmed. Please, come with me.'

'No. I'll stay here, at home. I'll be fine.'

'Lucy ...'

'I'll be absolutely fine. We can phone often. Go and sort out your problems, I know you're troubled. I care for you too, so just go and sort it all out and go to your meeting. I'll be fine here.'

There was no persuading her. Marc would be away for two nights. They wouldn't tell anyone, so no one would know that they weren't both at home as usual. Marc would be back by the weekend ready for the next field event and barbecue.

Reluctantly Marc stowed his bag in the boot of his car. Lucy came out to see him off. They hugged and he got into the car. 'Please be careful, I'll be back soon,' Marc said.

'Of course. Enjoy your trip and I hope you get it all sorted. See you on Friday. Bye.'

'Bye.'

Marc drove up to the gate, turned down the lane and disappeared.

* * *

MAGGIE WAS SITTING at a window table in the cafe drinking coffee as she spotted Marc turn by the bridge and up the road leading out of the village. She noticed he was alone. *Ah*, she thought, *Lucy must be at home. I'm going to have a word with that little madam and find out what she's up to.*

She finished her coffee and left the shop to walk up the lane to Beliton Manor. As she walked, she thought about what she was going to say. By the time she reached the front door and pressed the doorbell, she was really worked up.

Lucy opened the door. 'Hello, Mum,' she said.

'I want to have a word with you, you little madam. You think you're so superior living in this place, what have you been doing to Dick?' she said, fuming.

Lucy was taken aback. She stepped outside and said, 'Let's go and sit down there,' pointing to the decking.

'Proper little lady of the manor,' said Maggie, snarling. 'What have you said to Dick?'

'Why? What's wrong with him?' said Lucy as they walked to the sofas.

'He won't tell me,' said Maggie.

'Oh, you do surprise me,' said Lucy. 'It would be hard for him to admit to you what he's been doing to me for years. I tried to tell you, countless times, but you refuse to believe me and you always defend him. I told you that's why I ran away. You didn't care. You've never cared about me. Ever.'

'What have you said?'

'I told him to leave me alone and stay away from me. Because despite that whatever you think of him, however much you worship him, he started again. The day of Joan's funeral to be precise. So does spelling out reality test your cosy little version of him?'

Maggie was livid. 'You lying little bitch. Why are you trying to break us up?'

'I'm not trying to break you up. If you are truly happy with him, then good luck to you. But he just can't help himself. He thinks he's so special—irresistible, and women can't turn down his advances. Conceited bloody narcissist! Yes, he's got you and he seems good to Marty ... And how lucky Marty is, knowing who his father is. It's something I've never known...'

Maggie, still seething said, 'So you lure him away to get back at me? Not getting enough from Marc?'

'Don't be so ridiculous. I was working late in the school office when he sneaked in and cornered me. Luckily Jim was around still and he heard me scream, otherwise I don't know what would have happened... It's just like the times he used to swan into the bathroom whenever I was in the shower, or the times he came into my bedroom while I was asleep and he started running his dirty fingers up the inside of my thighs. I'd scream but you never came. You'd just put it down to him playing a game and that I was screaming with ... with ... fun. Well, it wasn't a game, he terrorised me, as I told you many times, and you didn't care. And that day I ran away, he'd pinned me to the bed and roughly groped me, he intended to rape me, but he heard you come in downstairs, so he said he'd get me another time.'

'I don't believe you. What have you said to him?'

'I told you ... to leave me alone. I'm happy here. I have a loving home. Joan cared about me and did so much for me, and you were happy to hand me over. Sums us up, doesn't it? You don't care. You never have.'

'But I'm your mother, you should love me,' Maggie whined.

'No. I understand exactly how you feel about me. My presence brought you shame. I spoilt your fun when I was tiny, you couldn't go out with your mates doing what they were doing. Your parents made you face up to your responsibility of getting pregnant at fifteen ... and for me, not even knowing who my dad is ... how do you think that's made me feel all my life? And now you think we're mates and you can make up for lost time. You don't even see me as your daughter ... I. Am. Your. Daughter.' Lucy deliberately spoke slowly.

'Of course, I know you're my daughter. But I must make sure I'm alright—that I've got a home, job security, money, and I've got Marty ... and we're a family...'

'Exactly, you've got what you want. A home, a family ... just leave me alone to make my future and keep that horrid man of yours under control and away from me.'

Maggie went quiet.

Lucy thought, *the truth spelt out has perhaps hit home—just a bit. She's been a useless mother to me. She knows Dick can be rough and he yells, often accompanied by slaps and punches when he doesn't get his own way. She puts up with it so she has a home, for herself and Marty. She just puts it down to his nature.*

Lucy went on. 'I never knew what it felt like to be loved until I met Joan and she loved me like a mother. Then I understood. Eventually I learned confidence in my abilities, instead of all the put downs, and I could build a career. And now I've a lovely friend in her nephew who cares about me ...'

'Friend?'

'Yes friend. We house share ... amicably. We're best friends.'

'Is he gay, or something?' said Maggie.

'No, he just treats everyone, especially women, with respect. He doesn't force himself on anyone or cross their boundaries. He's polite and caring, kind and empathic to everyone. A gentleman. In fact, he's shown me how kind men can be, because I never really had a positive male role model until I met him. Yes, Grandad was around when I was very little, but he was probably so ashamed of what you did, and I was a constant reminder. I expect that's why they moved away, and you moved us in with a monster, not caring about me. I was just excess baggage.'

Maggie had calmed down and now felt regretful. 'Okay, don't remind me. I'm happy that you've found happiness and you're building a good career. Marty tells me you're a good teacher and the kids think you're great. I am proud of you ... of what you've achieved.'

Lucy felt better for getting all the anger, shame, and resentment out into the open and talk about it. She said, 'And you came here to have a go at me?'

Maggie felt sorry for Lucy, for all her pent-up frustrations. 'I'm grateful that Joan took care of you. I could see you progressing and she gave you more than I could ever have.'

'Well, that's got that out of the way. Just do better for Marty, he's a nice little boy, despite his father's genes.'

'Will we ever be a proper mum and daughter?' asked Maggie.

'I don't know. Too much has happened but ... maybe ... one day. Just keep Dick away from me.'

'Don't know how I'll do that; he just goes off. Disappears for a while leaving me running the pub. I don't know where he goes.'

'Well, make sure he's got his fair share of work to do instead of just sitting drinking all day, bragging to anyone who'll listen, and treating you like a slave. So why do you think I had something to do with it? What's changed with him?'

'He's gone quiet. I know he saw you and Marc,' said Maggie.

'I bet he didn't tell you he tried to punch Marc.'

Maggie gasped. 'No, he didn't mention that. Was Marc hurt?'

'No, luckily Marc knew how to defend himself, and all Dick was left with was a bruised ego. We just told him to stay away.'

'Ah, so he's stewing on it.'

'Yea well ... just keep him busy.'

'I'd better go, I've a pub to run.' They stood up. 'You should have told me all this before. I've got a lot to think about,' said Maggie.

'I did tell you, but you didn't want to hear it. Perhaps now you're ready. I'm still dealing with all my baggage before I can move on. I'm getting there. You need time to process it too, but most of all ... be a mum to Marty.'

Maggie was now sheepish. 'You're not jealous in the slightest, are you?'

'No. What happened, happened. The only way forward is to deal with it, rationalise it, leave it behind and move on.'

'Thanks, Lucy.'

They briefly hugged and Maggie turned to walk away, back up the drive. 'Bye, Lucy.'

'Bye, Mum.'

CHAPTER 16

Lucy felt slightly better for the talk with Maggie, but she wondered whether it would make any difference. She had no reason to trust her mum, except she saw that she'd changed from the angry woman who arrived on the doorstep, to a more reasonable person. Her anger visibly fizzled away.

Bertie arrived. 'Hi Lucy,' he said. 'I've come to mow the lawn and potter about. There's always something to do.'

'Hi Bertie, how are you? And Emily?'

'I'm fine thanks and Emily is okay now. She's just enjoying some time with the children. They're doing some propagating, for the field.'

'Ah, good. Oscar takes after you. He's keen and works hard, for one so young. Would you like a coffee? I was just going to get one.'

'Thanks. I'll just get the mower out and make a start.'

A short while later Lucy returned with the coffee and they sat on the decking talking. 'Is Marc busy?' asked Bertie.

'Um, yes. He's a bit tied up today,' said Lucy.

'Pity. I wanted to talk to him. Where's his car?'

'Bertie, I can trust you, can't I?'

'Of course... he's not here, is he?'

'No. But I don't want anyone to know that I'm on my own here. In case it gets back...'

'Back to who?'

'Just keep it to yourself.'

'Okay, no problem. I just wanted to chat about the field, that's all.'

'We'll be there on Saturday. Can it wait?'

'Yes. And don't worry I won't say anything.' Bertie wondered why she didn't want anyone to know, but respected the request. 'In fact, I can come tomorrow too, if you like, I'm planning some hedge trimming.'

'Fine. I can help you if you like. No harm in learning. And your company would be welcome.'

'Sure. Everyone is fired up about the field. It's starting to look good now it's ready with organised beds for planting. The plants the children have propagated will soon be big enough to go in.'

'And what about the barbecue on Saturday?'

'It's all organised. Marc's okay, is he?'

'Yes, he's just gone for a work meeting at head office, that's all.'

'Thanks for the coffee, I'll carry on with my work.' Lucy picked up the mugs and went indoors. She had some work to do.

Meanwhile, Marc had a pleasant drive to Barry's house. He was looking forward to having a discussion with him and hopefully make his final decision. He quite expected Barry to say he was too soft, as his own parents would, and that he should just do what he needs to do without taking the tenants feelings and opinions into consideration. However, Marc knew he had a conscience and he wanted to sleep at night.

Sat nav: You have reached your destination.

He drew up outside Barry's house and got out of the car. Barry came out to meet him. 'Hi, Marc lad.'

'Hello Barry.'

'Come in.'

Barry led the way indoors, through the house, and out into the back garden. 'Hello, Marc,' said Pat, Barry's wife. She gave him a welcome hug. 'I've not seen you for a few years.'

'Hello, Pat. No, it's been a while.'

'A nice, chilled beer for you,' said Barry passing him a can.

'Thanks.' He opened the can and took a swig, savouring the refreshing coolness. 'Thank you for inviting me.'

'You're welcome. We miss John and Mary, and it's nice to see you. You look like your dad, you know,' said Barry.

'I used to get told that, all the time. The thing is though, as you know, I've a very different nature,' said Marc.

'Ah yes, quiet and thoughtful. I'm not saying John wasn't thoughtful...' Barry backtracked a bit. 'Your mum and dad were very proud of you, you know.'

'I sometimes think I was a disappointment for them. I'm not a sociable party animal like they were, as you know, and I worry that I didn't learn their business and that's why I'm struggling to make decisions now.'

'Yes, I agree. You were always quiet. Head in a book, or something. Your mum and dad knew you would do something different and, of course, no one ever considered they'd die together and so young, like they did, or they'd have arranged things more clearly for you. And I understand your worries.'

Barry continued, 'So, anyway, four of the houses were easy to deal with—the two newest ones flipped and the tenants buying two more. You've two apartments with old folks renting and the rest of them with tenants, yes?'

'Yes. And I feel I can't evict people just because I want to sell them, especially the old folks.'

'Not an easy decision, I know. Look, I've been doing okay recently, even with the forthcoming reforms to rental agreements coming in. How about I buy the two apartments from you? I've been and chatted with both tenants, the two old folks, just to see how they'd feel about a change of landlord. I think they liked me and were quite happy about it. The properties are in good condition still. They'd be simple to take on.'

'Really?' Marc gasped.

'Yes, the estate agent valuations for them were fair and I'll happily pay the price. I own other apartments in the block, so it makes sense for me.'

'Wonderful, thank you, that's two less people I have to worry about,' Marc smiled, 'I know you'll look after them.'

'The rest ... that's not so straightforward.'

'Hmm, and there's the inheritance tax. John, dad's accountant is working with Tim, the solicitor. They had a huge bill to pay before being granted probate. That's been paid from the estate capital amassed so far.'

'I understand. It must be horrendous. I have to say, your awful experience is making a few of us landlords think about how we may do something differently with our own estate planning. Put something in place in advance, maybe. It was always John's intention to review their Wills because they were written when you were really young, but he figured he had plenty of time. Well, you do, don't you? Getting to your mid-fifties is nothing. He was just allowing time for you to choose your path. John was planning to add a few more properties, but also to start enjoying life a bit. The idea was put on hold because of course travelling was limited because of the virus and the lockdowns...' Barry paused. Marc listened with interest and wondered what his dad could have done. Anyway, it didn't matter, the situation is what it is.

Barry continued, 'The demand for properties to rent is high and the terms are under review. Selling? Evict the tenants and the put them on the general market with the mortgage rates being increased doesn't bode well, right now. Selling them occupied, might reduce the value a bit as we discussed before, and a new landlord may want to charge different rents, etc. but I think it's the best option for you. You've seen the valuations and you've had plenty of time to think about it. I know you want to sell them and, in your case, I think you're right. You don't need the responsibility of trekking up here on a regular basis and I don't blame you.'

'It's just that I want to invest the money in some new and different ventures. I've brought some photos and drawings to show you if you're interested.'

Barry noticed how Marc's tone had changed. He sounded animated. 'Yes, show us, please. And then I'll understand.'

Marc fetched some papers from his bag left in the hallway and returned. He showed a photo of the house. Pat gasped. 'Wow! It's gorgeous.' She passed the photo to Barry.

'Fantastic! I can see why you love it there.' They looked carefully at more photos of the other buildings and Marc shared the sketches of what they could be when they're converted. Finally, Marc showed them Simon's drawing and plans for the shippon.

'How beautiful it will be,' said Barry. 'I understand completely why you want to develop the place. Your home will be enormous when it's done. Why didn't your uncle do it?'

'I think he came up with the idea not long before he died. He was ill for a while and the house, as it is, is plenty big enough for two.'

Pat picked up on the comment. 'You've got a lady in your life?'

'Sort of…' Marc went on to explain who Lucy is and why she's there and emphasised the house sharing.

'I see,' said Pat. 'Well, I hope it all works out for you.'

'Thanks.' Marc left it at that and returned to talking about the development plans and the considerations he must take into account with a historic listed property. 'In addition, I'm also considering ways I can introduce eco technologies. Houses as old as mine have evolved over the centuries and are a historical record of the building techniques of the times. I think, introducing technologies of our time is equally as important as preserving the past. It's important for future generations.'

'I can see why you want to know how you stand to invest in your very worthwhile project.'

'I've been welcomed into the community and met some interesting people. Well, the guys who drew these plans, for instance, and Bertie who is a garden expert. I've shown you what we're achieving in restoring the kitchen garden. I've become a governor at the school and I've handed over the use of a field to the school for the children to learn horticulture skills.' He went on to tell them about the school projects.

Pat noticed how he became very enthusiastic as he talked. It was much more than the house project; he was inspired by the whole village. 'Your mum would love to see you as you are talking about this. You are completely taken with the place and she knew that you weren't particularly happy in London.'

'You're right, I wasn't. It was a means to an end of setting up a good career and I accomplished that goal.' He went on to explain he was going to a meeting at head office when he left them.

'Well,' said Barry, 'I understand why you've been having sleepless nights... having so much to think about. Tomorrow we'll go and arrange your way forward. You need it done and dusted.'

Pat added, 'Despite you've had a very sad year, look at the wonderful opportunities you've been given to secure your future. You can create something you can keep on developing and enjoy ... with Lucy.' She winked at him.

Marc said nothing, but grinned and showed her his crossed fingers. 'Thanks for letting me run my thoughts past you.'

'You're welcome. I understand how we can approach the discussions tomorrow and why,' said Barry.

'Thanks, Barry, for helping me. I need your expertise to understand it all.'

'Happy to help,' smiled Barry, patting his shoulder.

'I want to come and visit you,' said Pat.

'You are most welcome. Any time.'

'I'll show you to your room,' said Barry. 'I thought we'd go out this evening for a meal.'

'Great,' said Marc.

MARC PHONED LUCY, he wanted to know she was okay. She told him about her day. A précis of the conversation with her mum and the chat with Bertie....

Lucy: 'Not sure what Bertie wanted to talk to you about, something to do with the field, but we're going to be busy hedge cutting tomorrow.

Marc: 'I'm glad you won't be completely alone. Have you heard anything from James yet?'

Lucy: 'No, I didn't expect to. You've been dealing with it.'

Marc: 'Okay. Well ... Barry understands my agonising now, especially that I have no one to talk to. He was a close friend of my dad's, so he knows what was in his mind. He's going with me tomorrow to sort it all out. Since I've shown him the photos and drawings of Project Beliton, he understands why I'm so keen.'

Lucy: 'Hey, I'm glad you've chatted with him and got another perspective. You might consider James and me a bit biased!'

Marc: (Laughed.) 'Biased? Nooo!'

Lucy: 'Well, it's good to hear you happy.'

Marc: (Concerned.) 'I hope you're okay and not too upset about the conversation with your mum.'

Lucy: 'I'm okay. I don't know whether what I said will make the slightest bit of difference though, except that she seemed to listen this time. She visibly deflated from seething to quiet. Maybe it's the right time for her to listen—I don't know. She was surprised that I was arguing less for myself than for Marty. I told her, that he has the advantage of knowing who his dad is and even if he's not a nice guy, at least he's got a relationship with him. I just told her to be a mum to him, and don't treat him with the same resentment she aimed at me. The circumstances of Marty's birth and mine are completely different, but I think maybe it sunk home about the way she's treated me.'

Marc: 'I'm so sorry to hear that. I think we both had a hard time as children, in different ways. In my case, they couldn't cope with me being quiet and studious, and packed me off to boarding school. It was probably the right thing to do really because they didn't have much time for me. The most fun I had as a kid was with my grandparents, and the few times I met Joan, and that's a bit sad. I think my parents loved and cared about me; they just didn't understand how to cope with me.'

Lucy: 'Yes, we do both have issues to rationalise. Once we've done that we can move forward.'

Marc: 'Anyway, how did we get onto this topic in a phone conversation? I'll be back on Friday evening and we can talk more then ... if you want to.'

Lucy: 'Maybe the telephone has put a distance between us and we're not being side-tracked by looking into each other's eyes, or reading body language, or something.'

Marc: 'Yes, maybe. I'll call again. If you need me, call anytime. Take care and don't work too hard tomorrow, but I expect you'll have a nice time with Bertie.'

Lucy: 'Good luck. I hope your meetings go well. Speak soon. Bye.'

Marc: 'Bye.'

The call ended and Marc stared at the fading phone screen for a couple of minutes thinking about Lucy. He missed her. He was snapped back to the present by a knock on his bedroom door.

'Are you ready? Taxi's here,' said Barry.

'Yes.' Marc stood up and slipped the phone into his jacket pocket and as he did so, his tummy rumbled. *Yes, I'm hungry.*

CHAPTER 17

James organised a meeting with Marc and Lucy. He said, 'I've been chatting with Ann, and she mentioned she'd really like to video call to chat with you, so I'm kind of mediating an icebreaker.

'She knew that Dick had replaced her with a young, single mother but she didn't know the child was you, Lucy. It troubled her. She knew Joan was using the threat of using the evidence to control Dick but wasn't sure what he was up to. And she was happy the threat was obviously enough because it worked up to her death.

'Ann was sorry to hear that he's been threatening you, Lucy, especially as a child. She knew Dick had some disgusting photos and that he visited websites where he could watch pornography, and she suspected he might have been a paedophile, or watching it. It was one reason why she ensured she wouldn't ever get pregnant with him. Once the initial magic in their relationship wore off, and Dick's charms tarnished, he revealed his true colours. She was scared of him, because he was often violent and abusive and, as we know, very controlling.

'Despite asking out of interest at the beginning, she was never able to get a straight answer about his past. She always felt he was spinning a yarn. Hiding something. She never met any of his family and never saw family photos or mementos, which she thought was a bit odd.'

Lucy felt sad. 'It sounds like she had a miserable time but was somehow resigned to it. Maybe, like mum, she felt she didn't have anywhere else to go, and no money of her own to be able to leave.'

'Pretty much, I think. I'll leave it to her to discuss details she's willing to share with you,' said James. 'Anyway, I did a bit of research to see if I could find anything about his past ... and I found out he's been in gaol.'

Lucy gasped. 'Well, that would explain him being cagey about his past to Ann. And maybe that's why he lost touch with his family. What was he in for?'

'GBH,' said James.

'No wonder the threat of releasing the evidence kept him under control,' said Marc. 'Clearly Joan didn't know about that though, the threat was enough.'

'Precisely,' said James. 'And when Ann went away it's not surprising the police wondered if he'd murdered her and took him in for questioning, despite the lack of any evidence to suggest murder and, of course, no body. Being held in gaol for a few days while they investigated was enough to give him some thinking time maybe?'

'I wonder why they never found the evidence that Ann knew about? The porn.' Lucy added. 'And do people change?'

'I don't know about change,' said Marc. 'But if he had a few days before the police called to see him while investigating Rita's disappearance, he could easily have burned paper evidence. As for the internet trail leading to websites ... maybe they didn't consider it. Didn't look. So, by the time he was schmoozing Maggie, a nice young female employee with a pretty daughter to watch, he'd chosen other options to get his kicks.'

'Yes, and now Ann knows about it, she's sorry it happened,' said James.

'It's not her fault,' said Lucy, 'she wasn't to know it would happen. She was busy protecting herself, understandably.'

'Anyway, she'd like to have a chat with you. She just asked me to fill you in generally about her position. You all now understand your different perspectives to make some decisions,' said James. 'I'll keep out of it unless you decide to take legal action.'

'Thank you, James,' said Lucy. 'Do I owe you anything for what you've done?'

James smiled, 'No, Lucy, I'm happy to help my friend and I did it in my own time. Ann is nice, you'll like her.'

'Thanks James,' said Marc.

'No problem. Right official talks done, are you guys free this weekend? Up for surfing again?'

'Yes, Sunday,' said Lucy.

'Brilliant. I'll organise the barbecue.'

* * *

MARC EMAILED Ann and told her James had been to see them, if she'd like to plan an appointment for a video call, they'd be happy to meet her. "Just let us know."

He went back to his work and almost immediately a notification pinged on his screen. "Later this afternoon? 5:00 pm?"

Marc replied: Fine :o) and returned to his work.

Lucy was outside on the decking reading, when Marc took her a coffee, and told her the news. 'Great,' said Lucy. 'Personally, I'd rather get the icebreaker meeting done and stop worrying about it.'

'I agree,' said Marc. 'This isn't really my business; it was only that we found out about it in Joan's journals that started us down this route of investigation. If you'd rather talk to Ann alone, I'll understand.'

Lucy looked at him in alarm. 'Marc don't say that. You're my best friend and I trust you implicitly. Up until I met you, I was actually quite scared of men. Not James, but I didn't really know him apart from the professional contact we had when Joan died. I thought all men were all misogynistic, narcissistic, egotistical, controlling bullies, because that was really the only enduring experience I'd had in my life. No real positive role models. You've changed all that—completely.

Smashed the nasty illusion. I know you'd never hurt me, or anyone else for that matter, verbally or physically. You're my best friend accompanying me on my healing journey. Just as I'm supporting you, I hope. That's what best friends do. We'll both chat with Ann.'

Marc thought about what Lucy had just confided in him and smiled. 'Thanks, Lucy, and yes, I'm grateful I have you to talk my problems over with. You care and understand. I'm grateful that we share a home and if that's all we ever have I'm glad it's happened.'

'I'm not ruling out more … later. Let's just take it slowly. We'll get there,' Lucy said, standing up. 'Finished your coffee? I'll take the cups in and tidy myself up.'

Marc stood up too. 'You look as beautiful as ever, don't be shy. Can we have a hug?' Lucy didn't say anything, she just put her arms around him and they hugged.

Breaking apart, Lucy picked up their mugs. 'I'll take my laptop downstairs ready,' said Marc as they walked up to the house.

A SHORT WHILE LATER, Lucy and Marc sat side by side waiting at the dining room table. At five the call came through.

Marc: Hi Ann, I'm Marc and this is Lucy.

Lucy: Hi Ann, pleased to meet you.

Ann: Lovely to meet you both. I'm glad James has mediated with the icebreaking chat. I thought if we talked and got to know each other we could decide the best way forward. Because I need a resolution too, for my future.

Lucy: Oh?

Ann: Yes. Since I came over here, I met a nice man and with him I've built a nice life and I have a daughter too. Pierre wants us to marry, for her sake, but he understands I cannot.

Lucy: Mum wants the same thing. She and Dick have my half-brother. Dick's always fobbed her off with the "wait seven years" fallacy because he has no idea about your whereabouts and from that hasn't tried to look. And she's had to accept the law changed this year and, as it stands, a marriage probably won't ever happen.

Ann: A divorce is the answer for her then too?

Lucy: I think Dick's happier without any legal commitment, so divorce would put the pressure on him. So yes, I'd say so.

(They laughed.)

Ann: I can see where your mum is coming from, she wants some security for her son and herself. I hope Dick's nicer to her than he was to me.

Lucy: He seems like a reasonably good dad to Marty, so maybe being Marty's mum helps her a bit. I don't know what's in her mind. We don't talk very often. We're not close. I'm a constant reminder of her murky past.

Ann: What a shame...

Lucy: I miss Joan. She showed me proper mothering.

Ann: Yes, she would have. Whenever we talked, she would tell me some things that a mum would say—how proud she was of you, how pretty you are, how hard you studied, what treats she was planning for you. She loved you. And I think you were exactly what she needed. You made her life complete, filled the gap. A family is what she and Simon had always wanted.

Lucy: I loved her too. I'm very grateful for everything she did for me.

Ann: So, what do we do? Joan protected you and kept Dick away from you and now he thinks he's free again? Well, no. I think, I need to come out of hiding and help you. You must be able to live your life safely, and be free to choose to do whatever you want to do. How would you feel if I came over?

Lucy: Delighted. We can make a plan. Make him suffer for a change.

Marc: Wonderful! Come and stay with us. Would Pierre and your daughter like to come too?

Ann: Thank you, but I'll come alone. Pierre will look after Angeline and will keep our business ticking over.

Lucy: I'm grateful.

Ann: Don't be. As I say, I'm doing it for me too. If I come sometime next week, would that work for you?

Marc: Fine. How will you travel? Ferry to Plymouth? Fly to Exeter? We'll meet you.

Ann: That's kind, thank you. I'll let you know what I choose and when.

Lucy: Brilliant. We'll look forward to it. Bye.

Marc: Nice to meet you Ann. Bye. They ended the call.

'That went well,' said Marc.

'Yes,' agreed Lucy, 'I can't wait to see Dick's face when he sees her. We'll look after her.'

'It will take the wind out of his arrogant sails,' Marc laughed. 'When Ann comes, we'll plan the meeting for the maximum effect. Perhaps with a pub full of people who remember Rita.'

'We'll plan something she's comfortable with, but I'm certain she's going to enjoy it too,' said Lucy. 'He'll get such a shock.'

'Initially, yes. I'm glad you have the end in sight,' said Marc. 'You can relax then and enjoy life.'

'Let's see how it all plays out. Once the Dick Problem is solved, I can work on the rest of the stuff in my head and leave the bad stuff behind. Dick made me feel … dirty. Worthless. They both made me feel bad, they blamed me for everything. It was my fault I was born. They constantly said, "That's not what happened." "You're lying." It was scapegoating and gaslighting. That's mostly what I must resolve. Accept that what I saw was what I experienced. Then I'll be able to leave the past there and move on.'

Marc put his arm around her shoulder. 'I feel sad that your childhood was so bad, and I'm here to listen any time. I will never question or dismiss whatever you say and it will be just between us. Okay?'

Lucy nodded, tears in her eyes.

Marc continued. 'I've realised I have past issues but nothing as bad as you had. My parents loved me, in their own way. They just didn't relate to me or understand me. I was proudly paraded, like a trophy, which I found really embarrassing. Excruciatingly embarrassing. But that's just the way they were—they celebrated achievements. I didn't. I don't. I just move on to the next thing. Maybe the lesson I must learn from the experience is, I must learn to stop and acknowledge achievements, give myself a pat on the back, relax and then move on to the next thing. Plan the next goal carefully and take the pressure off myself.'

'Yes. I've seen that. You've had a lot of unexpected situations to deal with this year. You arrived here grieving for your parents and this surprise landed on you, more grief, and in your mind expectations. You've chosen here, which is great, and you are planning Project Beliton, but you've been putting yourself under pressure and giving yourself sleepless nights because you want to get on with it. Get it done and create your vision. You'd definitely take the pressure off yourself if you stop, slow down and let what you must do happen, one step at a time. It really doesn't matter if you do the building conversions next year, or the year after. You might adapt your ideas and if they're not done in a hurry, you can incorporate the new thinking and developing technologies. Slow down and enjoy the process. You're young. There's no pressure. And you've become involved with the school and community projects. Just be kind to yourself.'

Marc paused, thinking before replying. 'Yes, you're right. There's no hurry. I guess I want to do the projects to persuade you to work with me to make it our dreams. Our future. Together.'

'It probably will be. I'd love to see it all happen. And I'll work with you to make it happen. Just. Slow. Down.' Lucy said squeezing his hand.

'Okay. We're on the road together and we might be getting somewhere. Let's cook dinner and wine would be welcome.'

'Couldn't agree more. Let's do it.'

CHAPTER 18

The next morning in the kitchen preparing breakfast, Lucy said, 'It's a nice day, let's go out. Brave the crowds and go somewhere, just us two.'

Marc smiled, 'That's a great idea. Where?'

'I'll take you and we'll just drive and see where we end up. I quite enjoy an adventure like that. We're up early and might find somewhere before it gets too busy with holidaymakers. We can probably find somewhere quiet and less well-known, perhaps, on the coast.'

'Okay, sounds like fun,' Marc grinned.

'Just put some options in the boot, such as picnic blankets, swimwear and towels, just in case, and we'll hit the road.'

Half an hour later, they were crossing the moor to the main road. 'I think it will do us both good to have a change of scene. If we stayed at home you'd be thinking of Project Beliton, or work, even though you're on holiday, and I'll be a tad apprehensive if I go to the village, even though I tell you "I'm fine!" And if we go the field and help there, someone will ask something. Or I'll be thinking of work and preparing something for next term,' said Lucy.

'You're right and yes, I agree, a change of scene is positive,' said

Marc, thinking, *And I get you completely to myself*. 'Where are you taking me?'

'I know a few beaches off the beaten track, which might not be too busy.'

'Great. Have you thought of any ideas for when Ann comes?' Marc asked.

'No, not really. We'll do whatever she's comfortable with. I think the simplest is just turning up at the pub when it's busy, like you said. With people around Dick won't say much and Ann will feel comfortable, especially if there are some of the community in there who she knows. The village doesn't change very much. Once people come here, if they weren't born here, most tend to stay for life.'

'Hmm, I can understand that,' said Marc, 'as an incomer. I know I've only been here a few months and I haven't experienced the winter weather yet, but it's a nice community and I love the changing scene of nature. It's made me feel like I belong. A novelty for me.'

Lucy thought for a minute, 'Yes, I understand what you mean. My only other experience was living in Greater Beliton, until mum moved us here when my grandparents left the area. But I suppose as I was so young, I didn't have a feel for the town. It was all I knew. Now I'm an adult I can understand the concept.'

'When I was younger, I got packed off to boarding school so I didn't build social networks at home. I didn't really know anybody; except the people my parents knew. At school I made a couple of friends, but as I wasn't very outgoing and didn't play masses of sports, I got bullied. I'd shut myself away in the safety of the library, or somewhere. I went to uni and house-shared with some people, but I didn't go for the beer swigging pub culture—not me, at all. And then I only went to London to get a good job. Means to an end. You know pretty much the rest. So, I've been drifting around and not anchored to anyone, or anywhere… until now.'

They went quiet, each lost in their own thoughts. Eventually, Lucy pulled up in a car park. It was only half full and the beach looked quiet. 'Is this okay?' she asked.

'Gorgeous. Let's find a nice spot to pitch,' Marc said, as he got their bags out of the boot. They wandered to the steps that led down to the beach and walked along the beach until they found a place they liked. Nice views, and not too many people around. *Perfect!*

Marc spread out the rug. They placed their towels on it and sat down admiring the scene. 'It's nice to just enjoy the peace, isn't it? I think I'll go for a swim. Are you coming?' said Marc.

Lucy was lying on her stomach reading a book. 'No. You enjoy it. I'll stay here.'

Marc changed and sauntered off down the beach to the water. Lucy put down her book and turned to sit up and watch him go. He reached the wet sand and started jogging to the sea—jogged right into it and as soon as he reached deep enough, he plunged in. *Don't blame you for that*, she thought watching him surface and stand, wiping the water off his face. With that, Marc set off swimming across the beach. Lucy turned and opened her book again.

A short while later, Lucy felt droplets of water on her back. 'Agh!'

Marc laughed, 'I thought you needed cooling down a tad.' He plonked down on his towel. 'That was ... refreshing.'

'Hmm, good word for it. I'm refreshed too, thanks.'

'Couldn't resist, you look beautiful lying lazing there.'

'Sweet talker!'

'Fancy a coffee? I noticed they sell take away coffee at the beach shop as we passed it.'

'Sure, thanks,' said Lucy.

'Okay, madam, I'll bring you a nice flat white,' said Marc, as he turned and left.

Once again Lucy watched him walking away towards the beach hut thinking, *He's fun. He's kind. He's amusing. He's a nice guy and he makes me feel safe and ... loved. Loved? Hmm ... yes loved. And I care about and love him.*

Marc reached the cafe, placed his order, paid, and waited. Lucy was still watching him. He took the cardboard drinks tray and small carrier bag from the counter, turned, and began walking back. She returned to her book pretending to read, instead she was still thinking, *I must still wait. We must wait. Heal. But there's nothing stopping us from building and enjoying our friendship.*

As Marc walked back towards Lucy, he was lost in his thoughts too. *She's beautiful, kind, and caring. I know I've fallen in love with her and I think she loves me, but I guess I must wait for a sign. She'll tell me, I'm sure. I'm enjoying her company.* He reached the blanket and sat down putting the tray between them. 'Lunch is served, Miss.'

'Thank you, kind sir. It's a little bit early, but that's fine. We have no agenda except of our choosing.' They started their picnic.

'Did you know there's a special full moon tomorrow? A Sturgeon Moon.' said Marc. 'How about we walk up Beliton Tor tomorrow night and watch it? And count the stars. We can take a picnic supper and just wait, in case some clouds come over. It'll be a late night, but hopefully worth it.'

'Sounds like fun. A midnight feast. Sounds like something you'd read in an Enid Blyton book as a kid. I've never done anything like that but would love to see it and admire the stars,' said Lucy.

'It's a date! Sorry, plan. Enid Blyton … that takes me back. The Five series,' said Marc.

They finished lunch, tidied up the picnic and relaxed.

In the late afternoon, they packed up their belongings, carried the litter to the bin and walked back to the car. 'Shall we go on somewhere else?' asked Lucy.

'I've got no plans. Do you fancy supper out?'

'How about fish and chips? Because I've an idea where we can go. But as it's early, we can go for a walk first and work up an appetite.'

'Okay, I'm quite happy, whatever you'd like to do.' They put their bags in the car and walked back to the beach for a stroll to watch the incoming tide and the sun dip towards the horizon, creating long shadows of the hills. Marc took several photos with his phone mentioning sketching and art.

'I'd like to see your artwork,' said Lucy.

Marc was embarrassed. He was never keen to show anyone and just stored them away. 'They're not good. I just do them for the enjoyment of painting, they never see the light of day. They're in a crate in the shippon somewhere,' he said fobbing her off.

'Why don't you show them to anyone? asked Lucy. 'You said you used to do art with Joan, didn't you?'

'Yes, when I was very little. Then as I grew up, I carried on practising in private. Grandma and Grandad encouraged me, whenever I saw them, but I stopped showing my parents. I think I probably got some patronising comment at some point, or they were too busy, or weren't interested, I can't actually remember. I know I stopped painting for years, then in my late teens I started again and hid them away.'

'Isn't it sad when children aren't encouraged to build their interests and follow their hearts? I had a friend who wanted to be a writer, but when she was out, or at school or something, her mother went through her stuff in her bedroom and some of her notebooks she'd start writing in vanished. Got taken away and destroyed probably. She'd learned not to say anything, but it wrecked her dream of being a writer. "Get a proper job that pays money," she was told. She felt utterly discouraged and trained for a career and got a job she hates. Sad.'

'Yes, I know the feeling,' said Marc. 'At least I got a job I enjoy, it makes me get up in the morning, and I've recently returned to art as a hobby. It was fun that day when we took Oscar and Gemma out and I could share a little of what I've learned. Receptive audience, I suppose.'

'And do you know the effect that had?'

'No.'

'I heard Oscar helping a friend in class one day, using your words to share what he'd learned. So, one kind guiding session has helped two children and will probably multiply.'

'Ah.' Marc felt embarrassed.

'I think I'd call it the kindness effect. Kindness spreads around,' Lucy smiled. 'Don't hide your talents, I'd love to see them.'

'Maybe, one day ...'

'I'm glad we're nearly back at the car,' Lucy said, 'it's getting chilly. I need my fleece now.'

Marc put his arm around her shoulder and they walked the rest of the way snuggled together. *That's nice*, thought Lucy, *I needed that.*

***

LATER THAT EVENING, showered and relaxing in front of the TV, Marc's phone pinged alerting the arrival of an email. It was from Ann: "Next Monday for a few days? Flying into Exeter at 14:20." Marc showed it to Lucy. 'Brill! We'll get her room ready.'

Marc messaged back: Fine. We'll be there. They returned to watching their film until it finished.

Marc said, 'I enjoyed today, thanks Lucy.'

'I did too. It was nice to go somewhere different and share it with you. I'm looking forward to our midnight jaunt tomorrow. We'll take some nibbles.'

'And a flask of hot chocolate. Talking of which, I'll go and make tonight's.' Marc got up and went to the kitchen.

Lucy smiled to herself. *I really hope everything will work out soon. Our time is coming.*

Marc returned with two steaming mugs of hot chocolate. He walked back out of the room and returned with a crate.

'I've dropped my reluctance to show anyone ... only to you though. Probably too much wine since we got back ...'

'Your art. Oooh, let me see.'

Marc sat down on the sofa putting the crate on the floor between them and lifted the lid. Inside was a mass of canvas boards and art books. Marc picked up a handful of them and passed them to Lucy. She took them and started going through the first book, slowly turning the pages. 'They're lovely. You're good. You should frame some and hang them around the house. She closed the book and began looking through the canvas boards. These are beautiful.' She put them carefully back in the crate and helped herself to some more, studying them as she went through them. 'I'm no art expert,' she said, 'but I know what I like. These are very good. We should frame and hang some.'

'No, I don't think so...'

'Oh yes!'

'Thank you for the vote of confidence, but they're staying in the box.'

'Okay, one day you might let them out.'

'Anyway, they're the wrong style for the decor here. I think, soon, we'll have to put our own style on the decor. Something a bit more contemporary.'

'Yes,' I agree. 'Joan used to say that, but never got round to it. You're expanding Project Beliton.'

'No, I've been thinking it for a while, but some structural changes need making too.' Opening it up, maybe? No hurry, and I need your input. You live here too. Then again, if the shippon was altered ...'

'We agreed to slow down. But yes, I'm on your wavelength. No quick decisions and consider all the options. This is liveable and will do a while longer. Anyway, thanks for showing me your art. Wait until next year for this, perhaps. You'll have done the winter here then too. I know what it's like. It can get a bit chilly sometimes,' said Lucy.

'Fair comment. Heated floor, with a heat pump might be the answer,' said Marc.

'No hurry. We'll make sure we have plenty of logs stored for the winter and that beautiful fire will keep the chill at bay. Right. Finished your drink? I'm off to bed if we're having a late one tomorrow.' Lucy picked the mugs up and headed for the kitchen. 'Thanks for a lovely day, Marc, I'm looking forward to tomorrow. Night, night.'

'Yes, thanks. Me too. Sweet dreams.' Lucy left the room while Marc turned out the lights and climbed the stairs to bed.

CHAPTER 19

*L*ucy and Marc were driving up the lane out of the village when they had to pull over and stop in one of the passing places to allow a lorry to squeeze past travelling towards the village.

'A removals lorry. I wonder which house has been sold,' said Lucy. She paused thinking, 'Ah, I remember … two kids from school, not in my class, were moving away. It'll be the big house opposite the pub.'

'I don't know. I've not really walked that way much except for going to James's. I haven't needed to.'

They carried on up the lane, through the tunnel of trees to the open moor. A big four by four was coming towards them. Lucy pulled over onto the grass to allow it to pass. The driver waved "Thanks" and carried on.

'The new residents, maybe? I don't recognise the vehicle. Let's face it with no through route to go somewhere, you don't go to the village unless you live there, or are visiting…'

'Or going for a hike.'

'True.'

They continued their return trip to the beach. Once again, arriving early meant plenty of room in the car park and the beach was quiet.

They chose a similar spot for the day and settled down for some quiet reading. After a while, Marc sat up saying, 'I'm off for a swim. Coming?'

'No, I'll wait here thanks.'

Marc stood up and walked to the water's edge, he waded in without hesitation, plunged in and began swimming across the beach. Again, Lucy admired the scene watching him, then turned back to her book. Predictably, on his return, he sprinkled her with water droplets again, before heading to the beach hut for snacks.

He returned and sat down beside her, putting the picnic between them saying, 'Madam, your refreshments are served.'

'Thank you again, kind sir. I could get used to this.'

'What? Having your snacks served by a butler?' Marc said jokingly.

'No, idiot! Just enjoying a quiet life with pleasant company and no rushing about. No demands.'

'Yes, but, if that was life it would get very boring. What would you do for days off then? Mooching is giving my brain too much thinking time.'

'Fair point. I know I deliberately keep busy so my brain is occupied. This is a really good book,' she said indicating her book. 'It's working its magic.'

'Well, I'm reading a murder mystery and it's not got me hooked yet, so my mind keeps wandering around.'

'Want to talk?'

'No, not particularly now. I'm at a stage where I'm visualising packing my past issues into a treasure chest, to leave it all behind. I'll know where it is if I choose to go there again and lift the lid. But I want to live for today.'

'Sounds positive. So, what are you focusing on? Which element of Project Beliton?'

'Predictable, aren't I? I think, converting the old stables first. With the greenhouse and garden tools storage underneath, the upstairs can be made into living accommodation.'

'For whom?'

'I don't know yet. If two other projects are aimed at holiday lets, then maybe a residential let. We'll need someone to help us run it all. Maybe offer it as live-in accommodation. The greenhouse would be great for propagating plants for the kitchen garden, which is looking good, don't you think? Now it's prepared ready to plant. The apple trees are loaded with fruit, despite being abandoned for years. We'll have a good crop in the autumn.'

'Great—stock up the freezer.'

'Talking of which, I think we should get a chest freezer. Put it in the shippon for now. The fridge freezer in the kitchen is nowhere near big enough if we're going to grow fruit and veg.'

'Uh huh, yes. Good idea. And yes, the old stables is a good place to start, as you've had the drawings done. It will be nice to see the building used for a practical purpose, instead of eroding.'

'My brain can focus on mulling that project over,' said Marc. 'I appreciate your endorsement.'

'Sounds exciting.'

'I'll ponder while you read.' With that, Marc lay back and promptly dozed off, while Lucy read.

'On the way home, they called in at an electrical superstore and ordered a large chest freezer and picked up their midnight feast goodies. 'There, see what my overthinking brain achieves,' said Marc laughing.

'Indeed. Was that while dreaming?'

'Errrr....'

'Only joking!'

'Hmm, yes, I know. See, I go by the theory if my brain knows what to do I act on a decision, rightly or wrongly. If it can't reach a decision, I wait until an answer presents itself.'

'I like that. Yes, I'm a bit like that too. I'm not a very decisive person. My heart guides me.'

They arrived home. 'I'll put our picnic, together,' said Lucy.

'I'll find other practical needs and put them in a backpack, such as a blanket. Despite that we know the route, I'd rather we walked up at sunset, wouldn't you?'

'Yes, good idea.'

When the sun started turning orange and began sinking behind the tor, Marc and Lucy left to walk up to the top. The walk was pleasant. They decided on Marc's favourite spot, on the flat rock, being a bit sheltered. They created a cosy nook, spreading out a blanket to sit on, and leaning back against another rock. It was quite comfortable.

The sun sank below the horizon and in the west a dark red sunset lit up the deep blue night sky. They looked south towards the coast and noticed a ship on the distant sea, its lights twinkling. Looking skywards the stars began appearing. Marc relaxed back and sighed. 'How lovely. Silence. Just the hooting of an owl somewhere in the distance.'

'Hmm, yes. Glass of wine?'

'Yes, thanks.'

Lucy poured two glasses and passed one to Marc and put the bottle back in the bag. She settled back too, leaning close to Marc enjoying his body warmth. Marc too was enjoying the sensation of her. He tried to distract himself by looking at the scenery. More stars appeared as the sky darkened. 'No light pollution makes such a difference,' he said to Lucy. 'Even living in an apartment, high up like I did in London, you still couldn't see much because of the light pollution. Obviously, the moon was visible, but never so many stars as this. I really don't miss the city life, to me it wasn't living. I value silence. There was always noise coming from somewhere; a plane overhead, a train rushing past, traffic noise, and people … so many people. And dogs barking. Never silence. I find it utterly draining. My brain buzzes.'

'I suppose some people enjoy it, but living in a town centre, let alone a city, would be awful to me too. I need space and fresh air and quiet. Is that why you chose to move here?'

'Not entirely. I met some lovely people I really relate to… Most especially a nice lady to share a gorgeous house with. It was a bit of a first for me, a lady who doesn't find me an indecisive quiet geek-type person.'

Lucy squeezed his arm. 'It is rather nice, isn't it?'

'What is?'

'Sharing a house. I feel safe with you and we're very compatible ... even down to the films we watch, unless you're just being nice.'

'It's compromise. We negotiate, then agree, that's the way we work.'

'And tonight, we're admiring nature's entertainment. Did you notice the bats earlier ... as we walked up.'

Marc shuddered. 'No, I'm glad I didn't see them.'

'They were only taking advantage of the insects at dusk for their supper.'

'Hmm, well, that's as maybe. They remind me of horror movies.'

They fell silent looking around and up at the stars. The moon appeared.

'The moon is quite large,' said Lucy.

'We should wait awhile; it's supposed to get closer to the earth in the early hours and look orangey. We don't have to wait up all night ... but a bit longer.'

'Is it nearly midnight?'

'Why? Are you hungry?' Marc looked at his phone. 'It's eleven fifteen.'

'Nibbles then. Some now, and more later.' She rummaged in the hamper and dug out a tub of olives and a large packet of crisps. 'Need a top-up?' She picked up the bottle of wine and unscrewed the top. Lucy poured and then topped up her own.

'Thanks,' said Marc.

They sat in silence picking at the nibbles and watching the scene. The moon appeared to get brighter. Suddenly they heard a noise which made them both jump. Marc turned on the torch in his phone and scanned across the area in front of them. He spotted a pony wandering in the ferns. 'Gosh, you made us jump,' Marc said to it. 'Don't you guys sleep at night?'

The pony stared back at them, as if to say, "What the hell are you doing here?" It put its head down and resumed grazing.

Lucy giggled. 'It probably hasn't seen many humans here at this time of night. I'm surprised we're alone. I thought with the special moon tonight more people would be out looking up at it. It's been mentioned on various news sources.'

'I suppose most sensible people will either glance out of their bedroom window, or be cuddled up under the duvet, sleeping. Talking of which, you're not getting cold, are you? I brought a spare blanket we can snuggle up under.'

'That would be good.' Lucy decided that although she wasn't particularly cold, the thought of a snuggle up with Marc would be very nice.

He delved into his backpack, pulled out a blanket, and wrapped it around them. 'Better?'

'Mmm, lovely.'

They fell silent again, still nibbling snacks and sipping wine, watching the sky and listening to the owl's hoots. Lucy placed her head on Marc's shoulder. 'Are you getting tired?' Marc asked her.

'A bit. Shall we have our midnight feast now?'

'Yes, it must be nearly midnight. Objective achieved then. Seen the moon looking pinkish and the picnic, then we can walk home.'

Lucy passed Marc a filled wrap. 'Thanks,' he said.

They sat eating, with the blanket wrapped around them. 'Not sure Enid Blyton had this in mind for the midnight feasts she wrote about. They were generally in a dormitory inside a boarding school. You went to boarding school—did you ever do one?' Lucy said, trying to visualise Marc as a child getting up to mischief.

'No. Not even shared a packet of biscuits at midnight. I think Ms Blyton just had a vivid imagination … or times have changed.'

Lucy laughed. 'Probably. Hot chocolate now?'

'Too right. It wouldn't be supper without hot chocolate.'

'And chocolate chip muffins…'

'Wonderful. If we only ever do this once, we'll do it properly.'

They returned to snuggling up with their treats. 'Good suggestion, Marc. This has been fun and it's a clear night. We've seen oodles of stars and just look at the moon. One to remember.'

'Yes, definitely.' Marc slipped his arm around Lucy and she nuzzled into him thinking, *how perfectly romantic this is.*

'Is it getting near the time for us to move on?' Marc asked, finishing the sentence in his head, ...*because I really want to kiss you.*

Lucy looked at him and gently kissed him on the cheek. 'Just a little while longer.' They stayed snuggled up, both savouring the moment.

'Are you ready to go home now?' Marc asked.

'Yes, I'll doze off if I stay here much longer,' Lucy said.

They gathered up everything they'd brought and carefully rolled up the blankets and put them back into the rucksack. Although the moon lit up the area well, Marc put on the torch again to have a final check to make sure they hadn't missed anything. 'Leave nothing but footprints and take only memories,' he said. There was no need for the torch to find their way to the track. The moon hung in the sky like a huge bauble on a Christmas tree and it lit their path all the way home.

* * *

THE NEXT MORNING, Lucy was awakened by her phone ringing. An unknown number.

The caller: 'Hello, is that Lucy Trethewey?'

Lucy: 'Hi yes, I'm Lucy.'

The caller: 'I'm Nick Owen. My family and I have just moved into Little Beliton.'

Lucy: 'Yes.'

Nick: 'I've been given your number because the headmistress at the school is currently abroad on holiday. I just wondered if you'd mind showing us around the school and give us a bit of info about it.'

Lucy: 'Oh, okay. When would suit you?'

Nick: 'This afternoon, perhaps. Two o' clock?'

Lucy: 'Yes, that's fine. I'll meet you at the school.'

Nick: 'Thank you. I realise you're on holiday, but I'm grateful. My girls like to get familiar with their surroundings.'

Lucy: 'No problem. I'll see you at two. Bye.'

Nick: 'Bye. Thanks.'

Lucy put the phone on her bedside table and lay back thinking about their midnight jaunt. She'd really enjoyed it and it gave her a warm fuzzy feeling. She smiled and got up and went to the bathroom.

A short while later she caught up with Marc enjoying a coffee in the kitchen. 'I think the mystery of the removals lorry is solved. I had a phone call from a man asking if I could do a sales pitch of the school and show his girls around. They've just moved here.'

Marc passed Lucy a coffee. 'It does sound like mystery solved. I'll walk that way with you and go and look at the field project.'

'You don't have to. I'll be alright.'

'It's no big deal. I want to go anyway. We'll go together.'

'Okay, thanks. I said I'd meet them at two.'

'Great, that's our afternoon planned.'

'This morning I'm going to get the room ready for Ann.'

'Need some help?'

'No, it's fine.'

'I'll go and make sure there's a clear space ready for the freezer when it's delivered.'

'Okay. That's our whole day planned.'

CHAPTER 20

*L*ucy and Marc arrived at the school at one forty-five. Lucy unlocked the door and they went in. 'I'll just hang around until they get here and make sure you're okay, then I'll go over to the field and come back. Perfectly reasonable as I'm now a governor.'

'Honestly, I'll be fine. Not everyone is like Dick, and do you honestly think the guy would ring me from his personal phone and then do something? He'd be easily tracked,' argued Lucy.

'No, well anyway, it's fine.'

'I'll go and gather some paperwork and forms.'

'I'll wait here. If they come a tad early, I can welcome them and introduce myself and give some of the community info. You never know, they might be people willing to join in.'

'Sure. You do the big sell.' Lucy walked off to the office that Marc found her in those few months ago.

A few minutes later a family appeared in the doorway. 'Hello, I'm Nick Owen. This is my wife Carole and my twin daughters Katie and Jenny. We've come to meet Lucy Trethewey.'

'Hello, come on in. I'm Marc Smythe. I'm one of the governors and part of the PTA and community. Lucy's just gone to get some paperwork for you.' The adults shook hands. Marc turned his attention to the girls. 'Hello Katie and Jenny. I bet you get fed up of people asking, but tell me who you are and give me a clue.'

'I'm Katie and I'm very slightly taller than my sister.'

'Hi Katie,' Marc said, shaking her hand, 'Hi Jenny,' he shook the other girl's hand.

'So, when did you move here?' Marc asked.

'Yesterday,' said Jenny.

'Ah, we saw your big lorry. I hope you're settling in alright. Welcome to Little Beliton school. We're very friendly here and there's always something fun going on in the village. Ah, here's Lucy ... Miss Trethewey. Lucy this is Nick and Carole Owen, Katie and Jenny.' He made sure he got them right.

'Hello,' said Lucy 'welcome.'

'I'm going over to see how the field project is going. Enjoy your tour.' Marc left them to look around and talk about the school. When he arrived at the field, he saw Bertie. 'Hi, Bertie, how are you doing?'

'I'm okay thanks. I just brought a load of cuttings from a job I'm doing to add to the compost heap. I thought it would help to give it a boost.'

'Ah, good. Is there anything needs doing here today?'

'No, the plants are doing fine. It's amazing how quickly we got it all going,' said Bertie. 'The children are keeping an eye on the parish hall garden too. The crop of tomatoes and lettuces has been magnificent this year. What are you doing here?'

'Just came for a look really. Lucy's showing a new family around the school.'

'Ah good. I'll be up to your place for the next two days.'

'Great. I'll see you then.' Bertie got into his truck and drove off. Marc took a cursory look around the field then left, closing the gate. He returned to the school where Lucy was still showing the family around, and the girls were looking at the outdoor projects.

Nick walked over to chat with Marc. 'It looks very much like the school is the heart of the village.'

'It most certainly is...' Marc went on to talk about the field project, the village hall and solar panels.

'Lots to be involved with,' said Nick.

'Everyone pitches in with the projects they are interested in and everyone is very friendly. Being involved with the school is a good way of getting to know people,' said Marc, 'and I should know. I've only been here a few months.'

'Really? You sound as if you've been here all your life,' said Nick.

'No, I'm the newcomer, but my relatives have lived here a very long time.'

'I grew up in Greater Beliton,' said Nick, 'but moved away with my family when dad got relocated for work. I went to college in Gloucestershire, so it feels a bit strange to be coming back to the area. I lost touch with people, of course. No such thing as Facebook and things like that to keep in contact when I was a teenager.'

'No, I can understand that. What do you do?'

'I'm going to be managing the big supermarket, Food Nation, in Greater Beliton.'

'That needs a variety of skills, I guess.'

'It does. Mostly people skills.'

'Anyway, welcome to Little Beliton, I'm sure you will be made as welcome as I was.'

Lucy and Carole came over to join them, while the girls played on the playground equipment. 'Are you happy with what you've seen?' Nick asked Carole.

'Oh yes, it's nice and the girls seem happy. Look at them.'

'Good,' said Lucy, 'we'll see you at the beginning of term, if not before. There's a community barbecue at the parish hall this Saturday, if you're interested.'

'Thank you,' said Nick shaking Lucy's hand.

The Owen family gathered and walked out to the lane, calling Goodbyes. Lucy and Marc watched them. The family crossed the road to the field and looked over the gate.

'I think,' said Lucy, 'I pick up a good vibe from them. They'll soon settle in just fine. Right, I'll lock up and we can go home.'

'Sure, do you need a hand, or shall I wait here?'

'I'll be fine. Just wait here.' Lucy went back into the building then reappeared a few minutes later and locked the door.'

They walked out to the lane. 'Let's go the moor route up the lane,' said Marc.

'Yes, it will make a change.'

They strolled up the lane, past the pretty cottages and the entrance to the farm, over the stile and towards the fields and the moors. 'When I was looking through Simon's papers, I noticed he was interested in buying an ancient woodland to preserve it. I don't know if he did, or if it's owned by the national park or the forestry organisation. Do you know where it is? I'd love to see it. I read these ancient woodlands have been in place since the ice age and they're full of old oaks covered in moss and are lovely gnarled oak trees. They're magical, evocative places where you wouldn't be surprised to find pixies or witches or something.'

'Luckily, they're usually off the beaten track and not easy to find. Too many visitors would ruin them. I think it's around the back of the tor, somewhere upriver. I've never been there and Joan never mentioned it. So maybe it was gifted toad preserved by a big organisation.'

'I was just curious, I've seen photos that's all,' said Marc. 'Maybe one day we'll go hiking and see if we can find it. It would be nice to see a real fairyland.'

'You are a big softie.'

'No, I believe in magic and round here is famous for fairy folk, isn't it?'

'Maybe. Or it's a mythology invented for the tourists. I'm not going to argue though, because sometimes magical things happen when you meet the right person.'

'Precisely.'

They walked quietly past the field with the beautiful cows, simply enjoying each other's company. When they reached the top of the lane, Marc said, 'It's just occurred to me, I'm no longer The

Newcomer to the village. The Owens are. Even he thought I've always lived here.'

'Hey, promotion! They're a nice family. The twins will be in my class.'

'Ah, nice that they've met you. They were cute.'

'I think we'll be seeing more of them. I felt a kind of … I don't know … a connection. Weird. They've only just moved to the area. Anyway, I'm up for a quiet evening and an early night.'

'Yea, me too.'

* * *

THE NEXT DAY Marc received an invitation from James to go over and join him for coffee. 'I'm having a bit of trouble with my computer, if you're able to help me.'

'Sure, I'll take a look and see if I can. It probably needs some updates, or cache clearing by the sound of it. I'll come over.'

Marc told Lucy what he was doing and left. Lucy was in a baking mood and quite happy working in the kitchen.

When Marc reached James's front gate, he saw Nick coming down the lane. He waited to speak to him. 'Hi Nick, how's it going? All your boxes unpacked?'

'Hi Marc. It's never-ending. Carole had a declutter before we packed up to move. Mind you, this house is much bigger so everything looks so clear and spaced out.'

'It takes a while to adjust to living in a new space. Good luck.' James came out of his cottage to join them. 'Hi James,' said Marc, 'this is Nick and he and his family have just moved here.'

James said, 'Hi Nick, welcome to Little Beliton.' They shook hands.

'Thanks,' said Nick. They stood chatting for a few minutes, Marc reminded him about the barbecue on Saturday evening, with a local band providing entertainment. Then he spotted Dick walking along the road.

'Lovely, we'll come along,' said Nick. 'Lucy mentioned it too.'

Dick walked up to them. 'If it isn't Mayor Marc making connections. Who's this then?'

Marc decided to keep cool and ignore the sarcasm. 'This is Nick. He and his family have just moved here. Nick this is Dick, landlord of The Fox on the Green.'

'Hello,' said Nick offering a handshake.

'Hello,' said Dick, ignoring it. 'Not seen you in the bar yet.'

'No,' said Nick, 'we're still unpacking boxes.'

'Might see you sometime then? Not that these two ever come in, especially Judge Joan's nephew...' Dick walked off.

'Friendly chap,' said Nick quietly, 'what's his problem?'

'He's got a problem with me,' said Marc. 'He doesn't like me.'

'Anyway, I'd better go. Carole's waiting for some milk that I've popped out to get,' said Nick. 'Nice to meet you, James. We'll see you and Lucy at the barbecue, Marc.'

'Bye,' said Marc and James.

'Come on in,' said James. 'I've made a pot of coffee.'

Marc followed James into the cottage and indicated a seat at the dining table where the open laptop was placed. 'I'll have a look,' said Marc.

'What was all that name-calling about?' asked James.

'I don't know. Clearly, he's got a problem with me. I mentioned to you he tried to punch me recently when Lucy and I left school one evening. He didn't succeed because I side-stepped and he staggered over, but it's obviously made his attitude worse. He's kept away from Lucy though.'

'Have you chatted with Ann yet?'

'She's coming to stay next week. We're picking her up at Exeter, on Monday.'

'Ah, good. How are you going to approach dealing with the problem?'

Marc paused, concentrating on the computer screen. 'We're going to support whatever Ann chooses to do. We'll decide when we get together. Here you go. I ran the virus search and updated it and it's just doing a clean-up. I think your computer will be okay then. We just need to wait for a bit. Let the software do its thing.'

'Brilliant. Thanks. Yes, good idea to decide what you're all happy with,' said James.

'Lucy and I are thinking maybe, just for once, a visit to the pub might be in order. He's hardly going to be difficult with people sitting in the bar.'

'That's a good idea …'

'Especially when some villagers will remember Rita,' said Marc.

'It will catch him off-guard and take the smug sod down a peg or two,' said James. 'I'll enjoy watching that.'

'Lucy is concerned about how her mum will feel.'

'I can understand that, but clearly he's not been honest with her either.'

'Anyway, next week. We'll invite you over to meet her. Here you go, your computer's fine now.'

'Thanks. I can get on with my work without any hitches.'

'My pleasure, I'll leave you to it. Thanks for the coffee.' Marc stood, walked to the door, and opened it to leave, when he noticed Dick hurriedly walking past, back towards the pub.

'Bye, James,' he said quietly, holding back, not wanting to attract Dick's attention again.

'Bye, Marc.'

Marc walked slowly down the garden path relieved to have not been noticed. He stepped through the gate and walked home.

When he arrived home, he heard Lucy crying. She was sitting on the sofa with her head in her hands. 'Lucy, what's happened?' he said quietly.

Lucy dropped her hands from her face to reveal a black eye and a cut. 'Dick came here,' she sobbed. 'I thought the doorbell was the postman or something and opened the door … and he punched me.' She covered her face with her hands again. 'He called me a tart … a harlot.' She sobbed again.

Marc put his arms around her and hugged her. 'Lucy, I'm sorry I went out and left you alone … I'm so sorry. I'll go and make a cold compress for you.'

'Marc, it's not your fault. We're at home and we can't live joined at the hip. We have to live our lives,' Lucy sobbed.

'Did he say anything else?'

'He just said, "Whatever you think you've got on me, you can't use it to control me like Joan did. Maggie told me about your conversation," then he hit me.'

'Where were you when this happened? Would the security camera I set up have captured it?'

'Yes … maybe,' Lucy replied.

'Just stay there a minute and I'll be back. I'll get you some ice,' Marc got up and hurried to the kitchen, placed some ice in a clean tea towel and returned to Lucy. She accepted it gratefully. He sat down beside her again and took out his phone to check the camera app. 'Yes!' he said, 'We've got the bastard. I'm calling the police.'

Lucy silently nodded in agreement and Marc made the call. Afterwards he checked to see how the compress was working and refolded it carefully around the ice cubes and Lucy replaced it. Marc put his arm around her and hugged her close. 'I shouldn't have left you alone,' he repeated, quietly as if scolding himself. 'I shouldn't have left you alone.'

CHAPTER 21

A police car pulled down the drive and stopped outside. Marc went to open the door. 'Hello, Sir. I understand you've had a problem. What's happened?' said the officer.

'Come in.' Marc stood aside inviting the two policemen to step into the hallway. 'Follow me.' Marc led the way to Lucy, still sitting on the sofa.

'Hello, madam, can you tell me what's wrong?'

Lucy removed the ice pack and showed her black eye and cut cheek. 'I had a visitor … and he did this.' She replaced the ice pack on her eye.

The policemen sat down. 'That looks painful,' he said. 'Who did this?'

By this time, Marc had opened the camera app again showing the attack and passed his phone to one of the officers. He watched it closely. 'Who's that?' he asked. 'He looks vaguely familiar.'

'Dick Taylor, the landlord of The Fox on the Green,' said Lucy.

'And why did he attack you?' asked the officer.

'It's a very long story, but basically, he's my mum's man and he thinks he can control me. He's been threatening and abusing me for years.'

'Why does he look familiar?' said the officer, thinking. *Dick Taylor ... Dick Taylor ... The Fox on the Green ....* He sat quietly, trying to remember and recall an old case. 'Anyway, why did he attack you?'

'My mum came over last week to have a go at me, as usual, and I spelled out a few home truths about my upbringing. I told her, yet again, what he tries to get up to with me ... yes, I mean abuse ... but she never ... has never, believed me, and always defends him. So, I told her to keep him under control and away from me,' said Lucy. 'And it seems, she told him about our conversation and he came here to have a go at me.'

'I can see that from your video. How come you've never reported him before?'

'He's been abusing me for years, most especially when I was a teenager. I was terrified, but mum never believed me, and she didn't protect me. So, I thought if I'd tried to report it to someone, no one would believe me ... and I just lived in terror.'

The officers listened silently, looking at Lucy sympathetically. 'Go on...'

'I know, now I'm an adult, but then I didn't have any solid evidence.'

The officer needed clarity. 'How long has this been going on?'

'Since I was ten, when I lived with my mum and then when I was in my mid-teens a kind lady ... Marc's relative, Joan, took me in and gave me a home here and kept me safe, but since she died, he started again.'

'We will certainly investigate this. Do you mind if we take a photo, for evidence? And we'll need a copy of that video you've got.'

Marc replied, 'I'll take the memory card out of the camera, for you.'

'It's okay, yes,' said Lucy. The second policeman took out his phone and took some photos.

'We'll need to take a formal statement. Can you come into the station to do that?' said the first officer.

'Yes, we can do that,' said Marc. 'Later today ... tomorrow?' Marc handed him the card.

The officer replied, 'As soon as you're free to come in and feel up to it. In the meantime, we will go and see Mr Taylor.'

'Thank you,' said Lucy.

'Did he do anything else today? Just that punch?' asked the officer.

'Just what you've seen ... the punch,' said Lucy.

'Out of interest, where were you sir? Was Miss Trethewey here alone?'

'I was out. In fact, Dick knew I was out. I'd gone to help a friend in the village with his computer, and Dick saw me as he walked down the lane. As I left, I saw him walking back towards the pub—although he didn't see me that time. I came straight home to find poor Lucy ... and phoned you.'

'Fair enough. You take care, Miss Trethewey. You should see a doctor and get checked over.'

'Yes, thanks. I'll get more ice and we can do that,' said Marc. 'Thank you, officers.'

Marc showed them out and then went to make a fresh ice compress for Lucy. He took it to her. 'Thanks, Marc,' said Lucy. 'Well, my secret is out in the open now.'

'I know it's hard and it's not what you wanted, it wasn't the way we were going to deal with it, except that now there's a police enquiry, and there is hard evidence for it. Depending on what Ann says, and is prepared to share, it could just be the end of Dick.'

'If only mum had listened to me and kept him away...,' said Lucy.

'No one will think badly of you. You're the victim in all this. You're the one who has been badly treated. Your needs were ignored. Your right to protection was denied. You have absolutely nothing to feel ashamed of,' Marc said reassuringly.

'Oh no, we're expected at the barbecue the day after tomorrow. I can't go looking like this,' Lucy said miserably.

'Let's go and get you looked at professionally first then we'll talk about the barbecue. Hospital outpatients? GP?' Marc asked.

'Can you call the surgery for me and ask? Maybe a nurse will be free to look.'

'Of course. It's about time I registered there too,' said Marc. 'Got the number?'

'Yes, here, use my phone.' Lucy unlocked her phone and handed it to him.

'Thanks.' Marc did his usual thing with phone calls wandering around talking. It deflected his phone phobia.

He came back into the room and gave Lucy her phone back. 'Just turn up and wait. Someone will look as an urgent assessment is needed. And I'll complete the forms and hand them in … before you ask. It feels like the final thing to do to be a real resident here. Permanence.'

'Ah, my suffering is proving to be a benefit,' Lucy smiled.

'Did you have to do something this drastic?'

'It's made you do it. I'll go and get ready and we'll drive over to Greater Beliton.'

Marc went out to the car park, as Bertie arrived. 'Hi Bertie, we've got to go out. I'll lock up, but you've got your key to the shippon for any tools etc.'

'No problem. I'll crack on. Hi Lucy.'

'Hi Bertie, how are you all?'

'Crikey maid, what's wrong?'

Lucy dropped the ice pack, from her eye.

'Blimey. How did you get that?'

'Dick,' Lucy replied.

'Why?' Bertie was concerned.

'We have some old stuff to settle and he decided that fists talk.'

'Crikey, maid. So, you're going to the docs?'

'Yes, we'll just wait until someone can see us.'

'I know Maggie is your mum and you two don't seem to get on, and I know you used to live at the pub, but I didn't know it was … this bad.' Bertie was shocked.

'Some day it might all come out. But for now …,' said Lucy.

'Of course, I won't say anything. The times you've helped us … I'm really worried about you though. Actually, thinking about it, I saw a police car in the pub car park when I drove past,' said Bertie.

'Yes, well, I'll think about how much I'm prepared to say, because as Marc says we can't miss the barbecue on Saturday.'

'Good for you,' said Bertie. 'That bloke is an arrogant shit at the best of times. Never parts with a penny to help the school fund. Never helps with anything. I don't know how his little lad is so pleasant.'

Marc intervened. 'Come on Lucy, get in the car. We'll see you later Bertie. Don't know how long we'll be.' Lucy got in the car and closed the door. 'Thanks Bertie. We'll talk later,' Marc said.

Marc drove carefully out of the village and up the lane to the moors and turned towards Greater Beliton. Once in the town Lucy directed him to the surgery. They parked and went in. 'Ah, Miss Trethewey, you can go in straightaway. Dr Coombes is free,' said the receptionist.

'Do you want me to come with you?' asked Marc.

'I'll be okay, thanks. You fill your forms out,' said Lucy. 'I'm sure I won't be long.' She turned and walked to the doctor's consulting room.

Marc completed the forms and handed them in, then sat and waited until Lucy returned. 'It seems nothing is broken, thank goodness, just badly bruised and the cut. I can tell the swelling is going down already. The cold compresses have done that. There will be a nasty bruise though.'

'So sorry Lucy, but it's good news that nothing is broken. Do we need to do anything else?'

'No, we've done all the right things. She just told me to rest and keep the ice pack on it.'

They went back out to the car park and got into the car. 'Do you want to go and give the statement while we're here.?'

'No. I want to go home. I could do with a rest,' said Lucy.

'Of course, I'll look after you. Bertie looked really concerned too.' Marc began driving home.

'Yes, he did. He's a kind guy. They're a nice family. I'm sorry they have a hard time with Emily's illness. I don't know what's wrong, but both kids are good carers when Bertie's not around.'

'They're lovely. Oscar's my little mate,' said Marc.

'He thinks the world of you. It's clear. I told you about the art conversation with his friend and that day with the draw tickets …'

'He was a right little charmer. He was doing the selling, I only supervised.' They went quiet and Marc reached the turning to the village.

Lucy broke the silence. 'What do I say about all this? People are bound to ask.'

'I think pretty much what you said earlier is honest and vague. Just that there's history with Dick to put behind you. Would people really be so surprised? Everyone seems to know what he's like.'

Lucy thought about it. 'You're probably right. Maybe all my shame is baggage in my head. It was gaslighting that does it. I knew what happened and mum would just say, "no you've got that all wrong" and present her version. I was always wrong. It's no wonder I've had self-esteem and self-confidence issues to deal with.'

Marc pulled off the road onto the grass and switched off the engine. He looked at her. 'Lucy, you are beautiful, intelligent, kind, hardworking, you're good at your job and the villagers all like you—especially the children, and you care about everyone and I, for one, know I'll love you for the rest of my life. You have endured the hardest start in life, harder than most people, and yet you give to everyone, and you still have so much to give. You take nothing—from anybody. You are a beautiful person with a beautiful soul.' Marc started the engine again, pulled back onto the road and drove home, allowing Lucy to absorb what he'd said.

He parked and they got out and walked to the front door. Marc opened it and stepped aside for Lucy to enter and he followed. Lucy walked to the lounge and sat on the sofa patting the seat beside her she said, 'Sit with me, Marc.' Marc sat down. Lucy had gone so quiet he wondered if he'd said too much. He clasped his hands together on his lap and looked down at them.

Lucy said, 'Thank you Marc. I know what you said came from your heart and you meant every word. I'm grateful that you're here with me and that you love and care for me as you do, every day. I'm grateful for your honesty and for everything you do for me. I know I can trust you implicitly and you will never hurt me. Thank you.'

Marc looked at her.

Lucy continued, 'And I know I will love you for life too, just please be patient a tiny bit longer and let's finish putting all this behind us. Me especially. We're almost there. Ann is coming, it will end then. It will be over. We can move on … together.'

Marc smiled. 'I can't wait.' They hugged.

'Thanks,' said Lucy, 'thanks for being my best friend.'

Marc stood up and persuaded Lucy to lie on the sofa making sure she was comfortable. 'I won't be far away. Have a rest and I'll fetch you a drink. Do you need a new ice pack.'

'Yea, that will be good thank you…'

By the time Marc returned, Lucy had drifted off to sleep. He put a blanket over her and left her in peace.

CHAPTER 22

Marc went outside for some fresh air. Bertie was still around somewhere as his truck was parked up. Marc needed some time alone to process everything that had happened. He went and sat on a decking sofa. He closed his eyes and took a few deep breaths.

The next thing he heard was someone stomping down the driveway. He turned to look. It was Maggie. Marc stood up and went over to her.

'What the hell has been going on?' she screamed at Marc. 'Dick's been arrested.'

'Quite probably,' said Marc 'he attacked and injured your daughter.' He emphasised "your daughter", rather than use her name.

'That's not what he told me,' Maggie was shaking with rage. 'Where is she? I want to see her.'

'Well, you can't. She's been medically assessed and she's resting,' said Marc.

'I want to see her.'

'No! But I'll show you a photo.' He took his phone out of his pocket and found the images and held the phone up for Maggie to see. 'There. That's what Dick did.'

Maggie's tone changed as she stared at the picture. Her anger instantly dissipated. 'How do you know it was Dick?'

'Because apart from I believe what Lucy says, the security camera caught it,' said Marc.

Maggie went silent, her mind racing. Eventually she said, 'And you say she's alright?', now clearly concerned.

'Yes, she's got an awful black eye, a cut cheek, and obviously she's shocked and distressed, but as I said, she's been checked over and she's resting.'

Maggie looked distraught. 'I caused this,' she said miserably. 'I told him what she said. He was furious. He said she'd always been a liar and ungrateful to him for providing her a home. That she's always trying to cause trouble…'

'Where's Marty?' Marc asked. 'If you're here and Dick's gone … where's Marty?'

'He's on a playdate with a friend.'

'Good.'

'I'm going to have to go and get him and tell him why his dad's not at home.'

'Yes, you need to explain it to him. My concern is Lucy and I'm looking after her. Do you know what amazes me most is, despite whatever Lucy has had to put up with, she always thinks of how it will affect *you*. She always considers your feelings.'

Maggie looked down at the ground crestfallen. 'Thank you for looking after her,' she said quietly. She turned and walked back up the drive. Marc watched her go. Glancing at the lounge window he saw Lucy standing there, she'd been watching. Lucy waited until her mum was out of sight and then joined him outside. They went to the decking sofas.

'I saw what you did, thank you,' said Lucy.

'No problem. My concern is you and I will always do what I can to protect you, although now I realise, I can't always do that,' Marc said, ruefully.

'No, we must be able to be independent. You went to help James. No problem. What was she so angry about?'

'They arrested Dick.'

'What did you say to mum?'

'I've given her something more to think about,' said Marc. 'I told her that despite everything, you always take into account her feelings.'

'I don't suppose it will do any good, she only thinks about herself. Anyway, let's enjoy some fresh air and relax for a while. You're as wound up as me.'

Bertie appeared through the gate in the hedge from the direction of the kitchen garden. He walked towards them. 'Oh my god ... Lucy. Are you okay? What a shiner!'

'I'll live. There's nothing broken. Take a seat, we'll talk.' Bertie sat down. 'Right, how are we going to explain this?' Lucy asked.

Marc said, 'I think, tell the truth. Dick did it.'

Bertie said, 'Yes, I agree. Quite honestly most people won't be surprised, they know what he's like. Over the years the pub regulars have seen and heard how he treated you when you were a kid.'

'Really?' Lucy gasped.

'People felt sorry for you, the way he yelled at you bossing you about. He might have thought taking you out the back made things private, but it didn't. He treated you like his slave—and your mum. When I was a teenager, having a few beers with my mates, we heard him. We heard he was the same when his wife was around. He slapped her about too. I think he was suspected of her murder when she disappeared, but they never got any evidence, or something.'

Lucy was taken aback. 'People remember that long ago?'

'Yes, not much goes unnoticed round here. Someone always remembers.'

'Oh,' said Lucy, 'that means the gossips are going to love this.'

'No maid, you've got that all wrong. They'll be really worried about you. Many have seen you grow up and rise above his bullying. You've done well, especially with Joan's help. It was only going to be a matter of time before he'd try and wreck any happiness you find.'

'Maggie just came and vented,' said Marc, 'Dick's been arrested.'

'Good,' said Bertie. 'About bloody time he got his comeuppance.'

'So, back to the barbecue ... we don't need to make anything up?'

'No, not at all. Don't stress. He's had it coming for a long time.'

'Ah, thanks Bertie, for keeping us up to date with the jungle telegraph,' said Marc.

'No problem. Always happy to help. I'll go now and I'll be back tomorrow, Em's feeling a bit poorly again, so I need to help her with the children.'

'Sure, if you need anything just let us know.'

Bertie stood up, 'See you tomorrow.' He walked up to his truck and drove off.

'It's nice to know that a lot of people were concerned for you. I suppose nobody knew how to help you back then, without interfering and making matters worse,' said Marc. 'Luckily Joan did.'

'It's going to be interesting to see the reactions when Ann's here. There will be quite a few who remember Rita, I think.'

'I suppose Dick will be back, out on bail by then, maybe? How long do they hold people?' Marc said. 'Anyway, he's out of your way for a few days. You can give your statement tomorrow.'

Marc put his hand around her shoulder and pulled her in for a cuddle. Lucy relaxed into it, savouring the comfort of body contact with him. She rested her head on his shoulder and closed her eyes.

* * *

THE NEXT MORNING, they drove to the police station in Greater Beliton. Lucy had found a pair of sunglasses with large frames, which mostly hid the injury.

The police officer who'd come to see them welcomed her, 'How are you today?' he asked, as they took seats in the interview room.

Lucy removed the sunglasses. 'Okay, thanks. It looks a lot worse than it feels … if I don't touch it,' she said.

'It looks nasty. You saw a doctor?' he asked.

'Yes. I got it checked and nothing is broken.'

They proceeded to discuss the event, creating the statement. He finished by saying, 'We'll hold him in custody while we put the case together. Not sure how long he'll be detained—at least over the weekend.'

'Right, thanks,' said Lucy, still feeling apprehensive about possible repercussions if he was released. She replaced her sunglasses.

He showed them out. 'We'll be in touch and let you know what happens next.'

They enjoyed a quiet drive home.

* * *

SATURDAY AFTERNOON ARRIVED and the team got to work setting up the barbecue. The awning, the fairy lights, tables for food, the barbecue was brought out of storage and the gas connected. An entertainment area provided space for the band, who were setting up their sound system. Tables and chairs were arranged indoors for anyone wanting the alternative, and the garden benches were cleaned off ready. The whole area looked attractive and inviting.

Lucy and Marc helped with the setting up. Lucy, wearing her sunglasses, didn't attract much attention as everyone was busy. Eventually most people, including Lucy and Marc, went home leaving the main organisers to it.

'It's looking good,' said Lucy. 'I'm sure it will be a great evening.'

'Yes, hope so, the solar funds should get a good boost. Did anyone ask you?'

'No, I didn't take my sunglasses off, which I expect people thought was a bit odd when I was indoors, but no one said anything. I just kept busy out of the way. I'll have to carefully apply my makeup tonight and tone it down a bit.'

'Beautiful lady! I don't understand these things.'

Early evening, everyone arrived at the village hall garden and family groups claimed their preferred bench. Lucy and Marc chose one on the periphery and reserved an adjacent one for Nick, Carole, and the girls. They poured their drinks.

Bertie came over, 'Can we join you? The only tables left are indoors and the children don't want to be cooped up in there.'

'Yes, of course,' Lucy said. Bertie waved Emily and the children over. Emily had been speaking to some friends sitting at a nearby table.

'Hi,' said Lucy. 'Feeling better?'

'Yes, thank you,' said Emily as she sat down and they got chatting. Marc high fived Oscar and Gemma, who ran off to play with their friends.

'How's Lucy today?' Bertie asked Marc.

'Better, thanks,' said Marc. 'She'll feel happier with you joining us, not having to constantly explain … well, until later on, when the sun goes down and she takes her sunglasses off.'

'I told Emily what happened and the children know she's had an accident, so they won't make anything of it,' said Bertie.

'Lucy will appreciate that. Thanks for your support. "Trouble" is out of the way for the weekend anyway, and Maggie will be running the bar, if she's got any punters.'

'Some of the old ones, playing cards or something. I feel sorry for the kid—Marty. He's in Gemma's class. She says he's quite a nice kid, but he doesn't get to socialise much and he doesn't have very many friends.'

'I suppose not if his parents are busy running the bar. Well, his mum anyway. Ah, there's the new family … I'll be back,' said Marc. He walked over to greet them. 'Hello Nick, nice to see you. If you're feeling a bit swamped in a sea of strangers, we've reserved a table next to ours for you. We can introduce you to some people.'

'Thanks, that's kind,' said Nick. They followed Marc across the garden taking seats at the next picnic bench and Marc made the introductions. Nick, being a friendly, extrovert type soon got talking to Bertie and was interested in hiring his garden services.

'Pleased to help. I'll come and have a chat,' said Bertie. Oscar and Gemma returned.

'Your little girl's sweet, she's made friends with Katie and Jenny already. Look,' said Nick.

Gemma said, 'We want to go over to the playground, Daddy.'

'Yes, go on then, I'll be there in a minute.' The three girls ran off with Oscar trailing behind them.

A few minutes later, Marc, Bertie and Nick joined them and continued talking while the children played. Nick was relieved to see his daughters busy chatting with other children and joining in. He worried that they were a bit shy and often stood back watching. No chance that was going to happen with Gemma around. Nick went over closer to the girls. There was another man standing watching.

Nick stood beside him, he said, 'Hi, I'm Nick. We just moved here this week. The twins over there are my daughters.'

'Ah, I thought I hadn't seen them before. How old are they?'

'Five.'

'And they're starting at the school in September?'

'Yes, Miss Trethewey's class. We went and met her this week and we were told about this event. Good timing for meeting people.'

'Same age as my daughter and they'll all be together in the same class. We'll make sure they get to know each other,' said the man, 'nice to meet you Nick, I'm Gerry.'

They continued chatting.

Meanwhile, Marc and Bertie watched Oscar and Gemma from a distance while they talked. 'Nice to see so many people here,' said Marc.

'This solar project has inspired everyone,' said Bertie. 'We're all worrying with the rising cost of energy, let alone the green issues reminders every time we turn on the TV. I know I'm dreading our winter bills, what with Em not being very well and I have less work in the winter, we'll struggle. Our rent is going up soon too.'

'I've something in mind that you might be interested in and it might help you,' said Marc. 'A business proposition.'

'Go on,' said Bertie, obviously interested.

'The stable block conversion. I'll get it started very soon and there will be a big three bedroomed flat on the first floor. So, I thought, would you like more work with developing the kitchen garden and greenhouse and live on site?'

Bertie looked at Marc. 'Really? That would be amazing. I'll have to talk to Em about it...'

'Of course. We can work at developing the kitchen garden together, donate some plants to the field project, maybe? I'm having solar panels installed to hopefully keep it all running economically, including the flat. We can work out how to do it—share the business profits, negotiate rent and everything. What do you think? You'll still be able to keep your other clients going too.'

Bertie was completely overawed. 'Gosh! What a proposition. Thanks, Marc. Thank you for thinking of us.'

'We'll talk later. I haven't told Lucy what's in my mind, but I know she'll be pleased. Oscar and Gemma will have plenty of safe outdoor space to enjoy too.'

Oscar came running up to them. 'Hey Dad, Marc, come and play football.'

'Sure,' said Marc, 'I'm up for a kick about.'

'Come on Dad! I want to be in goal.' Marc started dribbling the ball with Oscar towards the football pitch on the other side of the playground. Bertie went over to tell Gemma where he'd be and jogged across to join Marc and Oscar kicking the ball about. The three of them had great fun taking it in turns to kick goals, until it was time to go and get hotdogs and burgers and enjoy the music as the sun went down.

When they returned to the barbecue, Marc was pleased to see Lucy was chatting with Emily and Carole. She looked relaxed and happy. The girls were all happy sitting eating hotdogs with another little girl, and Nick was talking to Gerry and another family.

All going well, Marc thought.

Lucy wore her sunglasses until the last possible moment when it became too dark to see much, by which time the focus was on watching the band and dancing. The whole event hadn't proved to be the ordeal that Lucy had imagined and everyone was having fun.

It was approaching midnight by the time everyone had drifted off home and the bulk of the clearing away done. Lucy and Marc offered to help, but in view of Lucy's injury, now it was visible, they were sent away and left for their moonlight stroll home.

'What a week,' said Marc, 'whoever suggested that it's quiet and uneventful living in a remote Dartmoor village got it completely wrong. There's nothing sleepy about it.'

'And there will be more to come next week with Rita's return. Afterwards it will return to sleepy and uneventful ... for a while. I suppose that's why the slightest change keeps the community alive,' said Lucy.

CHAPTER 23

Marc and Lucy arrived in the airport car park in plenty of time to saunter over to the terminal building to Arrivals to meet Ann. They went to the coffee shop while they waited, watching the board. Eventually they saw Ann's flight number changed to "Landed".

They waited a bit longer, to allow for the walk through the terminal and passport control, before going over towards the door. It wasn't long before Ann appeared. They waved to attract her attention and she walked towards them.

'Hi,' Ann said, 'Nice to meet you both.'

'Hi,' said Lucy, giving her a hug and kissing her cheek.

'Hi,' said Marc, greeting her in the same way. 'Let me take your case.'

'Lucy, what happened to you?' Ann asked, spotting the mark beneath the sunglasses.

'Dick. Long story,' said Lucy.

'I'm glad I came,' said Ann, as they followed Marc out to the car park. He put the case into the boot and opened the door for Ann and she got in. Marc began to drive. 'Okay. What's the story?'

Lucy gave an overview of the last few days including that Dick was being detained. 'Although he might be released today. Spending the weekend locked up and alone to think might make him regret what he did. But I doubt it.'

'From what Joan told me, his regret didn't last long when I left … he soon reverted to his default behaviour. Sorry to say this Lucy, but your mum was lured into his web.'

'Yes, I know that. Dick knows how to turn on his charms to keep her there, especially since they have Marty, but he's often not nice to her. He's a complete narcissist. He's nice when he wants something, even if he's just demanding ego strokes, but he's also controlling and nasty. He says awful things about people and calls them names behind their backs, and yet he's smarmy and turns on the charm when they're putting money in his till, or he's drinking with them. Horrid man.'

'You're definitely right. So, what shall we do? Obviously attacking you last week has got him temporarily out of the way,' said Ann.

'Yes, but did you know he's been in gaol before?' Lucy said.

'Well, I know he was held and suspected of murdering me,' said Ann.

'No. Before that. He's got a prison record.'

'Noooo!' Ann was shocked. 'But that explains many things, like why he never mentioned his family background. How do you know?'

'James found it.'

'What was he in for?'

'GBH. So, my injury shows leopards don't change their spots.'

'I guess the police will have checked for a record this weekend too,' said Marc.

'I think … it's time to release what's lodged at the solicitors, don't you?' Ann sighed.

'If you're happy to do that. I couldn't prove what he was doing to me for years, not that I was old enough to understand "evidence" and "proof" when I was a kid, and he knew it. I was too scared to talk. I tried telling my mum and she'd dismiss me. Always defended him—took his side,' Lucy said.

'Marc, can we take a detour? To the solicitors?' Ann said.

'Yes, I can, but if I call James, he's been looking at the paperwork, since talking to you. He'll have the file handy and will bring it home this evening, if he's in the office today,' said Marc.

'Ah, right okay. I'd like to meet James,' said Ann.

'I'll phone him, as soon as we're back.' Marc continued the drive home. 'In some ways, I hope Dick is let out ... on bail. We can give him a real shock when I appear,' said Ann.

'We've been thinking that. He's hardly going to do anything with a pub full of witnesses,' said Lucy.

'We'll let you settle in first and then we'll decide how and when we do it,' said Lucy. 'I'm grateful you're here to help. We can put an end to him being nasty, for good.'

'As I said to you, I want a divorce, so it benefits me too.'

* * *

JAMES ARRIVED in the early evening. 'Hello Ann, lovely to meet you.'

'Hello, James. Nice to meet you too and thanks for your help.'

'This is yours,' said James, handing Ann a document folder. 'It's not pretty, is it?'

'No,' said Ann, 'it's not. And looking at Lucy ...'

'Yes, James,' said Lucy, removing her sunglasses.

James gasped. 'When did that happen?' He was concerned.

'Thursday, while I was with you,' said Marc. Do you remember Dick spoke to us when he went down the lane, and I saw him going back when I left your place? He did it then.'

'Crikey. Come to think of it, I saw a police car in the pub car park a bit later when I left to go to Steph's, I didn't think about it at the time.'

'We knew you were away for the weekend. And we were busy getting Lucy checked over by a medic and giving a statement.'

'What evidence did you have?'

'The security camera video.'

'Ah good. Sorry Ann, we've side-tracked the conversation. What's the plan with your folder?'

'Still not quite sure yet. I think we'll turn up at the pub first. I can't wait to watch his reaction when he sees me,' said Ann.

'The thing is, we don't know if he's back there yet,' said Lucy.

'Leave it with me, I'll find out,' said James.

* * *

DICK HAD BEEN BAILED and was back home at the Fox on the Green. The village news network was rife with speculation. James overheard people chatting in the shop while he was in there. He phoned Marc.

'Thanks for letting us know. We'll have a chat and let you know what we're going to do. More like when we're going…'

'Please let me know, I'm interested and you're my friends. I don't like what you and Lucy, especially, has had to deal with,' said James.

'Cheers, we appreciate your support. I'll let you know.'

Marc relayed the news to Lucy and Ann. 'So, when shall we go then? James wants to come too.'

'Let's get it over with,' said Ann, 'and go this evening.'

'Yes, I agree,' said Lucy. 'My eye is still looking bad enough but improving. Not sure it will have any effect on Dick, but mum might just feel a tinge of empathy and guilt. She's going to get a shock anyway.'

'Good,' said Marc, 'I'll call James back. What time? We'll call at his cottage on the way.'

'I'm thinking seven pm,' said Ann. 'I imagine it's a busy time still?'

'No idea,' said Lucy, 'we never go, but sounds alright to me.'

'I agree,' said Marc. 'I'll let James know. In the meantime, enjoy today and relax. Don't get wound up speculating about what will happen. We're all on the same side and Dick's completely outnumbered. And I imagine he's feeling quite vulnerable right now.'

Ann laughed, 'You sound almost sorry for him.'

'No, I'm not in the least sorry. He's had this coming for a very long time,' said Marc.

'I do feel a bit sorry for mum,' said Lucy, 'but she's got to live in the real world and see her wonderful Dick for who he actually is. A nasty slime ball.'

'Yep, in fact, she's got something to gain if she thinks about it. I want a divorce, so she's free to apply pressure—if that's what she really wants, if she thinks it will give her security, financial or otherwise,' said Ann.

'Yes, well, I'm not second-guessing about what she thinks anymore. I've seen her reactions to me lately, and the one Marc dissipated the other day. I really don't know what her problem is, but she's no longer my problem.'

'Well said,' said Marc. 'There's obviously something bubbling underneath, which controls her reactions and attitude, but it's not your problem. Not now.'

Lucy thought for a minute. 'Yes, you're right. I suppose it's been a case of loyalty, that she's my mum, but that doesn't give her the right to treat me like she does. I walked away for my self-preservation. I need to remember that.'

'It's none of my business, but as an outsider Marc's right. You've done extremely well to get past your problems, all you're trying to do now is rationalise them to move on. I get the feeling you're both holding back, but I can see you will move on … together.'

Again, Lucy went quiet, thinking. *Uh-huh, we both know we're sorting out our individual memories before moving on. It makes it simpler, getting it out of the way. Marc's just about there with his. This will sort out mine, once and for all.*

Ann said, 'I haven't told you my story, but I will. I met and married Dick when I was twenty and he was thirty, in 1993. Recently I wondered what I ever saw in him. I think it was because he was older than me, he seemed to be doing okay and I thought we'd be alright. As you say, he can work his magic when he wants to. We took on running the pub and it was doing alright at the beginning. We worked together, planning ways to earn a decent living after paying rent, etc. to the brewery.

'Ten years passed with the magic slowly losing its sparkle. He began slapping and punching me and I knew he was getting his kicks from looking at dirty mags and porn websites, but what shocked me worse was when I saw evidence of child porn. He was getting incredibly lazy leaving me to do all the work, he complained when it wasn't done his way, and he never gave me any money for myself. He was treating me like a slave.

'I met Joan not long after Simon died, in 2005. You know the circumstances; Joan had written them in her journals you read. I realised I'd met Simon once or twice because he used to meet friends in the bar, until he became ill. I felt empathy for Joan, he was a nice man. Larger than life, loved a joke, laughed in an infectious way and he was kind and sincere. Joan and I hit it off straightaway and we became good friends. She was lonely and had a gap in her life, and I was … well, in the situation I was in.

'Joan felt sorry for me and helped me through those bad times, as you know. She helped me save some money—usually the change when I did the shopping. She listened to my troubles, helped me to believe in myself, and encouraged me that there was something better waiting for me. I planned to get away and go travelling, or something … emigrate. I'd work as I travelled, and I'd do what I needed to get a new identity, as far as I could.

'So that's what I did, in 2008. I started my life again, in my mid-thirties. Joan gave me a lift to the ferry, in Plymouth, and off I went. A foot passenger into the unknown. Once in France I hitchhiked. I got myself casual work in bars and restaurants, or in shops. I picked grapes in the autumn. I thought I had to keep on the move or Dick might trace me. Imagine how surprised I was when Joan told me, by email, about how he was suspected of my murder but released because they couldn't find the evidence, and that almost immediately he'd employed a young single mother to take my place and she was living-in. It did cross my mind, ringing alarm bells, when Joan said "she's got a child", but I was glad to be out of the way. Free! He wasn't going to look for me.'

'It wasn't your responsibility to consider my safety,' said Lucy.

'By 2008 I'd settled into a happy life. I found a place to call home— a job I was happy doing, and a relationship with someone who really cares and loves me, and I was thrilled when I beat the post 40s rule and we had a child. A perfect, beautiful daughter. My life was finally as it should be. Joan and I kept in touch by email, and I persuaded her to come and visit me for holidays and the rest you know.'

'I'm happy you found safety and happiness,' said Lucy. 'You were brave enough to save yourself and live your life. It was different for my mum—she had a kid holding her back from choosing a different life. Me.'

'How come she was a single mum?' said Ann, 'if you don't mind me asking.'

'Not at all. She says she has no idea who my father is. She was fifteen when she had me. She wanted to give me up for adoption, but her parents wouldn't let her. They made her face up to her responsibilities and look after me, despite the shame of their daughter going off the rails.

'The shame was actually all in their minds, but hey. Eventually when I was ten, my grandparents decided to move abroad and have a new start. Not sure what changed, except that I remember mum having huge rows with them. I think, she wanted to go out and do what her friends were doing—partying maybe, and they refused to look after me. Or at least that's what she's thrown at me many, many times. It not only caused the fractures with them, but she grew to resent me even more. Lose, lose.

'So, she got the live-in job with Dick, which meant soon she was sharing his bed. It was an arrangement that provided a home for me too, if I kept out of the way and did as I was told. Which maybe included Dick getting some kicks for touching me up, etc. and that's why I ran away... and Joan found me.'

Marc had listened in silence and felt incredibly sad for both ladies, for what they'd endured, and the shame and emotional pain. He never thought he would meet anyone who'd been abused, as they had been. It wasn't in his sphere of experience. It happened to other people, surely?

Clearly not. Dick deserved to pay the price.

CHAPTER 24

James waited by his garden gate for Marc, Lucy, and Ann, and greeted them when they arrived. The four of them continued up the road to The Fox on the Green. They walked across the nearly empty car park and entered the building. A short corridor with a door to the left for the lounge bar and to the right for the bar. They chose the bar and went in.

Lucy took a deep breath and stepped through first. She was still apprehensive and hadn't gone back into the building since she left, nine years before. Ann followed, then James, and finally Marc. They chose a table with a clear view of the bar.

James and Marc went up to the bar to order the drinks. Maggie was serving. She looked sullen, but Lucy couldn't remember the last time she'd seen her mum smile, let alone laugh. She wasn't particularly friendly or welcoming, considering she'd never seen any of them in the bar before. The men returned to the table with drinks.

They conversed quietly, sipping their drinks. 'I wonder where Dick is?' said Lucy. 'He's not perched in his usual place on the bar stool with his back to the wall, at the far end.'

'I can see a drink on the bar,' said Marc.

'He'll be back,' said Ann.

A few minutes later, Dick appeared behind the bar through the doorway from the back rooms. 'Wait for it,' said James very quietly. Sure enough, Dick went around to his bar stool and climbed onto it. He picked up his drink and took a sip before replacing it on the bar. Then he proceeded to look around the room.

Finally, he looked across to the table where the four friends sat. His jaw dropped open and he went white. 'My god! Rita,' he gasped. 'Where did you come from?'

The quiet buzz in the bar instantly stopped and everyone looked around. First at Dick, and then at the table with the four friends. There were a few whispers, 'Rita. It's Rita.'

'Back from the dead, eh?' Ann said. 'You never thought you'd see me again, did you?'

Dick still stunned, put his hand on his chest and a look of pain crossed his shocked face. Maggie wasn't looking at Dick. She was looking over at the stranger sitting at the table with her daughter. She glared.

'Got nothing to say to me?' Ann said to Dick. 'Yes, I'm back to settle a few scores.'

Dick stared at her rubbing his arm. No one watching was sure if he was faking illness, to gain sympathy, or to try and control the situation. 'Why are you here?' He appeared to be struggling to speak.

'Oh, I think we have a few issues to sort out, don't we?' Ann replied.

Someone sitting in the bar called out, 'Welcome back, Rita, nice to see you.'

Another called out 'Hear, hear!'

'Hello everyone,' said Ann.

It was then someone saw Lucy. 'Crikey, what happened to you, maid?' called one man.

'Ask Dick,' said Ann, 'he might admit it.'

Maggie looked at Lucy, then across to Dick, who was still rubbing his arm and chest.

'Dick is unable to have a conversation without yelling, or forcing his opinions on others with his fists,' Ann added, 'as many of you might remember.' She glared at Dick, not sure if he was wincing in some sort of pain or still trying to turn the situation to his favour. Nobody went to his aid and Maggie stood still, looking between Ann and Dick.

One man stood and walked over to the table. 'Hello Rita, I'm so glad to see you looking so well.' He held out his hand out for a handshake.

Ann stood and took his hand and said, 'Hello Bob, how are you?'

'Well thanks. It's so lovely to see you. You're looking really well.' He returned to his seat.

Ann sat down again and took a sip of her wine and a quiet buzz started again, although people were still watching to see what Dick would do.

Lucy watched her mum. Maggie was avoiding looking at her. It was hard to read the look on Dick's face—shock, was it? Lucy turned her head to glare at Dick. She worked up the courage to speak. 'Yes, my face is a bit of a mess, isn't it? I bet you're feeling really pleased with yourself.'

Dick looked at her, still wincing, his hand rubbing his arm and he grunted. Lucy continued. 'They let you out then?'

'Rita.' Dick grunted again. 'You want to talk? In private?'

'Private? Not sure I can trust you. You still talk with your fists,' said Ann. 'I'd rather talk where we can be seen. It's safer. You can start by apologising to Lucy.'

Dick looked angry. 'No, she got me locked up for the weekend.'

'Just the weekend?' said Ann. 'Hmm, I suspect you might need to get used to a lot longer than that.'

'Why? I obviously didn't murder you.'

'You think you're so clever ... There's a bench seat outside in the car park. I'll talk to you out there—from opposite ends of the bench—and where people can see us.' Ann got up and walked out of the bar to the applause of the customers.

Dick scowled and followed her out.

Everyone watched through the window, Rita/Ann sat at one end of the bench and Dick plonked himself down at the other. One man turned round to speak to Lucy. 'Did that bastard do that to you? I saw you at the barbecue and didn't like to ask.'

'He did,' said Lucy.

'Why?'

'I don't want to talk about it. All I did was open my front door and I didn't expect it.'

'Nor would anyone. Oi, Maggie, keep Dick under control, he can't go punching your daughter,' said the man.

Maggie visibly shrank. She looked down at the glasses she was washing in the sink. 'Maggie, does he do that to you too?' he asked. 'We all know what he used to do to Rita. She was often bruised.'

'I'm saying nothing,' Maggie replied.

People were still watching the altercation and looking out of the window. Finally, Ann stood up and walked back into the building and sat back down with the others.

'Is everything okay?' asked Marc.

'Oh yes, fine. I think Dick and I understand each other,' said Ann. 'I will get what I came for, but I haven't finished yet. I have more business to sort out.'

'Would you like another drink?' James asked.

'No thanks, I think I've provided enough entertainment for one evening,' said Ann.

'We'll go,' said Marc.

They got up and Ann said to her audience, 'Thank you for your support, Ladies and Gentlemen, I'm sure we'll meet again.' They left the bar to another round of applause.

Outside Dick was still sitting on the bench. 'Had enough then, Mayor Marc? The nicest bloke in the village…'

'Shut up, Dick,' hissed Ann, 'that's always been your problem, calling people names, behind their backs. You aren't funny.'

'You think you're so smart, coming back, don't you?' Dick retorted.

'Just wait and see. I'm not done yet. You'll be hearing from my solicitor,' said Ann.

The four of them walked purposefully across the car park to the lane and turned to walk homewards. Out of sight, and nearing James's cottage, they began chatting. 'Phew! I had to work myself up for that,' said Ann. 'I always go out of my way to avoid confrontation.'

'Me too,' said Lucy.

'You girls were amazing. Really cool,' said Marc.

'Just the right amount of assertiveness, I'd say,' said James. 'Marc and I were merely moral support really.'

'I need to talk to you officially, James,' said Ann.

'Let me guess … divorce?'

'Of course. And how should I deal with the contents of that old file? Call at the police station and chat with the boys in blue?'

'I think so. They'll advise you.'

They reached James's cottage. 'Would you all like to come in for a drink? I'm sure I can lay my hands on wine.'

'Why not? Are you up for it Lucy … Marc?' said Ann. 'We'll celebrate round one, is it? Or two?'

'Two I think, I started the ball rolling when he was arrested,' said Lucy.

'Well, round three … is about to begin,' said Ann.

* * *

THE NEXT MORNING, Lucy took Ann to meet the police officer dealing with her case. Marc figured they didn't need him, so he stayed at home. Ann took the file with the reports, photographs and journal of the incidents she and Joan had created.

'Why didn't you bring this to us back then?' the officer asked, as he looked through it.

'I just wanted to get away and I was frightened he'd come after me. I created a new identity, as far as I could, and left. As it happens it was the right decision and I've built a nice life in France. I only came back to support Lucy when I heard about what he's been doing to her. It's the right time to share this "just in case" file, I think.'

'Thank you,' he said. 'We'll have a thorough look through it and we'll get back to you. You're looking a bit better now, Miss Trethewey,' he said.

'Yes, thanks,' Lucy replied. 'I'm feeling much better and less sore.'

The next appointment was for Ann to discuss with James, arranging the divorce. Lucy waited outside in the car park. She sat in her car musing over what had happened when they saw Dick. Was he faking illness with the chest and arm rubbing thing, she wondered. Nobody took any notice, so perhaps it was one of his seeking sympathy tactics, especially as he was still sniping sarcasm when they left. *Odious man!*

When she thought about it, she wasn't even feeling sorry for her mum. Despite that Maggie had heard what Dick did, and saw the photo, she still wouldn't apologise to Lucy. *Sod her!* Lucy thought, I *just feel sorry for Marty.*

She thought about Marc too. *He's been so kind and supportive to me. I know he was quiet yesterday, but this is not his battle. I had to work myself up to confronting Dick, and it was satisfying, after a long time coming.*

There seemed to be people in the community who knew what he was like and probably what he was getting up to, but maybe they didn't know how to help. Dick's always been secretive making sure he couldn't be challenged. I wonder if he's been bullying mum, and Marty too. Maybe that's why she kept so quiet. I don't know. I can't see inside her head; I don't understand her at all and I think she's pretty screwed up.

Eventually Ann came out of the office and got back into the car. 'All sorted?' asked Lucy.

'Yes, I think so. I'll probably have to return here again in a while, especially if Dick is charged and goes to trial.'

'Thanks Ann. I really appreciate your help and, of course, you're welcome to come anytime,' said Lucy starting the engine. 'Let's get back. Marc is cooking his lovely lasagne for supper this evening and he's going to invite James too. James often works from home because at the weekends he goes down to Cornwall and stays with his girlfriend.'

'If it's okay with you, I'll stay a few days more in case there is anything else I can do, then I'll go home,' said Ann. 'We'll keep in touch. You're both welcome to visit us anytime. Come and have a holiday.'

'That would be lovely, once we've got this all sorted out,' said Lucy.

Ann sighed and said, 'I can't help thinking you're both holding out on getting together. Just do it—life's too short not to enjoy it.'

'You're right. I know Marc would like us to move on. Now that everything is out in the open ...'

'Exactly. Enjoy life. He's a good guy. Joan sometimes told me about her thoughtful young nephew. He's had rather a lot to deal with recently, hasn't he?'

'Yes, he has. His parents estate is still being dealt with, it was a bit complicated and it took a while for him to make decisions. Hopefully it won't be much longer.'

'So now it's the right time for you two to move on. Honestly. What's stopping you?' Anne asked.

'Nothing now. I think you're right. Do you know, it's nice to talk to another woman. I know I can trust you and I think you've shown me that I didn't trust anybody, except Joan, and I thought it was just men I didn't trust.'

'I'm not surprised given what you've been dealing with, and now Joan's gone—your trusted mentor and mother figure. I know how important it is having someone who understands. Joan was a lovely kind, empathetic lady.'

'Do you keep in touch with your mum?' Lucy was curious.

'No. I spent my childhood in a children's home. I don't know my family at all. Not sure what's worse really, having my experience or yours—completely misunderstood and emotionally maltreated, from what you've told me. I know I'm unlikely to ever know who my family was.'

'Hmm, I just don't know who my dad is. Mum claims she doesn't know, but I doubt whether she was really such a wild teenager for that to be true. Who knows, perhaps she was a rebel. My grandparents were so prim and proper, bible bashing and totally ashamed of her, but made her "do the right thing". More like pay for her mistake, and I'm the one who suffered. On the other hand, I suppose I should be grateful, they could have had me put up for adoption ... oh, I don't know... What happened, happened. I just have to put it behind me and accept I have a mum who doesn't care.'

They pulled up in front of the house. 'Thanks for the chat, Ann. I said things I've not thought of before. It's been helpful. Thanks.'

'You're welcome my dear. You've found a lovely, kind guy in Marc. Go for it and be happy.'

CHAPTER 25

Lucy and Marc dropped Ann back at the airport one morning. They'd all enjoyed meeting and would remain in touch with mutual promises of visiting for holidays. Lucy and Marc decided to have a day out again, or at least go for a stroll somewhere and have a nice lunch. They chose a nice quiet restaurant by the sea.

'How are you feeling now everything is out in the open?' Marc asked.

Lucy thought for a minute, then said, 'I was surprised just how much the community suspected what Dick gets up to. The trouble is, I suppose, nobody knew how to intervene. If anyone reported it, it would have been dismissed as interfering, and it would have been denied, by Dick and mum. As always, they'd have dismissed me as a liar and going through a rebellious teenager stage.'

Lucy paused, then said, 'I have no idea what I would do if I knew someone was in the same situation. It's good to know people wanted to help though. Maybe I should have reached out to … someone, but who, I don't know. Sadly, it meant that someone had to get hurt first … Ann, then me. I still wonder about my mum, but she says nothing and is still defending Dick. I just don't get it. But it's her choice.'

'It's been dreadful for you, thank goodness it's all over now. He won't dare do anything, especially now the police are putting together a case,' said Marc.

'Yes, and I don't regret reporting him. As you said, I can't live in fear of him, for the rest of my life and short of moving away, like Ann did to be free, and giving up the life I'm building in the community I love ... I just can't let him win.'

'The life you're building ... please tell me you're happy to move on now and we'll build the life we want to live ... together,' Marc looked at her hopefully.

Lucy nodded, 'That's exactly what I mean, Thank you for waiting patiently. I can't think of anything I want more than to spend the rest of my life with you. I want us to build our future together.' She smiled.

Marc stood up and went to Lucy's side of the table, knelt on one knee, he took her hands in his and said, 'Lucy, I love you. Please will you marry me?'

'I love you too, and yes, Marc, I will marry you.'

Marc stood up and leant towards her and very gently kissed her. She stood up kissing him back. Then they hugged each other close and kissed passionately. The people sitting at tables around them in the restaurant clapped and called "Congratulations". They broke apart both smiling happily and took a bow of thanks.

Their waiter appeared carrying a bottle of champagne in an ice bucket and two glasses. 'Congratulations, please celebrate ... it's on the house.'

They sat back down. 'Thank you,' they said together. The waiter popped the cork and filled their glasses. 'Enjoy!' he said, leaving them to sip their drinks.

Marc felt himself grinning. 'We'll go shopping after lunch and you can choose a ring. Something you really like and want. I wasn't prepared for presenting a surprise.' The sensation of happiness gave him the now familiar warm fuzzy feeling. He said, 'You are a beautiful, lovely lady and I promise I'll always love you.'

Lucy laughed lightly, 'Beautiful? Nursing a black eye!'

'Which you've carefully disguised with your makeup ...'

Lucy smiled and said, 'Marc, I will always love you too. Together we make a formidable team ... there's nothing stopping us now.'

The waiter returned with their food and put the plates down in front of them. They thanked him and began their lunch.

Later that evening, with a diamond ring twinkling brightly on Lucy's finger, they sat cuddled up watching the sunset from one of the sofas on the decking. 'What a lovely day to remember—for always,' sighed Lucy.

'Definitely. So when shall we do the deed?' Marc asked. 'I reckon, as quickly as possible, as neither of us have anyone to plan around. Our friends in the community are our family.'

'Yes, they are. I know we're not church goers, but I reckon that's what we should do. Stay in the village and have a community barbecue party and invite everyone,' said Lucy.

'Sounds good to me, we'll go and arrange it tomorrow,' said Marc. 'Aim for the bank holiday weekend at the end of the month, maybe?'

'Yes, just before term begins. We can delay a honeymoon, to maybe half term?'

'Do you want the big white event?' Marc asked.

'I'll choose a nice sensible dress suitable for a barbecue, apart from that I don't care ... jeans and T shirts will do,' she smiled.

Marc laughed, 'I thought you might say that. And any little people to dress up for your attendants?'

'Oscar and Gemma ...'

'Oscar could be my Best Man, but perhaps I should ask James ... we'll work something out.'

'And tonight ...?' Lucy said winking at Marc, before they kissed.

'Tomorrow, we'll go down to Cornwall and go and surprise James and Steph.'

***

A FEW DAYS LATER, with most of the arrangements in place Lucy wanted to video call Ann to invite them over and to have a chat.

Marc went for a walk alone, he wanted to go to Joan's grave in the churchyard. He took a framed photo of Joan with him. It was usually standing on the windowsill by his desk. It was a photo taken long ago and in it she looked the way he remembered her. The graveyard was deserted. He stood the frame on her grave where she lay beside Simon and sat down. He sat quietly for a while, looking at the picture, thinking.

'Hello Joan,' he said quietly, 'it's about time I had a chat with you. I don't know if you can hear me, or not, it depends on what happens when we die, I suppose, and I haven't really thought about that. I'll go with the idea that you can hear me.

'Well, Joan, if you've been up there reclining on a cloud watching me, as I like to imagine, you've had some entertainment these last few months and I guess this week has provided the Happy Ever After so many stories deserve. But let's go back a bit first.

'Thank you for presenting me with the opportunity of a lifetime to choose a happy path into the future. I cannot believe how lucky I am. Please let Simon know, if he's not watching me with you, that I will take good care of his family's home and I'll adopt his ethos—it will be preserved for future generations. If he is watching me, he'll see and I hope approve of my decisions.

'Thank you for ensuring that I'd meet Lucy. I sometimes wonder if you were playing Cupid. Anyway, as you've seen we've become the best of friends first, and we love and care for each other deeply and we always will.

'Thank you for ensuring I learn a sense of belonging, for the first time in my life. This village community here is amazing. On one hand, many would say it runs on gossip, but if people are gossiping, they are at least connecting, and it shows they usually care, even if they speculate on details and get it wrong. But most importantly when something needs a team effort everybody joins in—it works. I used to worry about following the trail you blazed, could I keep up? Well, I don't think I'm doing too badly, do you?

'If you happen to see other members of the family, wherever you are, please say hi to Grandma and Grandad and tell them that all that sketching and house building is coming in handy. Please also tell

Mum and Dad ... Thank you for all they did for me. I know I didn't fit their mould and they didn't know what to do with me, or understand me, but they did their best and I'm grateful. Tell them, sorry I didn't choose to keep their business going. I wouldn't have run it well and I'm sure they will approve of what I'm choosing to do instead, with their help, so thank you. Also, tell them that I've found the love of my life. I'm sure they'd love Lucy, even if she's an oddball like me!

'I loved you all and I know you loved me. I'll be okay now I understand myself and I know I'm choosing the right path, and I'm with the right person. I'm living in a place I've grown to love. It will all be fine ... you'll see. Have fun at our wedding—celebrate with us. The whole village will.

'I promise I'll look after and love Lucy as we travel the journey of life together. We'll be absolutely fine. You'll see.'

Marc fell silent. He sat looking at the photo for a while longer, thinking about Joan, before he returned it into his backpack and walked home. He put it back in its place on the windowsill by his desk. He sat down at the desk and opened his laptop to check his messages and mail. There was an email from his parents' solicitor, Tim.

Dear Marc

You will be pleased to hear that I've finally completed your parents' estate. I've transferred the proceeds as per the details attached into your bank account ...

Marc finished reading the paperwork and sat back in the chair. *Oh, my goodness, it's done. Finished. I could cringe about the inheritance tax deducted, but I won't. I can only be grateful for the benefits I've gained to move on and live.*

Lucy walked past him. She stopped and stood behind him putting her arms around his neck and kissed his cheek. 'Are you okay?' she asked.

'Yes. I'm just letting something sink in...' Marc went on to tell Lucy the news. 'We're off the starting blocks for all the Project Beliton works. Our journey begins.'

Lucy said, 'Brilliant. And while we're talking about journey begins... I was thinking, instead of having a wedding cake, why don't we ask Debbie at the Cream of the Crock to provide a cream tea? Do you remember meeting her at Joan's funeral? It will feel like Joan's with us somewhere. Debbie would also do the salads and things for the barbecue too.'

'What a great idea! I'm pretty sure Joan will be around somewhere watching and grinning,' said Marc. 'We'll ask the main barbecue team if they mind cooking in relays, as usual. We'll provide all the food. I think some of them enjoy larking about being the chefs and as it's open to all the village to join us I don't think anyone will mind. Do you?'

'I've got one other thought, you just said "all the village" what am I going to do about Mum and Dick? Despite everything, I think she'd want to join us.'

'Of course. I guess it means we have to go and invite her,' said Marc. 'What do you think?'

'It's an odd situation. Who invites their attacker to their wedding? If I had a choice, I'd prefer that it was just Mum and Marty ... but ... and it won't be worth them opening the pub, will it?' Lucy was hesitant, thinking as she spoke. 'I'll arrange a meeting in the coffee shop with Mum and try and talk reasonably with her. Meeting in public, she'll hopefully not yell at me and make a scene.'

'Can I do anything to help?' Marc was concerned.

'No, this is something I must do. She is my mum, no matter how she's treated me,' sighed Lucy.

'I'll plan to be somewhere nearby, just in case.'

'It'll be okay. The worst thing Mum does is yell, she isn't violent. I'll be okay.'

'If you're sure. I arrange to meet Bertie and see if he'll organise the barbecue team for us.'

'Great, we can go and meet his family after I've met Mum, and I'll talk to Oscar and Gemma,' said Lucy. 'Anything else to arrange?'

Marc grinned. 'Best Man, check. Church and village hall, check. General invitations ... in process. Catering ... to ask.'

Lucy continued, 'Attendants, to ask. Clothes shopping, to do. We're kind of there, for a few days organising. Oooh, exciting.'

'Everything under control then, what could go wrong?'

Lucy gasped, 'Don't say that it's tempting fate...' she rolled her eyes.

Lucy sent a text message to her mum and requested a meeting, at a time to suit her. She received an immediate reply... "In an hour."

Oh gawd, thought Lucy. *She's mad at me.* She told Marc.

'Right, okay,' he said, 'get it over with. I'll call Bertie and meet him at the field, as it's only just up the lane. Go and get ready and we'll go.'

Twenty minutes later they walked down the lane to the village. 'Wish me luck,' said Lucy. They kissed, and Marc continued up towards the field to meet Bertie.

Lucy went over the bridge to the coffee shop. She entered the deserted shop and placed an order for coffee, with Jan. 'Mum's meeting me, so I'll wait until she's here, if that's okay.'

'Of course, I'll be around,' said Jan. Lucy went and sat at the table from where she could see the field. The next minute, the bell on the door rattled loudly as Maggie entered angrily and she banged the door shut.

'Hello Maggie, I'll bring the coffee over,' said Jan, calmly.

Maggie stomped over to where Lucy sat. She dragged out the chair opposite Lucy out noisily and thumped down onto it. 'So, when were you going to tell me then?' she said angrily.

'I'm talking to you now,' said Lucy calmly. 'It's hardly normal circumstances with a mother who's always disowned me, and her partner who's threatened and abused me and is now charged with assaulting me, is it?'

'Well, why so quickly. Are you up the duff or something?'

'No, I'm not. We just can't see any point in waiting,' said Lucy, remaining calm. 'Why can't you be happy for me? After all, you kept on suggesting I would be "alright with him", like I should go gold digging, or something. What we've built is something you cannot put a price on. Genuine love and caring. Is that something you understand?' Lucy remained calm, watching her mum's face. As always, she saw the anger dissipating.

'Hmm, well … anyway … can I come?'

'Yes. You are the Mother of the Bride after all. And Marty, as he's my half-brother…'

'And what about Dick?'

'Good question. I don't want my wedding day spoilt with his angry outbursts and violence. But I don't honestly think it's appropriate, do you? What would you do if you were me? Just think about it.' Lucy still marvelled at herself for remaining so poised.

Maggie stayed quiet, obviously she had to think. Lucy's reaction wasn't what she expected. In fact, she hadn't known what to expect. Jan brought over their coffees and quietly put them on the table and retreated. 'Thank you, Jan,' said Lucy.

Maggie was still deep in thought. At last, she said, 'Actually, I envy you. You've got yourself a lovely kind man who everybody likes, and he treats you like a lady. Everyone I've heard talking is happy for you and wish you well. They say you're made for each other.'

'That's nice to know.'

'And I'd like to come, with Marty as my escort. I expect Dick would rather perch in his usual position, drinking whisky, in an empty bar. That's his happy place. And just maybe a few people might drift in for a quick drink as they pass by. It's my daughter's wedding and I'm pleased for her.'

'Thanks Mum,' Lucy smiled, 'and quite honestly I'm pleased. Have you told Grandma and Grandad? Would they want to come?'

'I'll call them and see. They might.'

They drank their coffees in silence. Lucy said, 'I have to go now and meet Marc.'

'Okay, fine. I'm glad we've sorted that out,' said Maggie, as Lucy stood up.

Lucy bent to kiss her mum's cheek. 'Bye, Mum.'

The shop door opened quietly and Nick entered. 'Hello Lucy, how are you?'

'Good thanks. Have you met my mum, the landlady of The Fox on the Green?' Nick went over to the table. 'Nick, this is Maggie, Mum ... Nick. I'll leave you to get acquainted.' She turned to Jan, 'Thanks,' paid her and left.

Maggie looked up at Nick with a look of shock on her face. 'Nick ...'

CHAPTER 26

Nick sat down in the seat Lucy had vacated. 'Maggie. How are you?'

Maggie was in shock. 'Nick. I'm okay, and you?'

Nick looked over to Jan. 'Two coffees, please.'

'Coming up,' nodded Jan.

'Lucy is your daughter?' Nick asked. 'She's beautiful, like her mum. She showed us around the school the other day. Marc and Lucy have made us really welcome.'

'Us?' Maggie asked.

'Yes, my wife Carole and my twin daughters, Katie and Jenny. They will be in Lucy's class in September.'

'Ah nice. You're living in Little Beliton?'

'Yes, the house opposite the pub,' said Nick.

'Oh.'

'It's lovely to see you again. I never forgot you, you know, when my parents moved us away,' said Nick. 'You were my first love, after all.'

'Well, we were only just fifteen,' said Maggie.

'Fifteen. It seems like a lifetime ago. You're looking good,' said Nick.

'Thanks. Despite having a daughter who is twenty-four this year. It is a lifetime ago, Lucy's lifetime anyway,' said Maggie quietly.

Jan brought the coffees and took away the empty cups. 'Thanks, Jan,' said Maggie.

Nick went quiet. Maggie could see he was considering what she just told him. She remained quiet. 'Lucy is twenty-four this year?' he asked.

'Yes, her birthday is just before Christmas.'

'We moved away in the spring. It wasn't a good time to move schools just settling down to the GCSE syllabus,' said Nick. 'Are you trying to tell me something?'

'Hmm, yes. My GCSEs were rather messed up, and my life fell apart completely. I had Lucy when I was fifteen. Just imagine the grief I got, the shame I brought on my family and the pressure on me to tell who the father was. I never told. But then how could I? I'd lost touch...'

'Maggie, are you telling me that I'm Lucy's father?' Nick went quiet. 'You went through all that, on your own? And we only made love once, just before I left.'

'Yes, once was all it took. She's a lovely person and sometimes I can see she looks a bit like you.'

'You're absolutely sure I'm her dad?' Nick said quietly.

'Of course. I wasn't a little slut putting myself about, despite what the gossip mongers said at the time. I'd only ever been with you, until I went to work for Dick.' Maggie sighed. 'Who wants to take on a single mother in a relationship? I wrecked my chances of a Prince Charming sweeping me off my feet. Just once, to say goodbye... '

Nick looked crestfallen. 'I am really, really sorry that happened. We should have been more careful and taken precautions, but we were young and thought it wouldn't happen ... just once ... and it was rather nice as I remember.'

'Yes, it was,' agreed Maggie.

'What does Lucy know?'

'Nothing. The same as everyone else. She took on board everyone's attitude, mostly from my parents, that I'd been a teenage rebel and got myself in a stupid situation, brought shame on the family and Lucy's been told not to be a little tart like her mother.' Maggie looked sad. 'No, I haven't had a good life, but thank you for the compliment.'

'And Dick, your partner ... he's the guy who attacked Lucy, isn't he? I saw the awful black eye she got when we were at the barbecue. Poor Lucy. Why did he do it?'

'He's always tried to abuse her, since she was about eleven, but that time he was livid at an argument Lucy and I had. She'd spelt out a few things to me about my lack of mothering care and told me not to do it to Marty. I was upset. Dick asked what was wrong, and stupidly I told him. So that time, you might say he was defending me ... for once. But if I'd thought he would do that to Lucy ... I wouldn't have said anything. Stupid, stupid me.'

'Crikey, it's a bit of a mess then?'

'You could say that. And now he's going to court for hitting her, he'll lose the pub because he won't be around to run it, probably. So, I lose a home and a job, and I have Marty to care for. My life has fallen apart again.'

'Marty is his son?'

'Yes.'

'What a mess. Let's think of some solutions. What are you going to tell Lucy ... about me? Can you hold off until I've talked with Carole?'

'I'm not saying anything to Lucy right now. Her life has turned a corner and she's happy. I'm happy for her. And I don't want to mess up your life either. It's been my problem ... for always ...'

'Okay, we'll cross that bridge later. What can I suggest to you? Have you thought of taking on the pub yourself? You become the licensee. You run it. Your business,' said Nick.

'I hadn't thought of that. I know the business, I do all the work, except for dealing with the finances. Dick controls that. Why would the brewery take me on? I didn't even finish school with any qualifications.'

'You could go to adult education classes, learn bookkeeping, maybe.'

'That's an idea I can think about. Thanks.'

'It's about time I helped you, I think.'

'It is nice to see you again, Nick. I'm glad you're happy. Truly I am.' They finished their coffees and Nick put the money on the table to pay. 'I've got to get back,' said Maggie. 'I have some pondering to do.' Maggie stood up.

'Yea, me too. We'll chat again soon. I know where to find you,' said Nick.

'Not in the pub.' Maggie looked alarmed.

'No, okay, let's swap phone numbers. Give me a day or two. Lovely to see you, Maggie.'

'Nice to see you too, Nick.'

Maggie spoke to Jan on the way out. She waved. Nick waved back, then he stood up and went to find the items he'd popped in for.

* * *

Lucy, in the meantime, walked happily up the road to catch up with Marc and Bertie. 'How did it go?' Marc asked her.

'It was fine. Hi Bertie, how are you all?'

'Good thanks. We're just talking about your barbecue. It's a lovely idea and I'll happily talk to the chefs team, we'll sort it.'

'Can we come home with you? I'd like to ask Oscar and Gemma something.'

'Of course, Em will be pleased to see you too.'

They all walked together to Bertie's cottage around the back of the football pitch. Oscar saw them coming and ran out to greet them. 'Hello, Marc. Hi Miss Trethewey. Marc, Dad, can we go and have a kick about?'

'In a minute, we'll come and say hi to your mum and Gemma first,' said Marc.

'Okay,' said Oscar. He walked along happily beside Marc jabbering away until they reached the cottage where Emily was pruning plants in the front garden.

'Hi Emily, how are you?' asked Lucy.

'I'm much better, thanks. Would you like a drink?'

'Sure, I'll come and help you,' said Lucy, 'I want to have a chat.'

Bertie and Marc were playing catch the ball with Oscar, and Gemma came cycling along the road towards them. Emily and Lucy returned with a tray of drinks. Lucy placed it down on the garden table. 'Gemma, Oscar, come here,' said Emily.

'Okay,' they said.

Lucy said to them, 'We've had some fun times recently and I wondered if you'd like to do something special for us.'

'Yes, yes …' they replied enthusiastically.

'I would like to ask you if you'd be my bridesmaid, Gemma, and Oscar if you would be the ring bearer. Marc and I are getting married in a couple of weeks.'

'Yes,' said Gemma, 'does that mean I get to wear a pretty dress?'

'Yes,' said Oscar, 'does that mean I help Marc?'

'Oh yes, it's a very important job looking after the rings until we need them and Gemma, yes, we'll go shopping for some pretty dresses, maybe tomorrow, if you're free? I need one too and you can help me choose. That's what bridesmaids do.'

'Cool. Yes, yes, yes,' both children were very enthusiastic.

'Sorted! Thank you.'

They all spent the rest of the afternoon chatting and drinking and playing football with the children. It was early evening when Marc and Lucy walked home. 'What happened with your mum?' asked Marc.

'Once again, she arrived seething, but I remained remarkably cool and it evaporated. As you know, every time I've seen her these last few weeks, she's been hopping mad about something. Our relationship has spiralled down to the worst level ever. But by the end of our chat, it got much better. I flipped Dick's unwanted presence back onto her—in my shoes, how would she feel? She thinks he'll keep the pub open, even if it's empty, so she'd like to come and have Marty escort her. And that's what she's doing.'

'That's good, I'm happy for you. She is your mum, after all. She should be there.'

'You sound happy,' said Lucy.

'Why shouldn't I be? My recent troubles have all been solved. I'm marrying the nicest, most beautiful woman I've ever met, who I love with all my heart and I'm living in a gorgeous house in a pretty village, what's not to be happy about?'

'I've just got a feeling that fate's not quite finished yet, that's all,' Lucy said.

'What's left? I've reconciled my past. You're getting on better with your Mum, and Dick … we have to wait and see what happens, but he's lost any control he thought he had. What's left?'

'I don't know, really. But I feel there's something. I'm happy, I'm marrying you, the whole village is excited about celebrating with us. I'm truly happy and whatever it is, I can deal with it.'

* * *

IN THE MEANTIME, Nick was wondering how to discuss his news with Carole. He waited until the girls were in bed before broaching the subject.

'I had a bit of a shock today,' Nick said.

'Oh?' said Carole. 'I thought you were a bit subdued this afternoon. What's wrong?'

'You know I grew up down here before we moved to Gloucestershire…'

'Yes,' she said. 'And …'

'And I met someone today I knew at school …'

'That's nice. An old friend?'

'Actually, she's an old girlfriend. My first love.'

'Oh. Who's she? Married with four children?'

'Not exactly. What would you say if I told you she's the mother of a child I didn't know existed until today…'

'What? Are you trying to say, your child?'

'Don't be mad, I love you and the girls and always will. Nothing will ever change that.'

'Who's the child?'

'Lucy.'

'Lucy, really? She's nice.'

'She is, isn't she, and she has no idea who her father is.'

'Who's her mum?'

'Maggie at the pub, the landlady.'

'With the nasty bloke Dick, we heard about. The one who hit Lucy. We saw how injured she was at the barbecue,' said Carole.

'Yes, precisely. He's been horrid to her for a long time and made her life a misery.'

'She's so nice, kind, caring … like you are. And she has no idea who her dad is?' asked Carole.

'No,' said Nick.

'Poor Lucy. That's tough.'

'So, how would you feel if Maggie and I tell her? We could keep it quiet for a while, and get to know her, and we needn't tell the girls yet that she's their half-sister. It would be a bit awkward as she'll be their teacher, don't you think?'

Carole went quiet, thinking. 'It's a bit of a surprise, isn't it? If you'd been promoted and moved anywhere else in the country, you'd never have known.'

'No. And I think Lucy deserves to know, don't you? Wouldn't you want to know in her shoes? Not everyone is as lucky as us growing up in loving families. It's a kind of taken for granted thing that everyone knows who their parents are.'

'Yes. I think you're right; she should know. How are you going to do it?' Carole was curious.

'Maggie and I should sit down with Lucy and explain how it happened and why. She's been through so much,' said Nick.

'Okay, thanks for asking me. I know our family happiness isn't at risk and that's the main thing I'm concerned about.'

Nick gave her a hug and kissed her. 'Nothing will ever ruin what we have. Ever. I love you and the girls, so much. And we'll decide the right time to tell the girls about their half-sister. Thank you for being calm and understanding. Maggie and I were only fifteen and saying goodbye. We only did it once. It was bad luck really, except Lucy is lovely.'

'Young love, eh? Come to think of it, she does look a little bit like you. She's calm and kind, like you too.'

'Thank you, my beautiful, lovely, kind wife, for being so understanding,' said Nick.

'Tell her soon.'

CHAPTER 27

*L*ucy and Gemma went dress shopping in Exeter and were sitting having a burger lunch when Lucy's phone rang. 'Hello Nick,' she said.

'Hello Lucy, can I organise a meeting with you?'

'Of course, when? I'm out shopping right now.'

'Later this afternoon, in the coffee shop?'

'Sure. See you about 4:30, we'll be back by then.'

'Thanks. Bye.' He hung up.

Weird, thought Lucy. I wonder what he wants. They finished their lunch and returned to shopping for dresses and shoes. Gemma was having fun. 'What about Oscar?' Gemma asked.

'I think we'll let Marc, James and Oscar worry about that. They might want something traditional, or smart casual, or fancy summer shirts, maybe? We only need to be dressed up for an hour, and we all want to have fun at the barbecue.'

Gemma looked around the shop they were standing in, 'Oh, Lucy, you'd look beautiful in that one.'

'It's lovely. Let's find you a pretty dress too and we'll try them on.'

Lucy had to admit that she'd never had so much fun before either, with her nine-year-old personal shopper.

. . .

By half past four with shopping completed and Gemma dropped home with her new outfit, Lucy parked in the village car park and walked across to the coffee shop. As she crossed the bridge, she was surprised to see her Mum and Nick sitting in the window of the shop chatting. She entered the shop, greeted Jan, and went to join them at the table.

'Hello,' she said, 'you two are getting along I see. Good to see you making friends in the village Nick. Hi Mum.'

'Take a seat,' said Nick. Lucy sat down next to her mum.

'Nick and I knew each other years ago, we went to school together,' said Maggie.

'Wow! I thought you'd just moved to the area, Nick,' Lucy said.

'I have, but more accurately I've moved back. Carole and the girls had never been here until we came house-hunting. We just preferred the village to Greater Beliton and thought it would be a nice place for the girls to grow up in.'

'It is lovely here. A very friendly community and the proximity of the moors to explore from here on foot is priceless. A great place to grow up,' said Lucy.

'For most people,' said Maggie, 'but not so much for you.'

'I don't know, I had a nice time with Joan. I love it now,'

'Sorry I made your life such a misery,' said Maggie.

Lucy was taken aback, this wasn't her usual feisty, defensive mum. She sounded completely different. 'Nick, I don't know what your influence is on my mum, but I quite like the change.'

'Don't be hard on her Lucy, she had a pretty hard life after I knew her,' said Nick.

'And when was that?' asked Lucy.

'We said—at school,' said Maggie.

'Oh right.'

'Infants, primary…?'

'Secondary. We were fifteen when we last saw each other,' said Nick.

While Jan delivered coffees and cleared the empty cups, Lucy was processing what she was told. 'Thanks, Jan,' she said. Jan left them to talk. 'Are you trying to tell me something? Fifteen...'

'Yes,' said Nick.

'Are you...?' gasped Lucy.

'Yes,' said Maggie.

'How?' Lucy asked.

'In spite of what you were told, mostly by your grandma and grandad, I wasn't a little tart or being rebellious. It was a one-off thing, before Nick moved away,' said Maggie.

'And Maggie didn't know where I'd gone, so she couldn't see the point of mentioning it. She took all that grief, fundamentally paying the price for one mistake,' said Nick.

'Except you are a lovely mistake. I shouldn't have treated you like I did, especially recently. We had a bit of a break, with Joan's help, and now you're marrying her lovely nephew. And you're happy. And I've been jealous because you're getting everything I ever wanted. But none of it was your fault that I wrecked my life, and I blamed you. And I do understand the one thing you've always wanted to know is who your dad is.'

'And it's me,' said Nick. 'We could send off for a test, but I for one, believe your mum. She knows.'

'I don't know what to say, I must process this. But I am very pleased to meet you...' Lucy went quiet, thinking, 'Who knows?'

'Just us three,' said Maggie.

'No, I told Carole too. I talked to her. She understands you needed to know.'

'I never thought that I'd have both my mum and dad at my wedding. You are coming, aren't you Nick? With your family?'

'I'd love to. I hear you're inviting the whole community. It's a lovely idea.'

'We're not the usual couple with loads of family, so we're doing something different. I really must think about all this. I will talk to Marc.'

They finished their coffee, Nick settled up with Jan and they all went their separate ways. Lucy walked back to her car and drove home.

When she arrived, Marc was sitting outside on the decking with a beer. 'Hiya,' he said and went over to greet her.

'Hi Marc, let's go and sit down. I need to talk to you.'

'What's happened? I thought you'd have a great day shopping.'

'I did, Gemma and I had a lot of fun and chose some lovely outfits, but ...' Marc waited, 'but I went for a meeting with Mum and ... Nick. Long story short, it turns out Nick is my ... dad.'

'What? That's a shocker. How come?'

Lucy went on to explain the story. 'I knew, I just knew, there was something else about to happen. I just don't know what to think. It's an absolute shock. The one thing I've always wanted to know, and we're getting to know his family as friends, and I really like him ... and he's my dad.'

Marc gave her a comforting hug. 'I don't know what to say. I'm pleased for you; I'm shocked with you too. He's a really nice guy—I like him, and his family. How many people know?'

'Five. Mum, Nick, Carole, you, and me. It's the one thing I've always wanted to know and now I'm ... stunned to silence and don't know what to think. Mum even apologised for her behaviour towards me too. I'm gobsmacked.'

'Let it sink in. Sleep on it. Take as long as you need.'

'The strange thing is I could have my dad give me away at the wedding, as per tradition. But then again, the whole thing would be out in the open. And the other thing is I'll be teaching my half-sisters in September and I've already got a half-brother at school,' she rolled her eyes and laughed. 'I'm a bit of an oddball and unwittingly buck the trend a bit!'

'You're keeping the school numbers up. Just think of it this way, we started to get to know Nick and his family a couple of weeks ago and we really like them. He's friendly and getting to know everyone. If you could choose a dad, wouldn't you choose him, or someone like him?'

'Yes, and I don't have to choose.'

'Exactly. Just think it over and talk to your mum and Nick again.'

That night, Lucy tossed and turned, even though she had the benefit of the warmth and comfort of a cuddle up with Marc. She couldn't stay in this state of dilemma and realised she had to make a quick decision. The big day was only a few days away.

Let the secret out or not?

It was then it dawned on her, it wasn't actually her problem. The secret was a benefit to her because it answered her biggest question. The decision to reveal it was Nick and her mum's concern. Her mum's because it could aggravate Dick. Nick's because he'd have to try and explain it to his little girls. Arrange a meeting again, she told herself, flip this dilemma back.

Marc woke up, sensing her wakeful state. 'You're agonising, aren't you?' he said.

'Yes I was, but I've just come up with the answer—for me anyway. Turn it back on them. It's not my problem, I'm just the result of the mistake, and I've got the answer I wanted.'

'Yes, you're right,' said Marc, pulling her into a cuddle. 'Now get some sleep.'

'I'll try. Sweet dreams,' Lucy said, and finally she fell asleep.

The next morning, Lucy organised another meeting—late afternoon at the coffee shop. Jan put the three coffees on the table and left them to talk.

'Right,' said Lucy, 'the way I see it, the problem isn't mine. Mum has always kept the secret, and strictly it's none of Dick's business, but I understand mum's fears.'

Maggie nodded her head.

'Nick didn't know until a few days ago and none of us want it to spoil his happy family relationships. It seems Carole is nice, kind and understanding about it, and I figure the fear is telling the girls the truth. Might be a bit tricky for them to understand at their age. However, as it doesn't change their world, they'll probably only need minimal information right now and explain more later, when they ask.'

'Okay, I'll think about that,' said Nick.

'I have a few other thoughts,' Lucy went on. 'I never in my wildest dreams thought I'd ever have my mum and my dad at my wedding, so that impossible dream has come true. It's normal for a father to walk his daughter down the aisle, but so far, I thought I'd manage on my own.'

'I hadn't thought of that,' said Nick. 'Okay, I understand.'

'And the other thing is, as we all live in the village and not much gets past most people, there might possibly be speculation? If the truth was told immediately, it would stop it in its tracks. People are kind. They knew about Dick abusing, Rita, but probably not how to help—except for Joan, that is. They heard how he made my life a misery and Joan helped me, and gave me a home, and everything else. And as for you, Mum, they probably know more than I do whether it's worth staying silent about any abuse he's giving you, or not. He's a lazy, bullying creep as most people know. It's your choice.'

Maggie shrugged.

Lucy finished by saying, 'I was the only person to be affected by not knowing and I'm happy that I know now. What you do is up to you.'

Maggie and Nick sat silently for a few minutes letting what Lucy had said sink in. She was right, of course. It wasn't her decision. Nick spoke first. 'You're right Lucy. You've dealt with enough in your life, by the sound of it, and you are leaving the past behind and moving on. I wish you luck and happiness and I really like Marc. I'll talk to Carole and see what she thinks.'

Maggie said, 'You're right, it's none of Dick's business. I'll just tell him. It doesn't change anything in my relationship, except Dick is behaving himself right now and I'm okay.'

Lucy finished her coffee. 'I'll leave. You might want to talk without me around. I'll see you soon. Bye.'

Lucy stood up and went to pay Jan and left.

Nick spoke first, 'I need to talk to Carole first, then I think we should speak again.'

Maggie replied, 'Yes, I agree. It's more likely to affect you, let me know. I won't tell Dick yet.'

When Lucy arrived home, Marc asked, 'How did it go?'

'Good. I've left them to decide. As I said, it doesn't affect me. It's their decision. Oh, and I've thought of something we didn't think of. People usually organise a wedding present list. I totally forgot. I don't think we need anything; we have our home already and we're going to do it up our way.'

'Yes,' said Marc.

'So, I think donations to the solar project instead.'

'Lucy, you really are the nicest person. Yes, I wholeheartedly agree. We'll alter the invitation we're going to deliver to everyone. "Please come, enjoy the barbecue, and in lieu of any intended gifts, please donate to the solar project ..." brilliant. I got a phone call; the band is booked. Everything is just about sorted.'

'Oh really? When are you and James going shopping and take Oscar?'

'Ah right. New T shirts and jeans it is then,' Marc laughed. 'Dinner is ready, we'll do the invitations this evening.'

CHAPTER 28

The day of the wedding arrived. They were lucky that it was a stunningly beautiful day, clear blue sky, and sunshine. It was the only thing Marc had no control over and he was grateful it was so lovely.

The village looked pretty decorated with bunting and garlands of flowers. The cottage gardens in full flower made a lovely backdrop and the church had been dressed beautifully with garlands of flowers. As for the village hall garden, it was a lovely centrepiece for the festivities. Everyone joined in helping with something.

Marc got up and showered, he dressed in his wedding outfit and went downstairs to make coffee and returned with a mug for Lucy, while she showered. He went back downstairs and outside to drink his coffee.

Lucy finished showering and returned to the bedroom. She dried and styled her hair and carried on carefully applying makeup. She admired herself in the mirror. Not bad, she thought, her injuries now pretty much healed.

James arrived with Steph. She was looking pretty wearing a flower print dress and a few flowers pinned in her hair. 'Hi Marc,' James called. 'How's it going?'

'Good, chilled out,' said Marc.

'I was amazed you guys broke the tradition of not seeing each other before the ceremony,' said Steph.

'Well, that's us, we make our own rules and the whole event is breaking with tradition. It's what we want.'

'I'll get you coffee,' said Marc.

'I'll go,' said Steph, 'and I'll ask Lucy if she wants a hand.'

James and Marc sat on the decking sofas chatting. A few minutes later Steph returned with their coffee. 'Going to have mine with Lucy,' she said and disappeared back indoors.

'Well Marc, I for one am really happy the way things have worked out for you two. You two are made for each other. I saw the sparks twinkling when you met.'

'You did,' agreed Marc. 'Lucy was the sunshine that chased my black fog away. I knew right from the start what a special person she is and we'd be great together.'

'You waited patiently, and I understand why,' said James.

'Yoo-hoo!'

Marc looked around to see Lucy standing there looking stunning. He stood up without taking his eyes off her and walked towards her. 'You are absolutely beautiful and you look amazing.' He kissed her gently. 'I am the luckiest man.'

James wolf whistled. 'Beautiful.'

'I scrub up okay then?' Lucy smiled. 'And we haven't even had breakfast.'

'Wait a sec,' said Steph, returning a few minutes later with croissants and a bottle of champagne. 'You have to have a Wedding Breakfast!'

'Literally. Ah, thanks,' said Lucy laughing and giving her a hug. They returned to the sofas and the sunshine. Steph produced a camera and fun photos were snapped while they ate breakfast.

'Right guys, it's time to walk down in a few minutes. I'm going to brush my teeth,' said Lucy.

'Go for it,' said Steph, 'I'll clear up.'

Marc and James walked up to the drive. 'I love your break with traditions,' he said. 'This is going to be a whole lot of fun.'

A few minutes later the four of them were walking down towards The Green, admiring the village decorations, and greeting everyone they met. When they reached the church gateway, Marc had a flashback to when he last stood there waiting—at the funeral. This time Oscar and Gemma were waiting for them with Bertie and Emily. People walked past the group, greeting them with smiles and disappearing into the church. The florist presented Lucy with a bouquet and Gemma with a posy. Oscar was clutching a little velvet cushion as if his life depended on it. James pulled two wedding rings from his pocket and threaded them onto the ribbon and secured them. 'You're doing a grand job,' he said to Oscar, 'just a little while to look after these.'

Oscar looked very serious, 'Yes, sir, I'll take good care of them.' James winked at him and ruffled his hair.

Bertie said to the children, 'Do you remember what you're doing?

'Yes dad,' they replied. Bertie and Emily joined the others in the church. Followed by James, Steph, and Marc.

Lucy stood outside the church porch with Gemma and Oscar having a friendly chat, with the photographer clicking away. Next thing James reappeared. 'Just wait a minute or two longer please.' He disappeared back into the church and closed the door. Lucy was mystified, but the three of them waited patiently, enjoying the sunshine.

Inside the church everyone went quiet at James's request. Maggie and Nick stood at the front of the aisle. Nick spoke, referring occasionally to a sheet of paper he was holding. 'You all know Lucy's Mum, Maggie.'

The congregation sat nodding ... Yes.

'And nobody knew, even Lucy, who her dad is. Maggie moved here into the village as a single mother and got the job working in the pub. Maggie has kept her secret to herself and she didn't tell anybody until last week.'

The congregation sat quietly listening and looking puzzled.

'It's true,' said Maggie, nodding.

'Maggie and I bumped into each other. We hadn't seen each other since our schooldays, just before my family moved away. Maggie and I were dating at the time, and sad we'd never see each other again. It was when we did meet again that I learned the news... I am Lucy's dad.'

It seemed everyone listening gasped.

Nick spoke again. 'I am very grateful to my darling wife Carole and my girls Katie and Jenny for their support relaying this news, but I want to do the honours for Lucy and walk her down the aisle.'

Everyone applauded. Maggie took her seat and Nick walked back to the church door.

* * *

MEANWHILE, Lucy and the children waited outside, they could hear the applause. *I wonder what that's all about*, Lucy thought. Next thing the church door opened wide and Nick stepped outside. 'Lucy, will you do me the honour of allowing me, your dad, to walk his beautiful daughter down the aisle on her wedding day.'

Lucy's eyes began filling with tears and she smiled. 'Yes please, Dad. Thank you.'

'Don't cry, Lucy. You look absolutely stunning,' said Nick.

Lucy swallowed hard, composed herself and took a deep breath. 'Okay, Oscar and Gemma, are you ready? You know what you're doing, you'll be fine.' She tucked her arm into the crook of Nick's elbow and the children took their places behind them. Gemma clutching her posy and Oscar very carefully had the rings displayed on the cushion.

They stepped into the doorway and waited. Everyone turned around to look and applauded again. The organ started playing, the applauding stopped and the group began walking slowly to the front of the church where Marc waited with James beside him. James winked at Oscar who grinned. Marc smiled warmly at Lucy and was pleased she looked so happy walking beside Nick.

The service proceeded with Gemma and Oscar performing their duties perfectly. The group walked back down the aisle followed by Nick, Carole and the girls, Maggie and Marty, and James with Steph.

Outside everyone enjoyed taking photographs. Lucy would get the traditional photos with both of her parents, and half siblings, and Maggie had ensured her parents, George and Julie, came to see their granddaughter on her big day. Lucy was amazed and pleased to see them.

Nick stepped forward. 'Lucy, I have a surprise for you.' An older couple joined them, 'Meet your paternal grandparents, Michelle and Doug.'

Once again Lucy was overwrought and tears welled in her eyes. 'I'm pleased to meet you,' she said kissing them both.

Carole said quietly to Nick, 'There isn't the slightest doubt, is there? Lucy looks a lot like your mum.'

'She does,' smiled Nick. 'We've all got some catching up to do.'

The next surprise was for Marc. Barry and Pat greeted them. 'Your mum and dad would be absolutely thrilled and we're here representing them. Congratulations!'

'Thank you so much for coming,' said Marc greeting them with hugs and kisses and introducing them to Lucy.

'We're very pleased to meet you at last,' said Pat, winking at Marc, 'Marc told us all about you.' They chatted for a few minutes.

'By the way, did you notice the late comers enter very quietly?' James said to Lucy.

'No, I think I've been a bit distracted,' Lucy said.

'Surprise!'

Lucy spun around. 'Ann! Oh, how lovely, you made it.'

'Our flight was delayed, but I organised the surprise with James. Meet Pierre and Angeline.'

'Hello, pleased to meet you,' Lucy said, kissing them on both cheeks.

'We are pleased to meet you,' said Angeline, in perfect English. 'Yes, it is useful learning languages from birth with two natural speakers.'

Ann said, 'I'm so happy for you two. You are two of the nicest people I've ever met and utterly made for each other.' Ann winked. 'We're so happy to be here celebrating with you.'

James said, 'We'll look after you Ann, you'll soon remember many people I think and get chatting. Come and sit with us.'

People began walking across to the village hall and the party began. Marc was glad of a quiet few minutes to talk to Lucy. 'Are you feeling okay? You've had rather a lot of surprises today.'

'I'm amazed. Absolutely amazed. I have relatives! I'm so happy. And most of all, so happy to be with you, my dear husband, Marc. We'll travel our life journey together and we'll be okay. I love you so much.'

'I love you too, with all my heart.' They kissed.

Marc glanced across the churchyard towards Joan's grave and swore he could see Joan standing there, smiling at him, nodding. She silently spoke so he could lipread, 'Be happy,' then faded from view. He smiled.

Lucy snapped his attention back. 'By the way, I love the Hawaiian shirt theme. Very suitable for a barbecue. Fun! Now we'll go and party with everyone else and we'll get to know my family.'

They walked across to the village hall. Marc momentarily glanced over his shoulder to the graveyard. It was now empty. Did he imagine it?

In the parish hall garden, Marc and Lucy looked around at the village community. Everyone was having fun chattering. Marc said, 'I don't think we could have planned anything better than this, could we? We have so many friends. We're so lucky.'

'You're right. And I am really looking forward to travelling our life journey together. We couldn't wish for a nicer community to be around us,' said Lucy. 'And no matter whatever happens, I know we'll work out any problems that arise together. I love you, and I'll love you for the rest of my life.'

Marc put his arm around her and gave her a hug. 'I love you too,

Lucy, with all my heart.' The band struck up as he led Lucy to the dance floor. 'Let's get this party started and have some fun. We'll begin our journey together—the way we mean to go on.'

The end

Unless you'd like to read the next story in the series...

LEARN AND MOVE ON

THE SEQUEL TO THE HEART GUIDES YOU HOME

Coming next...

A contemporary romance. Maggie has a dreadful life. She's hit rock bottom—no money and no home. She must create a secure and happy future for her young son, Marty, and herself.

Enter Peter. They become good friends, but Maggie resists love—she doesn't seek complications. Or does she?

ABOUT THE AUTHOR

Caroline Scott Collins, author of contemporary romantic fiction. She loves writing and fulfilled a lifelong dream when publishing her debut novel, *A Charming Bequest* (2022.)

Caroline loves where she lives, in a pretty market town steeped in character and history, on the western edge of Dartmoor, England. It is situated not far from the river Tamar, with easy access to the whole of the southwest peninsula. The beautiful beaches, the pretty villages, the rugged, wild beauty of the moorlands all fire her inspiration and connect with her soul.

Caroline writes stories her imagination creates resonating with truth, facts, and emotions. She deems it's important to offer readers enjoyment and believable escapism with her stories—honestly written. *(She will never use AI.)*

Website: www.carolinescottcollins.co.uk
Blog: MoorScribbles.wordpress.com

ALSO BY CAROLINE SCOTT COLLINS

A Charming Bequest (Second edition, March 2022 Published by Moor Publishing)

Sophie is young and building her career as a freelance writer. She's a good researcher, so her Great Uncle asks her to find out about his sister Sally's life story.

She begins with internet searches, and on a forum she meets Philippe who is looking for information for his grandmother.

Sophie visits Philippe and his grandmother in France, where she meets interesting people and gleans unexpected information—far more than she imagined.

She returns home to uncover more of Sally's story, learns her true family history, and a surprise.

Available in paperback and ebook

Paperback ISBN 978-1-8384594-1-3

Kindle ISBN 978-1-8384594-0-6

CAROLINE SCOTT COLLINS A CHARMING BEQUEST

REVIEWS

This book was hard to put down once started. A very good, believable story. I'm looking forward to the next novel from this author!

Mrs M L Jones

A brilliantly written, intriguing, story. I've read it several times and still enjoy it. Waiting for the next book by this author.

Nanny

www.ingramcontent.com/pod-product-compliance
Lightning Source LLC
LaVergne TN
LVHW031538060526
838200LV00056B/4552